Dear

LAST OF THE TASBURAI

***

May your path in life be illuminated in light

22/4/2017

REHAN KHAN

ISBN: 1497471389
ISBN 13: 9781497471382
Library of Congress Control Number: 2014906181
CreateSpace Independent Publishing Platform
North Charleston, South Carolina

For my family

AVANTOLIA
N
BLACK SEA
LAND OF THE MAGROG
PEARL CITY
Forest of the Free
AVANIST REPUBLIC
Pontik Mountains
KINGDOM OF DURIA
Durian Steppes
KINGDOM OF ATHENIA
Krake Hills
REPUBLIC OF KRAKONITE
Grasslands
River Sjorn
Boreale Forest
Sjorn Hills
Marshlands
Scandez Mountains
KINGDOM OF KRONNOBURG
KINGDOM OF PATHAN
FORBIDDEN QUARTER
Marsh Hills

LAST OF THE TASBURAI

Chapters

Prologue xi
PART I 1
1. Following Orders 3
2. Laying a Trap 8
3. Oblivion Prison 13
4. Highest Bidder 19
5. Last of a Kind 24
6. Charity 31
7. Kronnoburg 39
8. Remembrance 47
9. Tournament 54
10. Marching Orders 61
11. Confrontation 65
12. Sword 70
13. The Council 77
14. Good-byes 86

15. Child Care 91
16. Hunting Party 103
17. Hunderfin 108
18. Proposal 115
19. Protector 121
20. Trust 126
21. Krakonite 132
22. New Orders 139
PART II 145
23. Party Plans 147
24. Ifreet 153
25. Forbidden 158
26. Choices 167
27. The Key 172
28. Hawarij 178
29. Old Friends 183
30. No One at Home 189
31. The Reception 196
32. Daydream's Over 202
33. Dead Brass 208
34. Nightmare 214
35. Release 219
36. Plans 222
37. Guilt 228
38. Seeking an Audience 234
39. Seed of Hope 239
40. Fear 242
41. Rage 250
PART III 257

42. The Wall 259
43. Armoury 268
44. Mist 275
45. Loyalty 282
46. Hedging 286
47. Heir 292
48. Flow 297
49. The Lady Ligonier 301
50. Lady Luck 307
51. Close Attention 311
52. Heritage 319
53. Terms 324
54. Clash 329
55. Demon Blood 334
56. Old Friends 338
57. Letter 345

PROLOGUE

Courage. Elek invoked it. The hilt of his sword slipped in his hand. His boots slid on wet shingle, as his knees buckled. He couldn't see Father, but was certain he was close. The moonless sky cast a blanket over the shore. Thick fog rolled in from the Black Sea. He squinted through the murk.

Dark shapes leapt off longboats, swiftly moving from the edge of the water up the pebbled beach. His heart pounded as he swung his gaze right then left; he knew these were soldiers coming ashore. He could hear their boots trampling on shells. Hundreds. Heavily armoured. He wiped the sweat off his brow, as a voice inside pleaded for him to flee.

His Father was out there. *Hold firm.* Elek sensed they'd seen him, transfixed like a frozen bystander. A knot tightened in his stomach. There were too many of them. He turned to run, scrambling back up the bank, making for the lookout tower. He was short of breath and felt lightheaded but remembered what he had to do.

Shouts behind him intensified. He sped up. His foot jammed against a rock and he fell flat. The sword clattered to the ground. He was up once more, making a clumsy grab for the hilt, but it caught on a boulder; he'd have to leave it. Sounded like a wall of metal closing in on him. *Run.*

Elek was through the tower door. He dropped the deadlock before rushing up the stairs. Would it hold them for a minute?

Smash. The door held, rattled violently. Again. This time the door flew off its hinges. Ironclad soldiers swarmed in, broadswords raised aloft. The spiral staircase was too narrow for the pack - they'd need to come up one at a time. He scrambled up the stairs on all fours, like a wild animal with a hunting party on its tail.

Elek released the second deadlock door; it fell from a slender murder hole in the ceiling, cruel spikes protruding from it. This door was reinforced with sheets of metal, stronger and harder to breach.

He glanced around the circular room with its dusty floor. Threadbare, but for the fire, a healthy supply of wooden logs and coal and a brass tube the size of a man set within a metal frame in the centre of the room, connected to a chimney rising up and out of the tower. Seizing a pair of tongs he lifted the red-hot poker from the hearth. It would ignite the powder left by the pyromancers in the oblong tube. His Father had told him the resulting fire would be seen for miles. Neither of them had ever set it off. Not until today. Suddenly he felt calm. He was dead already.

Elek stepped toward the brass structure. The door rattled. The soldiers were trying to get in, but they wouldn't be able to, not before he'd sent the warning to the people of the Athenian archipelago.

An image caught his eye. A bloody red silhouette formed on the outer window, before bursting through it, sending thousands of shards across the floor. He stepped back.

Shaped like a man, yet flickering like a flame, the Ifreet's eyes glowed molten red, the tips of its fingers and toes tar black. Before he could react, the demon shifted, and stood before him, the tube behind it. Elek lunged, driving the burning metal poker at the Ifreet. As it pierced the demon's body, the metal melted like wax dripping over a roaring fire. He recoiled, removing what remained of the poker. A cruel smile formed on his enemy's face.

The demon gripped his wrist: searing heat made him shriek and drop his makeshift weapon. With his left hand he reached for the hunting knife strapped to his waist. The Ifreet was upon him, ramming him to the ground. His head hit the deck as the demon grabbed his ankles, yanking him out the shattered window. It leapt, hovering in mid air, before it let Elek slip from its burning grasp. The air rushed at his face and as he hurtled head first towards the rocks, his eyes caught sight of the Ifreet, poised like a leaf caught in a breeze, floating. *Courage.*

PART I

1

FOLLOWING ORDERS

It was a challenge running over rooftops in Avantolia. The vertigo was making Adan dizzy. The roof ended with only one way ahead: a narrow crossbeam to the other side. He looked down. His head was spinning, but he saw them stumble in the dark alley a hundred feet below. The three criminals kept glancing around. The rain lashed Adan's face, and the wind whipped around him.

It's just a piece of metal. Focus. A couple seconds, and it's over.

This time he gazed ahead, sliding one foot onto the crossbeam. The howling wind tugged at him, and his boots slipped on wet metal. He stretched his arms out.

Nice and easy. No need to rush. Shouting came from below. They'd spotted him. He looked down and wobbled.

Adan growled and ran the remaining distance over the beam. The brickwork on the roof's edge was loose, but he moved before it crumbled. The building ended. Another roof was far below. He remembered his master's words. *Never hesitate. Let your movements flow.* Adan leapt, arms out wide, robes flapping, and heart pumping. His feet hit the loose gravel on the roof. He rolled, stood, and ran again. Adan used the tower's internal stairwell to reach ground level. All he needed was to keep out of sight and follow the criminals until one of the masters showed up.

Adan heard footsteps and turned sideways. The criminals hurtled out of the narrow alley, crashing into him and knocking him over. The first one was at least six feet tall with broad shoulders and a face crisscrossed with scars. The second brute was bigger with an eye patch, close-cropped hair, and stubble. The warrant for their arrest said they were seafaring men. The third man was of medium build and wore an iron mask.

"Tasburai," said Scarface.

"Apprentice." Eyepatch chuckled. "Let's do him before the master shows up."

Adan might have been sixteen, not as well built, and not as mean-looking as these fellows, but he wasn't a pushover. His master said half the battle was in the preparation. His hand closed around the hilt of his sword, Tizona. The criminals froze, watching the blade forged from pure Orlisium steel. No, Adan could take them without Tizona. Master Suri-Yi would be impressed.

Scarface came for him. Wielding a large hunting knife, he was a blur of arms and legs. It was too late for the sword anyway. Scarface was on him. Adan shifted, catching Scarface's heel and shoving him into a heap of decomposing rubbish. If he had smelt like salty deck slop before, he was even more rotten now.

Eyepatch circled with upraised fists. He moved like an experienced prizefighter. Scarface rose, but Adan slammed a boot into his stomach, sending him sprawling deeper into the refuse and knocking him out cold. On the ground was a circular bin cover. Adan bent down, swivelled it in his hand, and threw it like a discus. It caught Eyepatch in the midriff.

The iron-masked man had shifted his weight one way then another, but hadn't moved. Eyepatch pulled a long strip of rusted metal from the scaffolding. Brandishing it like a crowbar, he came for Adan. "Come on, kid," he shouted, swinging it wildly over his head.

Eyepatch plodded forwards with heavy steps. Adan skipped, ran at him, and shot under his opponent's legs before he whacked Eyepatch on the backside, sending him flying into the air. Adan surveyed the sailors. The warrant said they were wanted for political crimes. Looking at them now, Adan found it hard to imagine. Still, it was his role as Tasburai to arrest criminals against the Avanist Revolution, and so were enemies of the republic.

The man in the iron mask retreated. His feet dragged on the ground as though terrified of a dark wraith. He was staring behind Adan. Adan spun just as Master Naram-Sin shot past him. Naram-Sin was lean and wiry, and rammed into the masked man.

"So you thought you'd get away from me?" said Naram-Sin.

"Please, I beg you. Release me from this mask. I can't live like this!"

"Only when you're in the Oblivion."

"No! Not that place, please! I'll pay whatever you want. Don't send me there!"

"I'm not interested in your money. Only your title." Naram-Sin kicked the man in the head. He grabbed his ankles, tied them together, and dragged him away.

"Coming...they're coming," the man in the iron mask mumbled.

Naram-Sin whacked him again and knocked him unconscious. As he went past Adan, he said, "Kill these two." Then Master Naram-Sin was gone, carrying the slumped form of the masked man over his shoulder.

Adan ran his fingers through his wet black hair and surveyed the two sailors. His instructions weren't to kill. He was just to bring them in for questioning by the Secret Police. The man in the iron mask had mumbled about someone coming, but who was coming?

Adan stared at the two for several minutes. He was still working out what to do when his master, Suri-Yi, bolted out from the alley where the criminals had emerged. As always she was dressed modestly in dark robes and a high-necked tunic. Her long, silky hair was tied in a ponytail and clipped in place by a ceremonial brooch. The emblem of a Tasburai master, a circle surrounded by four smaller ones, was etched into the skin of her right and left wrists.

"Where is the iron-masked man?" said Suri-Yi.

"Master Naram-Sin took him."

She clenched her fists.

"He's headed for the Oblivion," Adan continued.

Suri-Yi's eyes narrowed to small slits. He recognised that look. He gulped, knowing how her enemies must have felt in the moment before she attacked.

"What about these two?" Adan asked.

"Leave them." Suri-Yi turned and walked away.

2

LAYING A TRAP

Ylva crashed through the forest, feet slipping on moist leaves and damp, soggy ground. Her heart was pounding as if it was about to come out of her chest, and her arms were scratched up by nettles. She ducked late, slammed into a low branch, and fell in a heap. She felt naked without a weapon and easy prey for the horsemen riding up.

Father said it was best she not carry weapons when they captured her. Too right, she reckoned, but it didn't make her feel any safer. She, a sprightly young'un, surrounded by men on horseback? She'd heard a nasty tale or two of what happened to girls like her. Still, her old man had a knack for knowing about things others could only guess. He wasn't headman for nothing.

The Nostvekt horsemen were all around. She could see their mounts through the trees. They were laughing at her—a timid teenage girl ripe to be put to work and too easy to catch. She knew she had the better of them, but showing off was for another time and place. Get to the castle city of Kronnoburg, her old man had said.

A soldier trudged towards her, his bright boots getting sloshed up in the mud. Net in hand, he expected to snare her like a pheasant. *Shall I let him? No. Father didn't say nothing 'bout making it easy like for 'em Nostvektians.* She wanted a bit of fun first.

So Ylva lunged wide, rolled through brambles, got more cuts on her shoulders, jumped up, and ran. She skidded on her knees, sliding on the ground. The net flew high and past her. She turned, gave the soldier a cheeky smirk, and sprinted away from him.

Two more riders came over the ridge with spears in hand. They weren't going to use weapons on her. She was too precious. They wanted her for selling in the market, and there was no need to damage her before some wealthy widower paid a handsome fee for her. She sped up. The soldiers exchanged glances. A boulder was ten feet ahead, dry enough to leap off. She hit it plumb, launched into the air, and took the closest rider by surprise. Yanking his neck with her porcelain-coloured hands, she shimmied herself into the saddle behind him.

The soldier lost his grip and thumped to the ground like a sack of potatoes.

This is more like it! Now she was going to enjoy them chasing her. Father wouldn't mind.

"Yah!" shouted Ylva. The horse responded to her command and galloped down the ridge, leaving behind the Nostvektian soldiers.

The mare was strong. It ran well. Ylva put half a field between herself and the pack. It was like the training she'd done with Father time and time again. He was a man of method and made sure she practised regularly. There was a deep gorge ahead about fifteen feet wide. She'd moseyed around it earlier in the day. She debated whether to jump it or not. Racing downhill with the land before her opening up, she turned to look. At least a dozen Nostvektian soldiers were on her tail. *Good. I have their attention.*

The wind pushed back her mousy brown hair as she clutched the reins and dug her heels into the horse. The mare leapt, sailing over the gorge. Half the soldiers pulled up. *Cravens*, she thought. The others made the jump. They would be spitting mad when they caught her. They'd probably want to sell her first before the other slaves. She was too much bother for them. They'd find some fat, rich nobleman who could do with her as he pleased.

She steered her mare towards Castle Kronnoburg's great walls. The soldiers would want to stop her from reaching the castle and save themselves the embarrassment in front of the guards in the turrets. Those who had jumped the gorge were breathing heavily, pushing their horses, and shooting murderous glances at her, but she knew they wouldn't act on impulse. Nostvektians were too prim and proper.

Ylva was grinning. It had been a while since she'd enjoyed herself like this. The past few weeks had been filled with training, instructions, and map memorisation. The maps showed the interior of the so-called impregnable Castle Kronnoburg. Her father tested and pushed her on every detail, forced her to undergo additional physical training, and taught her to fight without her precious weapons. She felt lost without the sword hilt, bow grip, or spear handle. She longed for them like a lover, but she'd have to do without until the ruse was over.

The valley dipped, and Castle Kronnoburg disappeared over the horizon. She rode hard, urging her mare down the green hill. She loved the breeze on her neck and cheeks, and the sun upon her head. A few moments later, she looked around. The soldiers hadn't come over the ridge. She pulled up her horse, jumped off, and sent the mare on her way. Ylva took up a position on the ground and held her ankle. As the Nostvektian soldiers rode down the slope, they slowed.

"Mercy!" Ylva cried out, one hand on her ankle and the other raised in submission.

"Ha, stupid girl, what were you thinking?" shouted one of them.

Another grabbed her by the elbow and pulled her up. Ylva cried out, mimicking a searing pain, and she collapsed into the soldier's arms.

"No better than an animal," said the soldier. The others burst out laughing.

A soldier tied her arms and feet and hauled her stomach first onto his horse. She'd ride into Kronnoburg in this sorry state, but she kept reminding herself it was only a role. Ylva looked carefully at the soldiers' faces. She didn't want to forget. When she was reunited with her trusty weapons, she'd pay a visit to these men and see who laughed last.

3

OBLIVION PRISON

Adan despised this place. The stone walls were cold, and the air was lifeless. Mostly he hated the smell—damp as though soaked in fetid water. The familiar pain ran up his neck as he entered the Oblivion Prison. It gripped him every time like a clamp upon his spine, and it wouldn't let go until he left this infernal place. Adan glided along the labyrinth of corridors leading to the lower cells. Master Suri-Yi was by his side, and they followed Master Naram-Sin.

The tunnels were charcoal grey and poorly illuminated. The walls were bereft of windows. Suri-Yi had accompanied hundreds of men and women down these corridors. That's what happened to opponents of the

Avanist Revolution. They disappeared into the Oblivion Prison, or the Pit as it was better known. They were condemned by the republic, captured, and incarcerated by the Tasburai Order. Looking at Suri-Yi now, Adan couldn't see an ounce of remorse. Why should she be remorseful, though? She was Tasburai, and they were above the law.

The Revolutionary Guard, the Copper-Tops, accompanied them. Dressed in black, their helmets glinted like newly minted coins. Their soft leather combat boots squeaked on the shiny surface as they marched in unison. None paid him any attention, but they never did. Maybe it was better that way. No one wanted to be reminded of this grisly business. Each visit to the Oblivion Prison left Adan feeling guilty, as though an infection had crawled into his mind.

Deeper and deeper their little party went, wheeling a sealed casket through unidentifiable passageways. The thumping from within the casket had almost petered out. They reached the vault door. Adan held his breath. The door was a circular armoured-steel structure with vicious spikes. Two Copper-Tops stood on either side. Batons in hand, their faces were half hidden by masks. They were protectors of the entrance to the Pit.

"Tasburai confirmed," barked one of the guards.

The vault door swung open. As always the clerk was there. He sat behind a small desk in the centre of the enormous hall. He was a thin man with round spectacles and a fluffy moustache. He was immaculate in his high-collared crisp grey uniform. The accusing look came first. Then he recognised Naram-Sin and Suri-Yi, and his facial expression softened a touch. Armed Copper-Tops stood every ten paces around the hall, gazing straight ahead like statues.

The clerk was shuffling paper. He was always flicking through sheets and rolls of it, files and records of citizens who had disappeared to protect the republic.

"Master Naram-Sin and Master Suri-Yi, a pleasure," said the clerk. The first time Adan had heard those words, he'd actually believed them. He knew now pleasure didn't register with these servants of the republic—these keepers of the Oblivion Prison.

Suri-Yi merely nodded to the clerk. She had told Adan early in his apprenticeship that the less he said before other servants of the republic the better. She had warned that any idle statement could be used against him in the future. "Guilty until proven innocent" was the republic's mantra, and it was indoctrinated into its loyal subjects.

"Sealed casket?" the clerk asked.

"Yes," Naram-Sin replied.

The clerk rose, and his chair screeched over the marble floor. Smacking his lips, he approached the casket. Like an officious head teacher, the clerk wanted to ensure standards were maintained, so an inspection of the prisoner was a must. He'd never turned anyone away, though.

"Slide open the casket viewer," he instructed the guard.

The metal section of the viewer was pulled away and revealed a glass interior. The man in the iron mask stared back. He began thumping the glass. His words were lost behind the seal.

"An iron mask? My, you have gone to some lengths with this one," said the clerk.

"I want him in the Pit. Not a cell. Lower him in the casket. We'll throw in the key afterwards. Maybe one of the other prisoners will unlock it. If not, he'll rot inside," said Naram-Sin.

"His crime?" asked the clerk.

"Member of the subversive movement the Shining Fist. Wanted for political crimes against the republic," he replied.

"Approved," said the clerk.

"I want to question him first," said Suri-Yi.

"No," Naram-Sin replied.

"I believe he has information about merchant ships disappearing in the Black Sea. It could be a sign. *They* might be returning."

"Ha!" Naram-Sin snarled. "We killed all the Magrog. You oversaw it. *They* will not be returning. Enough of this nonsense."

"And if you are wrong?"

Naram-Sin laughed. "The world has moved on, Suri-Yi. You should too. There are now more important priorities."

"Such as?"

"Spreading the Avanist Revolution," said Naram-Sin, turning to look at the clerk.

"I still want to question him."

"No!"

The clerk and Adan looked from one to the other. The clerk clapped his hands. The enormous wooden door behind them swung open and revealed a chamber. The Copper-Tops wheeled the casket through.

"Naram-Sin, you do not have the authority," said Suri-Yi.

"I act upon the directives of Chancellor Sargon. You would defy the chancellor?"

Immediately the Copper-Tops turned to face Suri-Yi. Their hands were on their weapons. Adan's breath quickened. He'd been here dozens of times to deliver prisoners to the clerk. What was going on? Suri-Yi swung her gaze around the chamber.

"Do it your way," said Suri-Yi.

"I wasn't asking for your approval," said Naram-Sin.

The Copper-Tops lifted the casket and placed it into a wire cage tied to a pulley. They hauled it over the lip of the Pit, which was a circular opening in the ground shaped like a well. It spanned the distance a horse would run in three strides. As the cage began its descent, the thumping from within the casket grew louder. From within the belly of the Pit, Adan could hear faint voices crying out.

Adan stood at the edge of the Pit and looked down at its smooth circular walls. It was a self-run prison. The inmates decided who lived and who was not useful. No guards patrolled it. No one had ever escaped. It was said to be the size of two cornfields chiselled from the rock face below. Adan didn't want to know and had no intention of visiting the infernal place.

Naram-Sin removed the key to the casket from his robes. He looked across at Suri-Yi, smiled, and threw the key into the Pit. Adan never heard it reach the bottom. The rope lowering the wire cage was still running along the pulley. They waited in silence. Eventually the rope stopped moving.

"Your heart is cold, Naram-Sin," said Suri-Yi.

"I learnt from the best, Suri-Yi."

Adan became aware of the clerk studying Suri-Yi closely. She took a step back. The clerk was staring at her with those cold, hard eyes. She held his gaze, and he turned away.

Suri-Yi swirled around, striding for the vault door. Adan hurried after her. Naram-Sin remained stationary beside the clerk.

"Master Suri-Yi," said the clerk.

She froze, turned slowly, and faced him. Adan did the same but was desperate to leave. "Yes?"

He studied her face again. "Nothing. You may go," he said.

When Adan was back out in the corridor, his heart pounding, he realised Suri-Yi's hand had been around the hilt of her sword, Shamshir.

4

HIGHEST BIDDER

The slave ring of Kronnoburg was the nicest Ylva had been to. She'd done this act in other well-guarded cities, but none treated her as well as the Nostvektians. They got her to market, and she was washed, brushed, provided with a clean set of clothes, and fed a dish of crushed barley and meat. She was close to falling asleep when they called her onto the stands. It was her time to be sold.

Up she went, still pretending she had an ankle sprain. She had to be sure the right customer purchased her. Ylva didn't want to get stuck with a young buck. The crowd milled about before the podium. Ylva watched their thick, round, well-fed faces. Father was right. This lot was ripe for a bit of plucking, and most wouldn't even know they'd been swindled. By the time they did, it would be too late. She'd be long gone.

The crowd of men, some with wives by their sides, gave her a once-over. Ylva wondered what they were thinking. Scrawny girl, fifteen maybe, mousy hair, strong-looking arms, pleasing to look at, but could easily be missed in a crowd. No. More like damaged goods. Sprained ankle, scowl, and horrid temper.

Where was the old fellow? Her father said he'd be wearing a wrinkled hat with the image of the sun and moon on it. Ylva couldn't see him in the crowd. Father had said he'd be there.

The bidding started without him. The price reached fifty before the bidders were narrowed down to two—both young men in their late twenties. Neither wore a wedding band, and both gave her vulgar looks. The auction master, a wispy old fellow dressed in velvet robes, glanced from one bidder to the other as the price escalated.

"Fifty-five," the auction master said and paused.

A finger went up.

"Sixty from the gentleman in the red waistcoat."

A nod followed from the other bidder.

"Sixty-five from the gentleman with the grey hat."

Ylva was fidgeting, wringing her hands as she glanced around.

"Still sixty-five." He glanced at the man in the red waistcoat, but the bidder seemed spent. "Going once..."

Ylva was now sweating. *Oh, Great Spirit, protect me.* This hadn't been part of the plan. Everything had gone like clockwork. Father would be distraught she'd fallen into the clutches of a young Nostvektian. Her mind started to plan her escape. Once she left the slave market with her buyer, he'd have her tied up as they travelled to their final destination. When she escaped, the alarm would be raised. Nostvektians didn't take kindly to escaped slaves. If caught, she'd be thrown in the dungeons beneath the city. She tried to remember the escape route she'd learnt before coming to Kronnoburg. Was it the northeast or northwest gate she was meant to leave from?

"Going twice..."

"One hundred!"

Heads turned to see an old man wearing a tall, pointy hat with an image of the sun and moon stitched onto it. He wore long blue robes and leant on a wooden staff.

"One hundred," announced the auctioneer, and he stared at the man with the grey hat, who shrugged and walked off in disgust, his face a mask of disappointment. "One hundred. Going once...going twice...gone to the man with the blue hat and robes."

Ylva breathed a sigh of relief. Uncle Albertus had come through at the last moment.

Once they were away from the prying eyes of the slave market and into the narrow alleys of the walled city, Albertus untied her bonds.

"Sorry about that, dear. The first minister's tax inspectors turned up just as I was about to leave. Rumours are the Nostvektian merchant fleet didn't return from the Black Sea shipping route. The treasury is trying to squeeze more income tax from citizens. Most unsatisfactory."

"You had me worried, Uncle," said Ylva.

"Spirits of the forest protect us. Your father would be distraught to know what almost happened," said Albertus.

"Our secret then." Ylva had a twinkle in her eye.

"That's my girl. You always were my favourite niece," he said and ruffled her hair.

The alleys narrowed. Building roofs touched one another as they sloped upwards. The cobblestone paths were free of crowds and eventually emptied as they progressed further down winding alleys. She lost count of the right and left turns they took. Crudely painted on many walls was a statement: Rise up! Avanism is the light!

"What's Avanism, Uncle?"

"Oh that. Avanism is an idea to build a fairer world."

"What us tree folk practise."

"Not quite, my dear. The idea sounds the same, but unfortunately the Avanist Revolution in Avantolia and Krakonite merely replaced one king and queen with another, and they turned out to be far crueller to their people. My bones shudder when I think about the awful things they have done. We don't want that here."

"If you say so, Uncle. Are the others here?" she asked.

"Yes. And well into rich pickings."

That was a shame. She had hoped to get a head start, but it sounded as if the rest of the gang had already plucked the fat geese—rich merchants, wealthy widows, and young couples busy swanning around town. Still, she knew the really hard places to break into offered the best rewards. She'd need to be choosy.

The uncle and niece stopped at a green door. It was just taller than Ylva and extremely narrow. Albertus produced a chain of keys and slid one into the lock. The room within was dark. Albertus lit a candle, and it illuminated a larger red door on the other side of the storeroom. Once through and down the stairs, they entered an underground cellar.

"There she is, lads!" cried out a familiar voice. It was Hallbjorn the Bear, a longtime friend of her father's. With him were Eydis the Green, Sigrun the Hidden, and Brynjar the Blade. The entire gang sat in the midst of the loot they had burgled. They were the best thieving gang in the world, and they had been sent by her father, Olaf the Generous, to rob the rich of Kronnoburg.

5

LAST OF A KIND

Sweat trickled down Adan's back. *Ignore it.* Cordaro was retreating. *Press him now. Finish it. He's running out of ideas and space.* Their blunt practice swords danced in the air, sparks flying as the blades crossed. He wasn't expecting much resistance from his opponent, not with the level of competition left at the training school. Standards weren't what they used to be. Suri-Yi said he was an exception. Cordaro stumbled to the floor and pushed out his long legs to catch Adan, who leapt into the air. Adan descended with a smooth stroke aimed at the apprentice's fingers. Cordaro did what Adan anticipated. He panicked. His sword clattered to the ground.

"I yield," Cordaro sputtered.

Adan felt like apologising to Cordaro. The diffident older boy lacked the footwork and swordplay to face Adan. Cordaro might be suited to the close protection team of a politician, but he was a long way off the standard of a Tasburai warrior. Adan sheathed his weapon and offered his hand to Cordaro.

"Again!" Master Naram-Sin barked across the yard. This yard dominated the central quadrangle of Hamara, the Tasburai fortress on the banks of the Jungta River. "This time with Raven and Fur too." Naram-Sin gave Cordaro a look as though he wasn't worthy of holding a sword let alone being called an apprentice.

Raven and Fur jumped off the wooden parapet where they had been perched. All three boys were two years older and stronger than Adan. *Take it easy on Cordaro,* he reminded himself. Raven and Fur were, in the words of his best friend, Saphira, Naram-Sin's low-level muscle. When coercion was required or ears had to be pulled, they made it happen. They were lapdogs and well schooled to do their master's bidding. Adan offered his hand again to Cordaro, who took it reluctantly. Raven and Fur lumbered up beside him.

"Need some help, Cordaro?" Raven flexed his broad shoulders and rolled his tree trunk neck from side to side.

"Feeling lonely?" Raven continued, mocking Adan. He swished his sword around like an experienced circus performer.

Showing off is easier than fighting.

"Missing Mama?" Fur teased.

They all knew he was an orphan. *This is what we've become—petty juvenile criminals like Fur. People dressed in Tasburai garb but with little understanding of its noble traditions.*

The three boys fanned out. Fur was behind him, Cordaro was to his right, and Raven was ahead. *Take Raven out first. The others will back off.* Adan was about to strike when Fur lunged with his sword for Adan's neck. The weapon was blunt, but a blow like that was still likely to cause damage. Adan didn't turn around but went down on one knee and angled his sword horizontally over the back of his head. Fur's weapon clattered against it. The move startled Fur, who seemed to freeze. This allowed Adan to take out Fur's legs and put him on his back. Adan realised he'd forgotten about Raven, and he rolled instinctively. Raven's sword hit the dirt where he'd been a moment earlier.

"Move it, Cordaro!" Raven bellowed at the reluctant apprentice.

Adan could see Cordaro's heart wasn't in it. Cordaro struck half-heartedly at Adan's body. It was an easy block. Raven seized the moment to aim a vicious blow at Adan's knees. Adan somersaulted back and over the two simultaneous sword movements, and he avoided both. Landing with his sword ready, he snapped Cordaro's weapon out of his grip.

Cordaro fell to his knees and clutched his hand. "He broke my fingers!"

Raven retained a self-satisfied grin, but he wasn't as sure-footed as before. They circled one another. Raven swung a heavy head blow, but Adan saw it coming. He ducked under it and leapt straight at his opponent's chest. Kicking with his right and left legs, Adan sent Raven reeling backwards. The older boy lost his footing, and Adan used the flat of his weapon to strike his opponent's forehead, knocking him to the floor. Adan pointed the sword tip at Raven's chest.

"Yield," Adan said.

Raven glanced at Naram-Sin and then looked back to Adan and nodded. Adan offered his hand. It wasn't accepted. Fur followed and also refused. Adan took a deep breath and surveyed the yard.

"Enough," Naram-Sin said, rising from his seat. His pale skin didn't take well to sun, and he had red blotches about his face.

"A performance of great élan and elegance. You are ready for sterner examinations, Adan de la Vega," Naram-Sin pronounced to all who could hear in the yard. He then swept back his robes and left with most of the apprentices. Adan wasn't part of that favoured group, so he remained. He'd given up looking for a group long ago. He'd been alone ever since his parents disappeared.

Adan trudged back to his halls through empty corridors. There was a time when they'd been full of teaching and learning Tasburai. The place had been one of the world's greatest forts built to master the way of the

Tasburai, a path of martial and spiritual arts. Becoming Tasburai in those halcyon days had been a great honour, and it had taken years of dedicated training and commitment. The Tasburai Order had defended all Avantolia from the Magrog and their demons that had sailed across the Black Sea. Only the very best had become Tasburai, and only the elite of those had attained the rank of master. Adan longed to have been born in that age. Being a Tasburai today was a thankless task. The citizens of the Republic of Avantolia feared the Tasburai because they didn't understand them. The criminals feared the Tasburai because they didn't want to end up in the Oblivion Prison. Only the council found use for their unique skills.

Adan toyed with the ring on his finger. According to Suri-Yi, it had belonged to his mother. Suri-Yi had found it in his baby basket when she'd stumbled across him whilst on a mission. There was a note asking for the ring to be passed on to him when he became an adolescent. It didn't even look like a proper ring. It was more like something broken from a bigger piece. Adan felt as incomplete as the ring. He didn't know who he was. He only knew what he'd become.

Adan's thoughts soon returned to the Oblivion Prison. There was tension between Suri-Yi and Naram-Sin. They hated one another, but it had never come to blows. It was unheard of for two Tasburai masters to confront one another. The image of the man in the iron mask filled his mind. What information did he have? Could it really be the Magrog? Were they going to return?

"Hey, you!" Adan turned to see Saphira's beaming smile. As one of only two female apprentices, she got her way with Naram-Sin, who rarely spoke to her but didn't bother her either. The girls shared a vast living chamber in the highest tower and came and went as they pleased. There was concern in Saphira's chestnut-coloured eyes as she stopped beside him. "Naram-Sin hates you, doesn't he?"

"Hates Suri-Yi more. I just remind him of her."

"Is it worth it?" said Saphira, drawing close to him. Her expression became sombre.

"What do you mean?"

"Can't you see it? Aren't we just wasting our time with all this ancient training? Everyone in Avantolia despises the Tasburai. Master Naram-Sin says the Tasburai must change with the times."

"Since when have you believed what he has to say?"

"He has some bold ideas about reforming the Tasburai. He's been talking in his classes about a metamorphosis of the order."

"Into what?"

"A force for the times we live in."

"But if the Magrog and their demons return, the Tasburai must be ready. We are protectors of the people."

"Are we?" said Saphira.

"What?"

"We don't protect the people. Our purpose is to hunt down counterrevolutionaries and banish them to the Oblivion Prison. But most of these people are just citizens who haven't done anything wrong."

"Careful, Saphira." Adan placed a hand upon her shoulder and looked about furtively. "We're the last of the Tasburai. We have to keep the faith."

6

CHARITY

Ylva couldn't believe what she'd seen in Kronnoburg. The plump, well-to-do Nostvektians craved life all right. This lot's appetite was the same as a herd of cows in pasture: faces down and grazing all day. She'd never seen such a waste of food. *It's right bleedin' criminal.* The Nostvektians didn't eat like ordinary folk. They stuffed themselves on meals that came in parts, which they called courses. Starters, main courses, desserts, drinks, and on it went like gushing waterfalls filling their insides until they popped.

Then there were the theatrical clothes the Nostvektians wore. There were too many layers of fabrics, upturned high collars, and flouncy silks poking out from sleeves and shirts. No one could walk very far in it, and one certainly couldn't ride a horse. Fighting was out of the question. The person would trip and be skewered on his or her own sword. The Nostvektians weren't suited for much beyond living the high life, reckoned Ylva as she prowled the rooftops of a wealthy neighbourhood.

After Uncle Albertus brought her back from market, she'd met the rest of the gang. Hallbjorn the Bear had given her some tips as to the juicy areas where a bit of thieving wouldn't be noticed. Tonight, however, she was paired up on a job. Ylva and Sigrun the Hidden had a head for heights and sure-footedness to go with it, so the gang agreed to send them scouting overhead whilst the others stayed on the ground for easy pickings. She liked Sigrun. He was thorough, didn't easily get bothered, and had been with Father nearly ten years. Sigrun had two sons, still young'uns, whom he was apprenticing in the art of locksmithing.

Sigrun wore a utility belt over his grey overalls. It had every type of tool he might need to break in or out of a building. With Sigrun by her side, Ylva knew getting into any place wasn't going to be a problem. Choosing the right building was.

The gang followed certain rules when pinching. Ylva liked to think of it as their code. There was no point in giving thieves a bad name. They'd snag easily replaceable items, and the money they made they'd pass on to some needy family. The gang would also lift rugs and warm clothes, which could be given to folk in distress. Ylva and the gang knew never to take too much. Only taking a smidgeon from each place meant less inconvenience for the homeowners and less attention to their visit.

Father said the best people in their profession were like shadows—unheard and unseen in the dark. Ylva always liked to remind herself of this before a job. Her old man was never short of a few words. He'd been leading the people and helping the poor in the villages between Kronnoburg and Krakonite for so long that he'd earned a reputation as first amongst equals. He served the poor from the excess of the rich and called it redistribution of wealth. The little they took from the well-to-do citizens was barely noticeable to the rich but made a huge difference to the poor. Was it right? She didn't know, but it put smiles on the faces of many children in the villages.

"Look at that." Sigrun pointed to a finely decorated chariot being pulled by two white horses and surrounded by a troupe of the Royal Guard. A young, beautiful woman was perched in it like a stuffed parrot. Her long, elegant neck was stiff as a drainpipe, and locks of her wavy hair swept down and across her shoulders like a golden waterfall.

"It's Princess Elsta Mik. Custodian of the Forbidden Quarter," said Sigrun.

"Lovely as lavender," said Ylva.

The procession moved on. Rattling down the cobblestone path, they passed the folk of Kronnoburg, who tipped their hats, bowed, or curtsied as the princess went by. The people were all smiles even after the princess had left. *They love her like my folk love Father and me,* Ylva thought.

"Rise up! Avanism is the light!" was scrawled on many walls in the street below. Such inscriptions had become as common as muck. Ylva and Sigrun shimmied along the rooftops, and then Sigrun stopped and pointed to a row of darkened rooms in a building clad with mosaic tiles.

"How 'bout that one down there, luv?" said Sigrun.

"Looks empty." Ylva glided off the roof edge and floated down using a rope. Sigrun was soon beside her and worked the lock on the windowsill. They were in.

Entering through the kitchen, they saw the room was pretty empty: a loaf of crusty bread on the worktop, and an empty clay pot from the evening meal soaking in the sink. Steel plates and utensils were neatly stored on a shelf. It didn't look like a fancy dwelling, but even limited experience had shown her that sometimes the dingiest places hid the biggest loot. She'd made off with some very nice pieces from the homes of stingy old gits who wouldn't spend any money on decoration, though they could afford it. It wasn't right they stored up their wealth and took it to their graves. What was the point of that? Father would always remind her that sharing was caring, and if these miserable fogeys weren't going to do it by choice, a little encouragement never hurt anyone.

The hallway led off to three rooms. The first was a store cupboard with flour, wheat, and some old vegetables. Whoever lived there hadn't filled the store for some time. Sigrun shimmied to the second room and froze at the entrance. Ylva skipped over to him. Sleeping bodies littered the floor. Ylva exchanged a sideways glance with Sigrun. He motioned her to check the third room.

It was the same story. Ylva guessed there must have been at least thirty people living in this two-bedroom apartment with one kitchen and toilet to share. Sigrun tugged her elbow and shook his head. They headed back into the corridor.

"Didn't know there were hard-up types 'ere," he whispered.

"How much you got on you?" Ylva asked.

Sifting through his pockets, Sigrun found twenty and handed it to Ylva. She added her thirty. It was enough to feed this lot for a week. Ylva tipped the money into a leather pouch and crept back into the second room. She'd seen a baby basket where she could leave their little donation courtesy of Olaf the Generous.

Ylva didn't know if the spirits could hear her so far away from the forest in this great concrete city, but she prayed. "After hardship, ease."

* * *

"How much you eagles swag?" asked Hallbjorn the Bear when they returned to the floor beneath Uncle Albertus's shop.

"Few bits 'ere. Take a look," offered Sigrun. He emptied his bag on the table. Hallbjorn, Eydis the Green, and Brynjar the Blade gathered. Ylva always felt excitement at this moment—a sense of pride at having pilfered the best stuff they could lay their hands on. She even enjoyed the nervous wait before the rest of the gang gave their approval.

"Nice watch," said Brynjar, fingering a gold timepiece.

"Decent silverware," purred Eydis as she admired her feline features in a silver plate.

"How much money, me lovelies?" asked Hallbjorn.

Ylva looked across at Sigrun, but he'd started unbuckling his utility belt. He was removing tools and examining them as if he'd never seen them before.

"Fifty," said Ylva.

"Excellent," said Hallbjorn.

"Which we gave away," added Ylva.

"What?" they all screeched at once.

"If my niece gave money away, she did it for a good cause. She is her father's daughter," said Uncle Albertus from the doorway.

"It was, Uncle. We found 'bout seven families crammed into a tiny apartment. Stark poor as poor can be."

"Refugees have started arriving already. Thought it might be a few more weeks," said Albertus, surveying the others in the room. By the looks on their faces, they knew what he was talking about. She didn't.

"Refugees from where?" asked Ylva.

"Villages between here and Krakonite. Word is General Volek has been readying an army to move out of Krakonite and sweep across the land. He's been mobilising mercenaries, and they're headed this way."

"Why?"

"Power, my girl. These Avanists are an extreme lot. They push their revolution onto all around them, whether people want it or not," said Albertus.

This was the first she'd heard of it, but if Volek's army was coming out of Krakonite on the way to Kronnoburg, they'd be using the Merchants' Road. That ran next to the forest—her home.

"Our folk are in their way," said Ylva.

"Not if they know what's good for 'em," said Brynjar the Blade.

"Olaf does know how to marshal a defence. He'll be ready if they attack. But let's hope it doesn't come to that," said Albertus.

"Someone needs to stand up to them," said Hallbjorn. "Olaf's a good a man. He can do the job and fight for the people of the forest and the villages round it."

"He is a good man, but good men need more friends than he has. We don't know the size of Volek's army, but from the rumours, it sounds...sizeable," said Albertus.

"We have to go back and help them fight," said Ylva.

"Olaf needs you safe behind these walls 'til he sends word," said Albertus.

The others imitated Sigrun and began fidgeting with newly discovered keys, coins, and blades—anything to avoid looking at her. They all knew. They must have. Father had sent his most accomplished fighters to look after his little princess in the second-most secure city in the world. The thieving at Kronnoburg and all that training had just been a ruse to bring her here. Father knew she wouldn't have come of her own accord. Ylva would have insisted on staying to fight.

7

KRONNOBURG

The warm fragrance of summer emanated from the manicured lawns of the royal palace of Kronnoburg. Banks of flowers and swaying chestnut trees lined the grounds. A soothing wind blew down from the north. It flapped through the garments of hundreds milling around and chattering amongst themselves. They were mostly hangers-on who were glad to have been admitted to such a fine place. Princess Elsta Mik certainly thought them to be leeches. She surveyed the little people of Kronnoburg from her throne, which was set up on a podium and overlooked the beautiful lawn. The commoners had come to attend her late father's memorial service. She didn't need their condolences, but she'd thought it best to entertain her ministers' request to hold a day of remembrance for her father, whom the people had loved.

The courtyard and lawns to the rear of the palace were a happy place for Elsta. She had spent sunny afternoons there playing with her older siblings as both parents watched. Now she was the last of the House of Mik. There were only strangers before her with fake smiles. They were eager to please and desperate to be invited to court.

Elsta sat back on her throne as the chamberlain read out the attendees' names. White silk banners arched in the breeze around her. Songs were sung, sonnets were written, and prayers were uttered for the late king.

Elsta had sat poised for two hours. She had played the model hostess, but her patience was at an end. Her closest advisers, old men she had inherited from her father, milled about her. They were spineless and frail, but all the same, a queen could never rule the Nostvekt. She would govern through her king—a man her father had chosen before his death.

First Minister Karlsen mounted the dais. A crooked face and a cunning smile had been the first things Elsta noticed about him. The impression hadn't changed in the past year. Though he grinned from ear to ear, his unsmiling eyes betrayed him. They were uncaring whenever she spoke with him. It was as though the very effort of listening to her was a complete waste of his time.

"May the soul of our late king reside with his forefathers in the Palaces of Ujithana, and may he ride upon steeds of light as he looks down upon us from his throne," said Karlsen. He had a habit of ending each sentence with his upper lip pouting out and covering the lower one. She despised it. It made her queasy.

"Thank you," she replied with a courteous smile.

The minister of the treasury came next. Reider was a bent cripple and vile to look at, but he possessed the most gentle and caring eyes. He'd had the unfortunate experience of being tortured by pirates and held within their keep on an island in the Black Sea. This had lasted nearly six months, but he never broke the king's trust. In the end only a hefty ransom saw him released. As soon as he was well enough, her father had reinstated him amongst his most trusted. Elsta didn't need kind men around her, though. She needed men of action, substance, and loyalty.

"Thank you for coming, Minister Reider. Father loved you very much." Elsta held his hands when she spoke to him.

"As I loved him. None can replace King Usk Mik the Magnificent," said Reider. A tear welled in his left eye, and he moved on before it trickled down his cheek. Maybe not all the old men would need to go.

The minister of defence, Harald Skarko, approached. A man of shadows, he had dark marks below his eyes, a stern face, and a thick moustache covering his upper lip. He was adorned in ceremonial armour. Though he was never known to go into battle himself, he liked to dress in the garb of a war leader. Skarko was responsible for defending Kronnoburg and ensuring its many enemies did not destroy the Nostvektian way of life. *His is a difficult job, but he is a man I must learn to trust.*

"Your Highness, he was our king and will remain forever in our hearts," said Skarko. He clicked his heels and marched on.

The remaining nine ministers of the king's cabinet followed. Elsta struggled with their names. They were as bland as potato soup. What roles they performed remained a mystery.

Military officers lined up and approached. General Ulfheart was, according to her father, a fine man. He was near retirement, tough as nails, and a real war hero. He had held the line in the last defence of Kronnoburg. *Now here is a man to trust. A man of substance.* He'd done great deeds. He hadn't merely spoken about doing them. General Pineshaft came next. Grossly overweight, his gregarious manner was at odds with his position. He looked like a baker who would be at ease kneading dough and cooking sugary cakes for ladies to eat with their afternoon tea. *He also must go.*

The majors came next—Ulrik, Code, and Nurthwa. The captains queued up. Immaculately dressed, they puffed out their proud chests as they approached. Elsta deliberately paid little attention to these so-called dashing, handsome young men whom women her age swooned over. Yet there was one amongst the crowd who did stand out. His locks of golden hair shone when the sun caught them. Captain Rikard Navrosk had been her older brother Tromor's sparring partner. He was just a commoner, though, and didn't have an ounce of noble blood in him. She had to admit he was pleasing to look at and was quite the swordsman, if the stories from her handmaidens were true. A commoner was just that, though—little better than a servant.

"Captain, it is good to see you," said Elsta.

"Your Highness," said Navrosk.

"It has been too long since you last came to the palace. You should visit more," said Elsta.

"Duty calls, Your Highness, and since the passing of Tromor, well...I have no reason," said Navrosk. He maintained a respectful distance and poise before her.

"Am I, your soon-to-be-crowned queen, not good enough reason?" said Elsta. Her too-welcoming tone surprised her.

Navrosk sensed her overtly friendly gesture and shuffled his feet. "Yes, of course, Your Highness. I didn't mean it that way. I just didn't think it right to impose upon your valuable time."

Of course, and that's the right answer.

"Not at all, Captain. My dear brother's friend will always have a place in the House of Mik," said Elsta.

"And I am and shall always be at your service," said Navrosk and bowed gracefully. He'd spent so much time with Tromor he had even learnt the correct royal etiquette. He could almost pass for a prince's squire. He'd only been granted access to the palace because he'd saved her brother's life, and her father had taken a great liking to him. She never understood, though, why her father would show so much concern for one from such low social standing.

Elsta's attention soon turned from Navrosk to Captain Klas Hakar. Now *here* was a man with potential—noble by birth, handsome, an accomplished swordsman, and one who had definitely been on the shortlist of suitors. Hakar hailed from a loyal family, many of whom served in the armed forces. This included his older siblings. His father had been the minister for protocol in her father's cabinet. It had been a minor role but one granting him unparalleled access to the royal household. She had seen Hakar accompany his father on numerous occasions around the royal palace.

"Captain Hakar, how is your father?" asked Elsta.

"Well, Your Highness. He seems to spend his time away from Kronnoburg in his retirement. He's on the islands off the Durian coast."

"Good weather, I hear."

"Yes, Your Highness," said Hakar with a smooth smile.

"And what has kept you busy, Captain?"

Hakar raised a perfectly manicured eyebrow and replied, "Duty to my future queen."

"Tell me of this duty."

He pondered for a moment and then puffed out his chest once more. "The rigour of the army, Your Highness. It involves horse guard parades, combat simulations, war-gaming, and infantry drills to keep the commoners in the army in good order. They fall back into bad habits too easily. I put it down to poor breeding. Anyway, I'm sure these are boring matters."

"Oh, I always appreciate the efforts of true soldiers," said Elsta.

"It's a pleasure to be of service, Your Highness." Hakar saluted and strode away.

Minister Karlsen came back with a dashing young man by his side. *This must be him!*

"Your Highness, I would like to introduce Prince Theodorus Theseus of the Athenian Archipelago," said Karlsen.

Elsta had barely heard of this small group of islands off the Durian coast, and she had never met any royalty from Athenia. Her fiancé, however, was tall, broad, and immaculately dressed. He had a chiselled jaw and a shock of black, silky hair groomed down to his shoulders. His deep brown eyes were enchanting, and he had a smile that could melt the ice at the summit of Mount Urg.

"Your Highness," said Prince Theseus, taking her hand and planting a gentle kiss on it. She had dreamed of what he might look like but had never expected him to be so handsome.

"Your Highness," replied Elsta, blushing.

"All in Athenia were great admirers of the late King Usk Mik the Magnificent. His eminence was a light on the horizon. It radiated across the lands of not only Kronnoburg but the great court of Heraclius in Duria and further across the sea to Athenia. My father used to speak of him in the highest regard."

My, what words! He must be a poet. "Thank you. You will join me for the tournament, Prince Theseus?"

"If it pleases Your Highness, I will."

"I look forward to it," said Elsta.

Her fiancé bid her farewell and was gone. His red cape billowed in the wind behind him.

8

REMEMBRANCE

"My Shufi, I seek your counsel," said Suri-Yi.

The old Shufi mystic sat cross-legged to Adan's right. His eyes closed, he was rocking gently side to side. He was dressed in plain white robes, and his straggly white beard rested on his chest. His head was bowed down. He was in a trance, but his lips were moving.

Flickering orange tongues leapt from a thousand white candles floating on the channel of water that snaked through the Tasburai Temple of Remembrance. Kneeling at the altar, Adan wished the cold marble floor were warm. He was reciting his prayers, and his lips formed the familiar words. Everything flowed from muscle memory. Master Suri-Yi sat motionless beside him and waited for the Shufi to reply.

"What troubles you, Suri-Yi?" said the Shufi.

The daily remembrance in the temple was an opportunity for the Tasburai to safely seek the Shufi's opinion away from the all-seeing eyes of the republic. The revolutionaries had not disrupted the sanctity of the temple. It was the last place in Avantolia where the Secret Police did not have eyes and ears. Adan had rarely seen any Tasburai ask the old Shufi for advice. He couldn't even remember the last time Suri-Yi had broken the morning silence with a request for advice. He turned to observe his master.

"My choices trouble me," said Suri-Yi. "I feel no satisfaction or pleasure in what I do. The guilt of my past actions weighs me down. The harder I work the more I lose sight of my true purpose."

Adan had never heard his master speak with such candour before.

"Suri-Yi, I have known you from when you were a girl entering the Tasburai Order. You were a happy child who brought sunshine to every person you met. The years have clouded and darkened your horizons. Yet your core remains," said the Shufi.

"What am I to do?" Suri-Yi asked.

"Remember, the ones who will prosper in the hereafter will be those who journey to it with a sound, thinking, loving, virtuous heart," said the Shufi.

"Thank you for reminding me, my Shufi."

Casting amber on the stained glass windows, the first rays of the morning sun lit up the red, blue, and yellow glass. Crisscrossing beams of light reflected off tessellated pathways around them and streamed a spider web of colours throughout the temple.

The mystic turned to Adan. "Do you have a question, Apprentice?"

"I do not," said Adan.

The Shufi smiled. "We all have a question, Adan de la Vega. Only you know what yours is. When you are ready to ask it, I will be here."

The Shufi departed with an elegance that belied his years. He walked as though a draft had lifted him off the ground as a gust of wind would carry a fallen leaf. The temple was silent once more.

"Master?" asked Adan.

Suri-Yi remained silent. Then, with gracious ease, she turned to him like a mother would to her child.

"Yes?"

"Who was the man in the iron mask?"

His master took a deep breath. Suri-Yi gazed at the black Wall of Redemption. The nothingness of it was designed to remind the Tasburai of their temporary state in this world.

"He was important enough to be silenced but not important enough for me to know his name."

"As Master Naram-Sin dragged him away, the man said they were coming."

"They?"

"Yes."

Suri-Yi became silent. A frown appeared upon her face. "They might be the Magrog."

"The Magrog were destroyed. You told me."

"Yes, I had a hand in it," murmured Suri-Yi. "But can you ever destroy a race as resilient as the Magrog? I do not know. They reappear throughout history, coming again and again. They mass like dark thunderclouds on the horizon."

"Can we trust Master Naram-Sin?" asked Adan. His master shot him a look of annoyance. It surprised him.

"He is a master of the order. Why ask such a thing?" said Suri-Yi.

"I am sorry, but I thought...well, at the Oblivion. I have never seen you and Master Naram-Sin so openly hostile."

Suri-Yi rose and bowed one last time towards the Wall of Redemption. Adan followed.

"I am sorry. You are right to ask, Adan," said Suri-Yi. "I have been asking myself the same question for a long time now."

"Master, behind you, we are not alone!"

"I know."

Adan saw a line of dark-robed figures. Swords drawn, they were staring them down. *They are not Tasburai.*

"What are you?" Suri-Yi asked. Her back was towards the eight warriors.

"Hawarij," replied one with a voice that grated like steel on stone.

"I don't know the Hawarij. I am of the Tasburai. This is a place for those in search of solace," said Suri-Yi.

"Yours is a dead way. We are the future," replied the Hawarij with the grating steel voice.

"Who sent you?" asked Suri-Yi.

"Your executioner."

The Hawarij advanced, raising their weapons—swords made from Orlisium steel. *They use our tools.* Adan's hand gripped the hilt of Tizona. He would not draw it from its scabbard until his master gave permission. She was still facing the wall. The Hawarij advanced closer. Crossing the open courtyard, they fanned out in a semicircle.

"You have one last chance to leave peacefully," said Suri-Yi.

The dark robes of the Hawarij fluttered in the morning breeze. Weapons drawn, they were not going to yield to Adan's master. There was only one way to end this.

"Shamshir," whispered Suri-Yi. The name of her sword ignited her into activity. She whipped it from its scabbard and spun around to face the Hawarij. It was the only signal he needed. Tizona became an extension of his hand as he flicked it out like a serpent's tongue.

Orlisium steel clashed as sparks lit up the chamber. Adan rolled under the first blade and rose to face the second attacker. Three more blades zipped around his head like stinging flies. *They are skilled in our method.* Half the pack occupied him. The others swarmed over his master.

The Hawarij were relentless, covering every angle. They had form and technique. Adan blocked, parried, counterattacked, leapt, rolled, and ran. Speed would keep them chasing shadows, so long as he didn't tire.

Adan glanced over at his master. Suri-Yi had taken out two Hawarij, and they hobbled away, trailing blood. *Focus.* A blade missed him by a hairbreadth. *Too close.*

Then Adan heard a fearsome voice in his head. Blasting with anger, it roared from the pit of his stomach, rose, and filled his body with rage. He was terrified of this uncontrollable thing. It went through his veins like lava. *Don't lose focus.* A Hawarij boot slammed into his chest and sent him reeling back. He rolled with it, righting himself as he landed. A red mist seemed to fill his mind, and he began to laugh. It was too late for control. Adan let out a shrill battle cry and propelled himself at the Hawarij.

"Come on," he hissed and dived under a murderous blade. Tizona opened the stomach of the first Hawarij. The second lost an arm, the third his left leg, and the fourth his head. Adan turned to look at his master. Two Hawarij pinned her against the Wall of Redemption. He leapt at them from behind, nearly splitting the first in half. Suri-Yi disarmed the last one. She took hold of the Hawarij by the scruff of his neck and threw him against the wall. The Hawarij collapsed face-first. Adan raised Tizona and brought the sword down towards his throat. *Whack.* Shamshir blocked the blow. Suri-Yi's arm held firm as their weapons crossed.

“No,” she commanded him. “There’s no need to kill him.”

The weight of Adan’s blade was still pushing down. Blood. He wanted to see it flow. Slaughter the Hawarij. Suri-Yi was like a statue. Each sweated as they pushed in opposite directions. *Damn them. Damn them to hell.*

“I said no!” Suri-Yi swung Shamshir upwards and lifted Tizona. She slapped Adan in the face. Tizona slipped from his grip and clattered on the stone floor. He fell to his knees. Panting, sweat poured from his forehead.

“I am sorry, Master. I lost control.”

Suri-Yi rested a hand on his shoulder. “Be still.”

Adan clutched his face in his hands, kneeling before the wall. “Forgive me,” he said. The anger ebbed away, and a sense of calm returned. The fog of madness left.

“Step into the light,” said Suri-Yi. She took him by the hand, and they walked outside. It was a beautiful dawn. Red turned to amber as the blood in his veins began to cool.

9

TOURNAMENT

Elsta arrived at the tournament held in her honour riding a mare whose saddle was the green of a cedar tree, which was the emblem of her house. It was a magnificent white beast, and it turned the head of every passer-by. Thousands came to attend the tournament in Kronnoburg's central square. Tents and stalls sprang up overnight. Seating hemmed in four sides of the arena. The organisers had done a splendid job, and she would have to thank them personally when it was over.

She took her seat in the royal gallery with the ministers. The Royal Guard rode by. Their cedar-green cloaks flapped behind them. They were all aged, chubby men who Elsta felt had rather outstayed their use. She remembered Mother telling her glorious stories of the Royal Guard and their illustrious accomplishments. If she remembered her history correctly, the feared Magrog had crossed the Black Sea, and they were only defeated by an alliance led by the king of Avantolia, the united effort of the cities, and the work of some mysterious order called the Tasburai.

The contestants competing in each discipline entered the arena. First came the archers with their glittering bows strapped to their shoulders. Next came the strongmen. Each neck was wider than her waist, and their oiled muscles rippled in the sunlight. How ugly they looked. The acrobats rolled by, balancing on wheels and one another. They were remarkable but entirely useless. The wrestlers followed. Some had legs like tree trunks. Others were wiry arachnoid freaks, as far as Elsta was concerned, but they at least amused her.

Elsta's attention perked up with the next batch of contestants—the swordsmen. This had been Tromor's discipline, and she had spent years of her childhood watching her brother and Navrosk practise duelling. Her healthy appreciation of weaponry saw her seek and gain her father's permission to practise with a real blade. Tromor had tutored her, and sometimes Navrosk assisted. All that had stopped with the deaths in her family. Sometimes, though, she still practised in her bedchamber.

Navrosk was in the centre of the contestants. His ceremonial armour was shining silver. All the contestants saluted her, including Captain Hakar, who stood to Navrosk's right. His resplendent armour outshone all around him. He was truly a noble lord amongst his underlings—aloof towards those about him and in command of his people. Good breeding went a long way.

"Your Highness." Minister Karlsen addressed her in his usual unctuous tone. He was behind her with an unfamiliar visitor, but from the clothes, it was easy to tell the stranger was from the province of Pathan. "May I introduce Akbar Mia. He is minister to the Maharaja Jagbir Singh."

Mia was tall, thin, and wiry. He had deep black eyes and well-groomed jet-black hair. He wore a ceremonial toupee and raised his hand to his head in the traditional greeting of the Pathans. "Your Highness, it is indeed an honour to represent the maharaja at such an auspicious event."

"Welcome to Kronnoburg," said Elsta.

"I am sorry the maharaja was not able to attend. It had been his intention, but he had pressing state matters," said Mia.

"I am most grateful to you for coming, Minister."

"And you have met Prince Theodorus Theseus," said Karlsen, introducing the Athenian prince, who had just come into the royal gallery.

"Yes, of course. Your Highness, please come sit by me," said Elsta.

Prince Theseus walked past Mia. He offered a curt nod and swept into the seat beside her. He looked even more handsome today, and the incense he wore smelt like jasmine.

The white horn sounded. The arena was cleared of contestants. It was time for her to open the tournament.

"Excuse me, gentlemen." Elsta made her way to the dais and lit the burning flame to commence the proceedings.

The archers started the games. They hit centre targets from what seemed an improbable distance. Maybe they weren't so bad after all. The strongmen huffed and puffed while rolling boulders, lifting four men over their heads on sheets of steel, and arm-wrestling. Elsta struggled to watch. Their bodies looked grotesque with their bulging arms and freakish builds. Next came the acrobats dressed in dazzling blue, shimmering white, and crimson. Elsta found it difficult to count exactly how many acrobats there were. The crowd roared in delight at the spectacle.

The wrestlers rolled in the dirt, grappled, and crushed their opponents into submission. The crowd cheered, and Elsta applauded but then looked away in disgust at the end of the spectacle.

The final contest of the day was sword fighting. The contestants came from the army plus a few of her Royal Guard. The contests became tougher as the tournament progressed, and there were no entrants remaining of the portly royal guards as the tournament entered in to the later stages.

The sound of steel on steel echoed around the arena. The cutting and swaying of the contestants quickened as the field was whittled down to the last four.

In the first pairing, Captain Hakar faced off against Lieutenant Kortal. Kortal was a brutishly large man who had bludgeoned his way through the competition and had received the vocal disapproval of the commoners. She could not blame them. The people wanted artistry and finesse from the swordsmen. Elsta hoped Hakar would make short work of Kortal. The other pairing was between the lanky but nimble Captain Looch and Captain Navrosk. Elsta felt a strange allegiance to the commoner.

Hakar and Kortol went first. Kortal rushed out. Shattering blows rained down upon Hakar, who could only parry and retreat. Hakar was hurt in the onslaught. The bigger man was relentless and chased Hakar to all corners of the fighting arena. Every time Kortal's blade struck Hakar's steel, it sent out a vibration Elsta felt from the stands. Her heart pounded. The crowd echoed her concern for Hakar's well-being. Hakar's legs wobbled as though he was about to go down. His free hand touched the ground for balance. Hakar's crawling spurred Kortal to unleash another series of powerful blows. The big man was beginning to tire, though, and his mouth was open and sucking in air. This series of blows sent Hakar scrambling onto one knee. Again Kortal came, but he was overstretching. Lunging as he did, he was slightly off-balance.

Hakar's slowness vanished. He easily dodged the attack and skipped away. He parried with his blade, keeping his arm firm as iron. He rushed around the bigger man and tripped him. In the same manoeuvre, Hakar flicked Kortal's sword away with a blow to his wrist. The crowd went wild as Kortal yielded. Hakar was barely out of breath when he offered his hand to help Kortal up, but his opponent refused and stomped off to the boos of the crowd.

"Feigning weakness before a counterattack—a time-tested strategy to lull the opponent into a false sense of security," said Akbar Mia.

"Quite." Karlsen squirmed in his seat beside the guests.

"Your Highness, should we wager on any particular contestant?" Mia enquired.

"Sir, you must understand I cannot have a preference towards any contestant, but I would say both Captain Hakar and Captain Navrosk have shown promise," she said.

A burst of applause from the crowd drew her attention to the arrival of Looch and Navrosk. The lanky Looch was clearly on the losing side of audience affection. Navrosk had always had a way with people. Wherever he went he easily made friends and brought smiles to their faces. Even when he had come to visit Tromor, the household servants had looked forward to it.

"Hakar, Navrosk. Hakar, Navrosk." The crowd stated its preference for the final pairing.

"The young captain has the support of the commoners," said Theseus.

"He has always had an easy manner about him," said Elsta.

"You know him?"

"Well, no. Not really. I mean, he was a...person whom my late brother used to train with, so I've met him on occasion."

Navrosk casually brushed away locks of hair from his forehead. Looch sprang the first attack, but Navrosk was fleet-footed. Her brother had said the only way to beat Rikard Navrosk was to stop his movement and hedge him into a corner. Looch lacked this insight, so he allowed Navrosk the space to skip away from his attacks. The contest was a pattern of cat and mouse. The crowd was beginning to settle into the prospect of a protracted duel, and then Navrosk gave a lightning-fast thrust. It went under the taller man's defence, causing him to stumble and hit the deck. With Navrosk's sword upon his chest, Looch had no option but to yield.

The crowd was on its feet and energetically applauding. Elsta was too. Her ministers followed, and the entire royal gallery rose to the delight of the commoners. Feeling embarrassed, Elsta sat back down. She was glad a break was called before the final, and the audience dispersed for refreshments.

10

MARCHING ORDERS

The private chaperoned Captain Rikard Navrosk and Captain Klas Hakar from their changing rooms to the officers' old mess hall. It was odd for Major Ulrik to have summoned them before drawing swords against one another in the final. Nervous energy popped around inside Rikard. One moment he had a stomach cramp. The next, a shot of pain came behind his eye and then a twinge in his neck.

Hakar appeared supremely confident. Chest puffed out and head tilted back, he was looking down at Rikard, though they were the same height. Rikard wasn't going to be fooled. He knew when a man was tense, and Hakar's nerves were as fraught and shredded as his. The man's mouth was permanently open and sucking in air.

Rikard couldn't have chosen a more noble and arrogant opponent. The man came from a distinguished line of nobility. His relatives had been close to the royal family for generations, and many had briefly held military posts.

The private left them at the mess entrance. The hall was empty inside except for a table where Major Ulrik sat. To Rikard's surprise, the decorated war veteran General Ulfheart accompanied the major. What did the general want? He rubbed the pain in his forehead.

"At ease, gentlemen," said Major Ulrik. "Please join us." Ulrik directed them to two seats on the other side of the table.

Rikard could never remember having been in the general's company. The man was legendary. He'd led the defence of Kronnoburg as a young major when a militant faction from Krakonite had breached Kronnoburg's outer wall. His valiant rearguard action saved the House of Mik and was taught at the academy as a textbook example of fortress defence. There were even stories he'd been involved in the last Magrog resistance, but Rikard wasn't sure where fact blurred into fiction.

"No doubt the question of why you have been summoned at this hour has crossed your minds," said Ulrik.

Rikard knew Ulrik well enough to bite his lip and listen.

"Tomorrow morning at dawn, both of you will leave as part of a small tactical force on an important mission." Ulrik glanced across at the general. "I can't divulge further information at this time. Your unit will receive instructions at a predawn briefing," he said.

Rikard thought this secret mission sounded exciting and full of danger. It could be just the excursion that made a little-known army captain into a military hero. Like General Ulfheart, he'd make a name through deeds of heroism and valour. *No, I'm getting ahead of myself.* He remembered his father saying, "The efforts of honest elbow grease will always be rewarded, but never expect people to thank you for it."

"Suffice it to say, being in the final presents a risk to the mission. You are the finest swordsmen in Kronnoburg, and we need both of you unharmed when the unit leaves in the morning," said Ulrik. "We need to give the people their champion, but we also need both of you for this mission."

Ulrik had been giving him the eye. Rikard didn't like the sound of this.

"Captain Navrosk," said General Ulfheart.

"Yes, sir," replied Navrosk. He almost jumped from his seat to salute the general when addressed.

"You will forfeit the match to Captain Hakar."

Rikard clenched his jaw and remained silent.

"I want you to stage the fight. Work out in advance the moves you will perform. Give the commoners a show they won't forget, but in the end, Navrosk, you will yield," said Ulfheart.

"Yes, sir," Rikard whispered.

"And don't injure each other when you're showboating. Dismissed." Ulfheart stood and left.

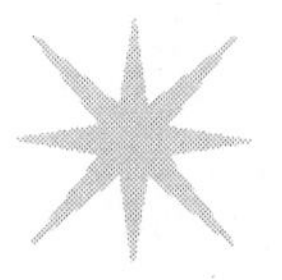

11

CONFRONTATION

I hate this place. Suri-Yi strode with authority through the Oblivion Prison. The guards on the outer passages saw her coming and gave way. Deeper and deeper she went, and as she did, Copper-Tops replaced the prison guards. They stopped her more than once and asked where she was going.

The tunnels leading to the Pit sloped downwards at awkward, slippery angles. The cobblestone paving made walking deliberately uncomfortable. Cries and moans came from the cells all around. The numbers incarcerated had swelled over the years. *When will it end?* Every time she went out now, it was to hunt counterrevolutionaries. In the early days she'd actually tracked down real criminals, but today, political crime was greater than any other crime.

She reached the cell where Naram-Sin was undertaking the interrogation. A Copper- Top waited outside. *Thwack!* Someone was thrown against a wall. Then the doorframe rattled as a body thumped against it. *Crack*. It was the unmistakable sound of a bone breaking. An anguished cry followed.

"I will see Grandmaster Naram-Sin," said Suri-Yi.

The Copper-Top stared. A sneer came across his lips. "He is not to be disturbed."

"Tell him it is Grandmaster Suri-Yi."

"I know who you are."

"Well then."

"He said he was not to be disturbed by anyone."

"I am not *anyone*."

The Copper-Top turned away from her. He stared ahead at the wall on the other side of the corridor. Suri-Yi gripped the cell door handle but was stopped from pushing it open. The Copper-Top grabbed her arm.

"I wouldn't do that," said Suri-Yi.

"Step away from the door," commanded the Copper-Top.

The pained cries escalated from within. The doorframe rattled again. The sound of scratching nails went from one side to the other.

Suri-Yi dug her thumb into a pressure point on the Copper-Top's wrist. Slipping her arm out of his grip, she pinched a nerve on the side of his neck. Instantly the man fell to his knees. A roundhouse kick to the back of his neck sent him face-first into the ground and silenced him.

"I did warn you," said Suri-Yi. She pushed down on the handle to enter the cell.

Naram-Sin was seated on a wooden chair, rocking back on its back legs. His feet were up on a wooden table. The chair on the other side was smashed in three pieces. A Copper-Top who seemed as wide as the doorframe had the prisoner pinned against a wall. As the Copper-Top strangled him, the prisoner gagged for air. The prisoner's bruised left eye was swelled shut, and his feet slid up and down the wall. He struggled desperately to break the ironclad grip of the Copper-Top. The prisoner's good eye momentarily lit up when the door opened, but when he saw her—another Tasburai—come in, despair visibly engulfed him, and his body went limp.

"I said no interruptions," shouted Naram-Sin, turning in her direction.

"It's me," said Suri-Yi.

"And?"

"Leave us," Suri-Yi instructed the Copper-Top. The hulk looked at Naram-Sin. The Tasburai master's lip twisted in a cruel smile.

"As the grandmaster instructs. We will continue with the interrogation later. Place him in isolation."

The Copper-Top loosened his grip. The prisoner crashed to the floor and was given a brutal kick in the head. The Copper-Top grabbed the unconscious man's heels and dragged him out into the corridor.

"Need I ask who he was?"

"The Shining Fist will receive no mercy," growled Naram-Sin. "Chancellor Sargon has instructed Shining Fist members, known affiliates, and sympathisers to be eliminated."

"Even a suspect?"

"All are guilty unless they prove their innocence to me."

"You have a true proclivity for violence. These are not the ways of a Tasburai," said Suri-Yi.

"Ha. Who are you to talk?" scoffed Naram-Sin. "Do you know what they used to call you in the war?"

She knew. She had heard it countless times, and every day she repented and regretted the things she had done. *The Shufi said to soften my heart. I am trying.*

"It was a long time ago," said Suri-Yi.

"People never change."

"Hawarij," said Suri-Yi.

"What?"

"They've returned."

Naram-Sin was silent. He knew of the Hawarij cult as much as she did. Her reluctance to acknowledge them in the temple had been to keep Adan away from this group of renegade Tasburai. Their puritanical literalist teachings seemed attractive to the young, and she had seen many Tasburai ruined by following their way. She didn't want that future for Adan. The boy was more important than he knew. The order elders had rounded up the previous generation of Hawarij and put them to the sword.

The elders had banished their teachings, burned their books, and eradicated their delusional ideology.

"My apprentice and I were attacked by a group of them in the temple this morning," said Suri-Yi.

"You survived."

"Should I have?"

"The executioner's blade was blunt."

Naram-Sin rose and walked over to her. He stood a nose length away. "It is good to know a Tasburai grand-master and her apprentice are still a match for eight Hawarij warriors." He turned away and left the cell, his hand was over the scabbard of his sword, Fire.

Suri-Yi's eyes narrowed, her gaze following him down the corridor. She hadn't mentioned how many Hawarij there were.

12

SWORD

Uncle Albertus said he'd get them into the royal palace for a bit of high-class thievery without Sigrun the Hidden's locksmith skills, and he did it. Her old uncle led the entire motley crew through the front gates, past the soldiers, under the watchful eye of the royal guards, and straight into the kitchen.

The kitchen wasn't the place Ylva would have chosen for entering, but her uncle knew a thing or two about these Nostvektians, and he hadn't been wrong yet. So she and the rest of the gang went in dressed as catering hands. The feast following the grand tournament needed extra serving staff, and the usual caterers weren't able to cope with the mouths to feed. Enter Uncle Albertus and his kitchen-hands-for-hire service.

Once they were all dressed and ready to go, trying to keep straight faces was difficult. One look at Hallbjorn the Bear, and Ylva burst out laughing. The giant was dressed head to toe in white with a cedar-coloured apron around his belly. It was enough to wake the dead forest spirits in a fit of midsummer humour.

"Here they are," said Uncle Albertus, announcing their group to a fellow by the name of Bjornd. He looked a right old git, but her uncle said he was a man of standing in the royal kitchen, so they best be nice to him. Uncle Albertus had taken the precaution of topping up their group with ten genuine workers with real catering nous.

"Right, you five girls with me. The others go down the corridor," snapped Bjornd, their governor for the evening.

Bjornd marched Ylva, Eydis, and three other caterers from their group into a hall next to the cavernous kitchen.

"Join this group." Bjornd pointed to a batch of fifty or so smartly dressed men and women queuing up in an orderly line. "Your aprons, gloves, and hats are over there. As each item comes out from the kitchen, take it to your table. You five will be looking after guests on tables forty-five to fifty. Spill or drop anything or insult any of the guests, and you won't be receiving a penny. In fact, we'll send you packing after a short stay in the dungeons below the eastern watchtower. To work, ladies!" Bjornd snapped his fingers.

Ylva couldn't tell what sort of beast she was serving—veal, mutton, or poultry. It didn't look safe. It was certainly nothing she'd chomp on. The nosh was so prettied up it could be sitting in an artist's workshop with a "do not touch" sign. The Nostvektians ate, spoke, and laughed all at once, and Ylva wasn't sure if the poultry was going into their gullets or if the beef they'd eaten earlier was about to reappear.

Ylva served a table to the rear of the great banqueting hall. Princess Elsta Mik and her folk sat on a raised podium. It was so far away at the other end of the hall that Ylva wasn't able to clearly see Her Royal Highness. Even so the princess sparkled like a jewel—a glittering diamond amongst a sea of grey old men. Only one other fellow caught her eye—the princess's fiancé. She'd heard Prince Theodorus Theseus was a dashing young Athenian. They'd make a fine, pompous couple.

Whack! Someone slapped her on the backside.

"Hey, you. Girl!" said one of the military officers at the table she was serving. One look at him, and she knew he'd had one too many drinks. "Sing for us, girl." Ylva smiled and moved away, but he blocked her path. "Not 'til you sing," the drunkard bellowed.

"Let the girl be," said an officer with thick golden hair.

"Shut up, Navrosk," the drunkard slurred. He grabbed Ylva's wrist and dragged her towards him.

Before he could crush her in a drunken embrace, Ylva's hand shot out. She took hold of a jug of ale and emptied it over his head. Cheers of laughter broke out from the other officers at the table. The drunkard let go of her but then lunged for her. Ylva backed off. The officer called Navrosk stuck a foot out, tripping the man, who crashed to the floor.

"Be away, girl," said Navrosk with a smile that left her tingling.

As Ylva hurried away, she thought that maybe all Nostvektians weren't so bad after all. There was Golden Hair for starters. Maybe he was the commoner version of a prince—the kind of fellow a girl like her might like to get to know.

It was time, however, to explore the palace for some rich pickings. She raced out of the banqueting hall, scooted past the kitchen where Bjornd was standing, and nipped around the corner before he could turn his head to spot her. She saw a stairwell leading down. *Best gear's always hidden underground.* She glided down the steps and came out into a dimly lit corridor. *I ain't afraid of the dark. I'm one of the tree folk and daughter of Olaf the Generous, the bravest man in the land.*

The corridors branched out like an ant's nest. There were locked doors along the way, and she wondered what loot was behind them. She needed to get Sigrun down here and decided to go back and find him. She backtracked but couldn't for the life of her remember how to get back. *Flamin' arrows. I'm lost.*

Father had once told her, "If you're not sure what to do, trust your instincts. They're as good as any, and I seen plenty."

What did they tell her now—left or right? She went right. The corridor sloped downwards, and she realised she'd gone the wrong way. *Hang 'bout. Voices. They might be soldiers guarding something precious.* She needed a closer look. As she got nearer, she realised the voice was a fellow singing his heart out and crying over some lost love. His voice was awful enough to crack glass.

Whoosh! The shot from her sling smacked Lovebird's forehead, and he keeled over. Using his keys, she snuck through the door and went down the stairwell. Firelight lit the darkened hall below. It was an enormous armoury but with weapons the like of which she'd never seen before.

There were rows and rows of swords. The steel shone in a peculiar way. Orlisium. Ylva had never fully believed her father's stories about Orlisium weapons, but these were surely them. He'd described the metal as a black pearl with depths within. When one stared at it, the metal was like a whirlpool in the middle of an ocean, taking the gazer deep down into something terrifying. She'd never realised a piece of metal could make her feel like that, but it was now obvious Orlisium was from another time and mired in magic. It was the only steel that could maim and kill the demons the Magrog sent. The Tasburai, whom Father liked to tell stories of, carried Orlisium weapons. "The hardest metal in the world for the finest warriors in the world," he had said. She'd never seen Tasburai warriors but had imagined them. When she was a young girl, she'd pretend to be a Tasburai warrior with her own named sword.

Other rows held spears, lances, shields, and even horned helmets made from Orlisium. It was as though an entire armoury had been forged to fight the Magrog and their demons. She reckoned the stuff must have been there for years. The Magrog hadn't been around for ages. Most people thought the Magrog never existed. They were just a story elders made up to put the shivers into children.

A grand oil painting caught her attention. It was a battle scene. Ylva guessed it was from long ago. In the background was the castle city of Kronnoburg, and defending its walls were legions of Nostvektian troops armed with Orlisium blades. They were nothing like the cowardly, spoilt Nostvektians of today. Opposing them were the dark forces of the Magrog army—enormous men in moulded black armour. At the front of their army were demons. Misty forms, they glimmered as though on fire. These were the Ifreet. Powerful creatures, they could move faster than any person, carry the load of ten men, and fight without weapons. Ylva felt the hairs on the back of her neck stand up. Looking at the painting long enough, the image seemed to crush her, and she was left short of breath.

Facing down the demons, on the side of the Nostvektians, was a small group dressed in dark brown and black flowing robes. Their Orlisium swords glowed in their hands. Tasburai.

"Anyone down there?" The voice came from the stairwell.

Stupid. I should have realised there'd be at least two soldiers guarding this place. The only way out was the stairs. Ylva grabbed one of the Orlisium swords. It barely weighed anything. Father had said it was the lightest but strongest metal in the world. Ylva raced back up the stairs before the second soldier had a chance to poke his face into the hall.

She was onto him in an instant like a fox out of its hole. His sword flew out of his hand as she sidestepped and cracked her blade against his wrist. The soldier let out a scared whimper. He looked as if he'd never been in a real scrap before.

"Don't hurt me!" the soldier begged.

Where are the real Nostvektian men? The type that stood up to the Magrog? Ylva wondered whether Golden Hair was craven like this fellow. She hoped he had a bit more backbone.

"Hey, what's that?" Ylva shouted and pointed behind the soldier.

By the time he'd turned back to look at her, she'd smacked him on the head with the flat of her blade. Ylva took once last look at the armoury and sprinted back up the corridor with her Orlisium blade. She hoped the rest of the gang had found something more useful to lift than an old sword.

13

THE COUNCIL

Grandmaster Suri-Yi rested back in her chair and peered out the window across the balcony. She gazed upon the building housing the Oblivion Prison. How beautiful it looked from the outside. A curving tower rose into the sky, and its glimmering facade reflected the rays of the sun. How different it was from the inside—cold and dark to its inhabitants. A falcon caught her eye. It soared far on the horizon, gliding over the towers of the inner district and flying by glittering spires, over streets crammed with citizens, and across rolling greenery that reached the ends of the defensive walls.

The only thing she hated more than the Oblivion Prison was this place—the grand conference room of the council. Political subterfuge was an art form here as decisions were made about the running of the Republic of Avantolia.

"Poll tax collection has been riddled with difficulties. My tax collectors have faced hostility from merchants, townsfolk, and even uneducated villagers. I'm sending tax collectors into areas with armed escorts," said Finance Minister Gyges—a wispy, bearded keeper of accounts. He struck Suri-Yi as sympathetic towards the Tasburai because he had never said a bad word against the order. Though, he had never said a good one either.

Yaram-Lim, head of the Secret Police, raised a hand. A reptilian fellow, he considered the Tasburai a historical leftover to be buried along with faith. At best he thought they should be displayed in the Hall of Antiquity. "My agents have broken up organised protest marches against poll tax collection which I believe are part of the subversive plans of the counterrevolutionary group the Shining Fist."

"It seems harsh," said Minister Nezullas. "Charging everyone, even the poor, the same amount for a tax. I've always been against it. It's not too late to withdraw the scheme. We can position it as a consultation exercise."

Finally, Suri-Yi thought. *A voice of reason.* Nezullas was a woman Suri-Yi had time for. She was tough but fair, and she never avoided speaking the truth.

"If people don't like it, they can leave," said Yaram-Lim.

"Collection for the treasury is important, but so is protecting the liberty of the people," said Nezullas.

"Who cares what the people think? They're all imbeciles anyway," said Yaram-Lim with a contemptuous shrug of his shoulders.

"How dare you!" Nezullas shouted, her face turning red.

"I dare," said Yaram-Lim.

Chancellor Sargon allowed them to squabble. His limpid blue eyes crackled with the energy of someone half his age. His cheeks were full, but he did not possess any excess fat upon his face. He did not have a sagging chin or jowls. For a man his age, he appeared in exceptional health. He could even be described as muscular. About his clean-shaven face, his snow-white hair flowed down and around his neck. His keen intellect was not in doubt, and though he treated her contemptuously, it all seemed a charade. Perhaps he knew more about the ways of the Tasburai than he revealed. She could see it in his intelligent expression. He was two steps ahead of everyone else.

Nezullas was on her feet and thumping the table. She woke General Serdar, who'd been close to dozing off. "I will not sit here and have the people insulted!" cried Nezullas.

"There's the door," Yaram-Lim said with a nonchalant wave.

"My dears," Sargon interjected.

How true to type. He always steps in just when matters boil over, entering as the peacemaker.

"Nezullas, I too love the people and am hurt by Minister Yaram-Lim's comments. Please be seated. It is not in the interest of the Avanist Republic for us to squabble like this. Yaram-Lim, your words do no good but cause ill feelings. The Republic of Avantolia is greater and more important than any one man or woman. We will make decisions on behalf of the people. We must. However, there is an etiquette governing our conduct, and we will adhere to it. I'm sure your comments were in the heat of the moment, and you meant no ill will to the people," said Sargon.

"You are right, Chancellor. I apologise for my conduct, Minister Nezullas," said Yaram-Lim.

Nezullas nodded curtly and silently.

"Nasu, what's next on the agenda?" asked Sargon.

"Kronnoburg."

Suri-Yi shot a sideways glance at Sargon. What was the old scheming politician up to now?

"Thank you, Nasu. It is time the Kingdom of Kronnoburg joined the Avanist Revolution and declared itself part of the republic," said Sargon. "The Nostvektians of Kronnoburg have laid claim as the custodians of the Forbidden Quarter for too long. The ancients were mad to give them such a title. No matter. I expect the masses will rise up and declare their love for Avanism with some encouragement from us. Activists have been in the city for weeks now, stirring up the masses and bringing our message to every street corner."

Chuckling to himself, Yaram-Lim added, "It'll work. It's a time-tested approach on the road to revolution and, ultimately, freedom."

"Suri-Yi," said Sargon, "I want you and Naram-Sin to travel to Krakonite and march with General Volek's army on Kronnoburg. I have already briefed the general and taken the liberty of keeping Naram-Sin fully informed of my plans. You've been distracted with other matters, it would seem. Naram-Sin will bring you up to speed. I want you there. You know the city better than most, especially the secret ways in and out."

"Chancellor, I believe there are more pressing matters that need the attention of the council at this time," said Suri-Yi.

"Oh really," Sargon shot back sardonically. A smirk appeared across his face. "What would our Tasburai representative like to discuss at the council?"

Suri-Yi addressed those seated around the table. "Council members, I have been receiving reports these past few weeks of merchant ships disappearing off the coast of Athenia in the waters of the Black Sea."

"Sailors mutinied and made off with cargo. So what?" retorted Yaram-Lim.

Suri-Yi pressed on. "Last week Heraclius, ruler of Duria, sent word to his admiral general to assign a fleet of naval warships to protect every sea route running along their northern coastline."

"About time the Durians did some policing along the coast. We always pick up the cost of doing it," said Yaram-Lim.

"Their naval warships have gone missing," said Suri-Yi.

There was silence. They looked at her and then one another. Sargon seized upon the silence. "Suri-Yi, my dear Suri-Yi. You love to live in the past, evoke your great battles against the Magrog, and hark back to when your heroic Tasburai saved Avantolia from the barbarians across the Black Sea. Do you seek to scare us with these stories of ships going missing? Is that what you want us to spend our time worrying about? No, our priority is to protect the republic from subversives, kindle the eternal flame of revolution, unite with Avanists across the world, and build a just and equal order for the people. We will never achieve this if we keep looking back to the glories of yesteryear."

"Chancellor, we should—"

"Enough." Sargon slammed his fist down on the table.

Sargon regained his composure and slicked back his thick white hair with his index finger. He forced a smile and looked at Suri-Yi once more.

"You and your little band are the last of the Tasburai. You are relics of history. Mystical warriors who have no use in the new world order other than hunting down criminals and depositing them in the Oblivion Prison—a role easily performed by the Secret Police. So don't speak to me about the Magrog threat. There isn't one. It's a figment of your imagination. Let me repeat once more, you will travel to Krakonite. Is that clear?"

"What if you're wrong?" said Suri-Yi.

"Then what difference does it make? We'll all be dead when the Magrog come," snapped Sargon.

The other ministers, especially Nezullas and Gyges, stirred in their seats. Nezullas stared at her.

"Chancellor Sargon, if what Grandmaster Suri-Yi says has even an ounce of truth, we should seek to investigate the matter," said Nezullas.

"Silence," Sargon hissed across the table. "Let me make it perfectly clear, Suri-Yi. You either follow orders in the name of the republic, or you disobey the will of the people and this council and so choose to be a subversive counterrevolutionary."

It was as though a fine layer of ice had settled over the council table, and a cold mist was forming before her eyes. Her mother had said that life was made of key moments, and when joined together, a pattern emerged. She wasn't sure what pattern was forming in her life, but she did recognise this as a key moment. Her response was going to determine everything that came after it.

"Then I choose subversion."

The meeting ended in commotion. Suri-Yi marched out of the council, and the ministers were on their feet arguing. Chancellor Sargon sat firmly in his seat with a smile in his cool blue eyes.

She had to brief Adan before she left. There was so much riding on the boy discovering who he was. Until the time was right, she would keep his secret from him and everyone else as she had done for sixteen years.

Adan was waiting where she had instructed—in the Hall of Justice. Adan looked up when he saw her and smiled. *You so resemble your mother.* Suri-Yi had only met her briefly, but the woman's features were forever etched into her mind. How couldn't they be? Suri-Yi had been with Adan's mother when she had died. Suri-Yi had killed Adan's mother when she drove Shamshir through the woman's heart. It had been the worst day of Suri-Yi's life, and every time she knelt before the Wall of Redemption, she prayed for forgiveness for the murder of Adan's mother and countless other souls she had blotted out.

"Master, what happened?"

Suri-Yi guided him by the elbow, and together they walked briskly along the corridor towards the exit of the building. "We don't have much time, Adan. Listen very carefully."

Copper-Tops passed them. Their suspicious gaze always honed in on every detail, conversation, and expression. They watched for nonconformist behaviour and were ready to pounce on the unsuspecting. She had been part of the original training programme for the Copper-Tops. This was yet another problem she had created for the ordinary people.

"I have severed my ties with the council. Sargon will declare me a counterrevolutionary. I must leave at once. I will travel to Duria and visit my old friend Heraclius. I fear dark days are set to return."

The boy looked at her with wide eyes.

"Sargon means to spread his revolution, but I know the walls at Kronnoburg will hold. General Volek's army will not be able to breach them. No army has. Once I go, they will ask you to denounce me. Do it."

"No, Master. I could never do such a thing."

"You must for your own safety. You will be on your own, and you must earn the trust of Naram-Sin. He will be sent to Krakonite then onwards to Kronnoburg. Make sure you are included in his party. Get to Kronnoburg. I will meet you there. If you want to know where you came from and who you are, the answer lies at Kronnoburg."

"What? I don't understand, Master."

"I will see you at Kronnoburg." Suri-Yi hugged her apprentice, stared at him one last time, and was gone.

14

GOOD-BYES

Suri-Yi knelt at the Plaque of the Unknown Tasburai—a memorial dedicated to her order in the centre of the eastern park. Few even knew of its existence, let alone understood its significance. The plaque was ultimately a symbol of sacrifice.

"I need to go, if only to return in better times. Change can only happen from the outside. You understand this, don't you? I pray for true intentions so they colour true actions." Suri-Yi placed her hand on the plaque. It was cold. She felt the same chill inside. The inscription read: Blessed are the pure at heart, for they shall meet the Creator with faces ennobled with light.

The park had a wide expanse of well-tended green lawns, an oval lake, and banks of multicoloured flowers in neat rows. The designers of Avantolia had created parks in every township. All the townships ringed the centre like flower petals. At the centre was the Oblivion Prison. Every citizen knew it existed but had never seen its insides. Those who did never saw anything else after. The Oblivion was like a foul smell permeating every nook of society. It was an unsaid word at social gatherings, an unwelcome visitor in every home, or a knock on the front door at midnight.

She was hand-feeding the place counterrevolutionaries, and as the late-afternoon sun cast a long shadow before her, it was little surprise every person walking in her direction changed course before reaching her. None wanted to make eye contact with her, pass before her gaze, or accidentally have to speak to her. Even walking in the shadow of a Tasburai engendered fear in the citizenry.

"Are you Tasburai?" a young boy asked her. She put his boldness down to not knowing any better.

Suri-Yi knelt down beside him. A smile crossed her face. "Yes."

"Do you kill people?" he asked.

Yes, it's my job. "I protect the people of Avantolia. Sometimes it means taking a life but only if I have to."

"Mummy says Tasburai are good killers."

Before the child had any further opportunity to denounce his parents, an older sibling dragged him away.

Good thing, thought Suri-Yi. One never knew who was listening. The clerk had ears in many places—an old lady feeding the birds, a man walking his dog, or a couple enjoying their picnic. So many eyes and ears couldn't be trusted.

There was a commotion near one of the park's entrances. People were running away, shouting, and pointing. Suri-Yi could see the men with black boots, batons, and copper-coloured helmets forming a line. They had come for her, and they had sent special forces from the Oblivion Prison. She wondered how the clerk had taken the news of her refusal to follow the chancellor's instructions. Was he glad to see her go, or was he a little sorry she wasn't going to bring him any more prisoners?

Suri-Yi unfastened the pin holding together the folds at the front of her robe. The two panels spread apart, and her hand went to the hilt of her sword, Shamshir. The Orlisium blade responded in her grip and glowed a gentle shade of green. Sword and wielder were one. The Copper-Tops fanned out before her. There were twenty at a quick count. Masks hid their faces. She wondered how many of these men knew her from the Oblivion. She reminded herself she wasn't going to take a life. She was only going to stop them taking hers. They were like her—blunt instruments of the republic. It was the machine she needed to stop.

They formed a circle, drew their swords, and positioned lances and spears. Suri-Yi stood immobile. But for the ebbing glow of Shamshir, she could have been a statue. Twenty elite prison guards with twenty murderous blades, and one Tasburai grandmaster with one sword. She felt sorry for the Copper-Tops.

"In the name of the One who is without beginning or end," Suri-Yi muttered under her breath.

The first wave of attackers came from behind. There were four by the sounds of the boots. In the split second that followed, she leapt at the five soldiers in front of her. They were unprepared for her attack. She took out the two strongest looking with slashes to their calves and sword hands. Both men crumpled to the floor. As the wave approached from behind, she bent down and somersaulted over them, landing behind the pack. Now they were two rows before her and easier to fight. She took out two more as soon as she landed. She removed them with blows to the kneecaps and the sole of her boot in their faces. The Copper-Tops regrouped and ran at her together.

A smile crossed her face. She leapt into their midst. Shamshir slashed high and low, thrust forwards, and reversed back into the Copper-Tops, breaking bones and fracturing wrists and ankles. Suri-Yi had always experienced inner calm in the centre of the maelstrom, and it came upon her once more like a yellow beam of sunlight on the crest of a rain-drenched hill. All extraneous sights and sounds were blocked out. She could only see the fighting circle and space around her. She could only hear the sounds and movements of her foes. She was aware of the cut and thrust of their weapons and the rising anguish and fear as they continued to fall. Wounded and maimed, they were unable to carry out their orders. She could only guess how many would be incarcerated in the Oblivion Prison for their failure.

It was done. All twenty Copper-Tops lay incapacitated. Crimson pools changed the colour of the stone pathways and green grass about her. She stood straight, sheathed Shamshir, and glanced about. The park was nearly empty but for a few people cowering behind trees and hedges. The little boy who'd spoken to her was there. His shocked expression said it all.

Suri-Yi ran for the park exit. She would leave the republic at this moment.

15

CHILD CARE

It must have been important for Master Naram-Sin to order a predawn assembly in the central courtyard of Hamara. Adan couldn't remember ever lining up at such an early time in his ceremonial attire.

"Tasburai," boomed Naram-Sin. He surveyed the line of students and other masters around him. "You have been gathered because one of our order, a grand-master no less, has been declared a counterrevolution-ary by the Avanist Republic. She has committed acts of subversion and will be excommunicated from the order. Each of you will now be asked to step forwards and denounce her," said Naram-Sin. He turned to

Raven. "Raven, you first. Repeat after me. I denounce the counterrevolutionary Suri-Yi. She is no longer a Tasburai."

Raven repeated Naram-Sin's words. Adan could see a smirk on the boy's face, and he threw a wicked smile at Adan when he rejoined the line.

Fur took a step forwards next. "I denounce the counterrevolutionary Suri-Yi. She is no longer a Tasburai."

The other students followed. To his surprise, Saphira took a firm step forwards and denounced Suri-Yi. What else was he expecting her to do? Before Adan knew what was happening, everyone in Hamara was staring at him. He hadn't stepped forwards.

"Vega, is there a problem?" asked Naram-Sin.

Of course there was. Suri-Yi was like a mother, an older sister, and a close friend. She had meant so much to him over his apprenticeship. How could he denounce her and be part of this repellent ceremony?

"Sympathising or showing affinity with an enemy of the republic is in itself a counterrevolutionary act. You all know this," proclaimed Naram-Sin. He turned his steely gaze back on Adan.

I can't do this.

He looked at Saphira. "Do it," she mouthed.

Adan stepped forwards. "I denounce the counter-revolutionary Suri-Yi. She is no longer a Tasburai."

The morning's events weighed heavily on his shoulders. Why had Suri-Yi done it? She had been close to the system, and a loyal servant. At times he felt her zeal for the work had been overwhelming. Suri-Yi's public denouncement had been followed by Adan receiving an assignment. He was to hunt down a leader of the Shining Fist, a counterrevolutionary movement gaining support in the Gallows. He'd heard about the Gallows. It was a semisubterranean city. Decent people wouldn't live in the Gallows.

When he reached the Gallows, he could hear the hum from the Oblivion Prison reverberating throughout the district. A subdued thunder, it made steel shafts vibrate and scaffolding shudder. The prison was close to this nocturnal place and served as a deadly reminder of what waited for dissidents and subversives who opposed the republic's will.

The listless forms of men and women shuffled past him. They hugged the walls of grey buildings as if moving too far away from these granite structures would be unsafe. Adan stepped over broken pathways and blocked drains.

His target, Ab Isaac, was up ahead—a bobbing head in the crowd. The street was crammed with people returning to their pest-infested dwellings. Brown water dripped from the underbelly of the Oblivion Prison onto the streetscape. Enormous exhaust fans built as outlets from the Oblivion generated artificial wind. This caused gusts of air to hit pedestrians in the face and send scraps of paper and rubbish rolling across the road. Adan looked up. A mesh of steel and iron covered the area where the sky should be.

On the rooftops across the street he saw Saphira. She skipped over obstacles and remained parallel with him. On the other side, Raven and Fur kept pace, leaping from one building to the next. Ab Isaac stopped. He purchased some food—milk, bread, and a slice of butter.

Saphira crouched like a tigress and surveyed the street. Something suddenly warranted her attention. Isaac walked on, and Adan followed, but Raven and Fur remained where they were. What were they looking at? Isaac's apartment was located in the next block. The location made for an easy extraction. There was an underground tunnel at the base of the building, so they could leave unnoticed. Adan went over the plan again in his head: *Follow Isaac into the building. The others will enter from the roof on the fourth floor.*

"Argh!" A scream from further down the street pierced the air. Adan glanced up. Saphira was shaking her head and gesturing to turn back. Why? He was so close to the target. Raven and Fur retreated. *Cowards.* He had to earn Naram-Sin's trust. He had to get close. Turning back was not an option.

A man with a crazy expression ran by. "What is it?" asked Adan.

"Reapers. Run for your life," he said, and he rushed away from the source of the commotion.

Adan remembered Suri-Yi telling him about reaper gangs terrorising the Gallows. They inhabited the sewers, mainly staying underground and hidden, but when their supplies ran low, they'd burst up to the Gallows, pillage and rob what they could, and disappear into the bowels of the earth. Police patrolled the nicer parts of the republic. They didn't come to the Gallows.

Ab Isaac. Stop the Shining Fist. Adan saw the horde of reapers. There were at least two dozen smashing property with crowbars, robbing anyone they came across, and swinging rusted machetes in the air. Behind this line of muscle came reaper scavengers. Running low to the ground, they were half stooping and collecting the loot. There were at least fifty. The reapers came in all shapes and sizes. They were filthy and dressed in rags. Cruel, arrogant grins were across the faces of the ones Adan could see. No one was going to stand in their way, and they knew it. The residents emptied the street. Some were caught, dragged to the ground, and set upon by reaper scavengers.

Half a dozen reapers broke off from the pack. They raced like ravaging dogs down the same alley Isaac had fled along. Adan hadn't come this far to lose his target to marauders. He was going to get Isaac first. Adan ran down the side street. He followed behind screaming reapers bellowing at the tops of their voices. Like a pack of feral dogs, they scared anyone who could hear them. *It's only noise. Even an ass can make a high-pitched wail.* Windows and doors shut, and people hid in the smallest crevices. The street narrowed into a winding alley with high walls on either side. They were slicked with water dripping from overhead gangways with rusted, fractured piping.

The reapers had cornered two young women and Isaac. The women were shaking and holding on to one another. Isaac was backed up against a wall. His head darted about. He made a run for it. A reaper jumped at him from behind, wrestled him down, and drove a knee into Isaac's neck. Two more reapers grabbed him by the legs and began to swing him like a sack of potatoes. They let him go, and he crashed into the wall. He crumpled to the ground moaning. A trickle of blood fell from his nose. The two women screamed. Fear bit at them, and the reapers closed in.

"You looking for a fight?" Adan shouted as loudly as possible and with as much authority as he could muster. He wasn't sure they'd heard him, but when the reapers swung around to stare at him with filthy, disfigured faces, he knew he'd gotten their attention. The tall, lanky one in the middle had greasy plaited locks of hair. He smiled. Half his teeth were missing.

"Get lost, kid," growled Greasy Locks.

Adan let the long trench coat and flat hat he was wearing fall to the ground, revealing his distinctive Tasburai robes. He pushed back the flaps and unsheathed Tizona. His grip on the hilt caused the blade to pulsate a low fluorescent blue. *Now I've got their attention.*

"Tasburai..."

It was a whisper at first, and then the reapers spoke the word more clearly. The two women looked even more scared when they saw Tizona. Adan's fingers wrapped around the hilt, and he raised Tizona so the blade angled sideways.

"Nice sword, kid. Mummy let you play with it?" said a reaper with a nose split in two.

"Haven't had Tasburai in the Gallows since...damn. I can't remember! We're honoured. Kill him!" ordered Greasy Locks.

The first came with a crowbar. A short, round guy, his weapon was as tall as him. The reaper spun the metal with considerable speed. Round it went, whooshing in the air. *Let him come just a little closer.* The reaper lunged, aiming the spinning bar at Adan's head. It was a clumsy manoeuvre. Maybe he wasn't as good as he first looked. Adan ducked. Tizona flicked out like a spasm in his arm, removing everything below the opponent's knee. The reaper fell on his bloody stump. Adan moved quickly. "Surprise should not be wasted," Suri-Yi had told him. He ran two steps up the alley wall and then flipped back in the midst of the five reapers.

Greasy Locks lost the hand holding his machete first. Two other reapers behind Adan crumpled to the ground as Tizona flashed across their midriffs. The two remaining reapers screamed insults and rushed him together. Adan felled the first to reach him with a powerful blow to his head with Tizona's flat side. He used the man's falling body weight to propel himself into the air. Adan kicked the remaining opponent in the stomach and knocked him unconscious with the butt of Tizona's handle.

All six lay moaning or knocked out around him. The two women cowered together. "It's okay. You're safe," said Adan.

Adan suddenly realised Isaac was no longer there. The man must have made a run for it when he was preoccupied with the reapers. If he was part of the Shining Fist, he wouldn't want to stick around waiting for Tasburai to question him. The Oblivion Prison would be his only destination.

Adan turned to look down the alley and saw two other reapers staring at him with dazed expressions. They pointed at him and then the felled reapers. "Tasburai... Tasburai..."

The reapers ran away, urging others further down the alley to flee. The main street was deserted when Adan emerged from the alley. His encounter with the reaper gang must have scared the other reapers off. It was nice to know Tasburai still struck fear in some tough quarters. Saphira, Raven, and Fur had held back. Where were they now? Isaac's apartment was across the road. He might as well check there first.

The Gallows residents were a rugged bunch, but a Tasburai in their midst made them uncomfortable. They avoided him, crossed the road, and didn't meet his gaze.

Isaac's apartment was on the third floor. The winding stairwell was deserted. As Adan stood outside the apartment door, he could hear raised voices inside. Had the reapers already come into the building? A woman screamed. There was nothing for it. Get in first and work it out later. With Tizona pulsating in his hand, he entered the apartment. It was surprisingly large, although the furnishings were rusty and broken.

"No!" It was the same woman's voice. It rang from the kitchen.

"Please, let the children be." It was a man's voice this time.

So Isaac had a family, and they were in the apartment with him. Adan hadn't thought about it, but now that he did, he didn't like the idea of arresting Isaac in front of his children. It wasn't right to humiliate a father in front of his children.

His stomach cramps tightened further when he looked into the kitchen. Isaac and his wife had their faces pressed down on a wooden dinner table in the centre of the kitchen. Raven and Fur stood over them with their blades at their necks. Beside the solitary window, Saphira held two sobbing children. They couldn't have been more than six and eight.

"About time, Vega. What kept you?" said Raven.

"Too busy hiding from the reapers," Fur mocked him.

His eyes met Isaac's. The man had a gentle, scholarly look about him. Locks of greyish-black hair reached down to his shoulders. He could picture Isaac sitting comfortably in a library amongst a pile of books and writing poetry. Perhaps he was the intellectual mastermind behind the Shining Fist. It was all the more reason to arrest him but not like this.

"Take them into the other room," Adan told Saphira.

"Please take care of them. Don't leave them on the streets. Not in the Gallows."

"They'll be well looked after in the central orphanage," said Adan. In truth he'd never been to the place and had no idea what it was like.

"Shut your mouth," said Fur. He shoved the mother's face once more into the flat of the table. "Shining Fist receive no favours."

Raven and Fur hauled the parents up, manacled them, and dragged them away. They'd be taken to the Oblivion Prison and questioned by the clerk and his inquisitors. They would use a number of inventive techniques to prise out the truth of their involvement in the Shining Fist and extract as much information about the group as possible.

As he was dragged away, Isaac dug his heels in. "Vega. Adan de la Vega."

"How do you know my name?" said Adan.

"I thought you'd be more like her," said Isaac.

Raven shoved him hard in the back. Isaac toppled over and lost his already-broken glasses. Adan bent down, picked them up, and placed them back on his nose.

"Who?" whispered Adan, trying hard to ensure the others around him couldn't hear.

"Your mother," Isaac whispered back.

Raven lifted him by the collar and hauled Isaac out of the apartment.

"Wait!" yelled Adan.

Raven shoved Adan back. "Beat it, Vega."

"No...wait," Adan said, and then he stopped. Isaac was shaking his head as if to say now was not the time. *If not now, when?*

"Fill my heart with light, my path with light," Isaac prayed as they took him away.

"My babies! Please take care of them. I beg you." They were the last words the mother spoke as Fur yanked her out and through the door.

* * *

The boy was called Jonah. He was eight. His sister was named Isobel, and she was six. Adan knew children of counterrevolutionaries didn't have a chance of survival. So rather than feeling good about his actions, he had a sinking feeling in his stomach as he stood before the admissions officer in the central orphanage. Was he about to condemn Jonah and Isobel for their parents' crimes?

Saphira handed the children their backpacks. They contained special toys and clothes they had packed before leaving the apartment.

"They won't be needing those," said the admissions officer. He motioned to an orderly, who forcibly took the backpacks from the children.

"We thought—" started Saphira.

"Don't. They will be issued regular uniforms and food rations. All children must be treated the same," said the admissions officer.

An orderly dressed in a white medical tunic, trousers, and white rubber shoes roughly took Jonah by the hand and marched off down a poorly illuminated corridor. An equally brash female orderly dragged Isobel down a grim corridor on the opposite side of the building.

Seeing the shocked look on his face, the admissions officer said with a wry smile, "Girls and boys are kept in separate buildings."

Adan wanted to protest what was happening. It felt wrong. How could they split them from their parents and then from one another? Adan had a dry lump in his throat as he watched the separation and did nothing about it. He reminded himself he was Tasburai—valiant, brave, protector of the people, and defender of the republic. Yet somehow protecting the people and defending the republic had become separate causes.

16

HUNTING PARTY

Riding on a stag hunt with the Royal Guard used to be so exhilarating. There was the parade, pomp, ceremony, chase, kill, and triumphant return. Elsta recalled that when the horn sounded upon sighting a stag, she'd feel the blood rush to her head, and the horses would rise to a canter and then into a gallop.

The horn sounded. "Stag!"

The hunting party of fifty moved with laborious slowness across the open field in the general direction of the stag sighting.

"We'll never catch it at this rate," said Prince Theodorus Theseus, riding up beside Elsta on a big black stallion. He was immaculately dressed, down to his soft red leather riding gloves.

"My sentiments as well," said Elsta.

"What say we give the beast a proper run?" he asked. He had a mischievous twinkle in his eye.

Finally. Some excitement. "What are you waiting for?" said Elsta. She dug her heels into her mare and shot away from the hunting party. A few of her Royal Guard sped up. So did Theseus. His stallion drew level with her within moments. They accelerated across the field with their steeds nose to nose and her hair billowing behind her.

The royal retinue was soon left behind as they hurtled across the field. Theseus drove forwards with his stallion leading the way.

Theseus veered right and into the forest. The trees were thinly spaced and barely slowed their breakneck pace. They ducked under branches and hurdled fallen stumps. Her cape caught and tore on a branch. It was no matter. She hadn't had such an outing for so long.

The trees thickened, and the sunlight diminished. He slowed his horse to a trot. *He must have sighted the stag,* thought Elsta.

"Whoa," said Theseus, yanking the reins of his stallion.

"What is it?" asked Elsta.

Theseus alighted, and Elsta followed. He placed his fingers to his lips. He crept towards a bush.

"Prince Theseus."

He disappeared inside the bush.

"Theodorus."

Everything went quiet. Suddenly Elsta realised she was entirely alone in a foreign part of the forest. The only sounds were those of the birds and insects around her. She couldn't remember the last time she'd been left alone like this. The bushes rustled, and out came Theodorus. He was clutching something behind his back.

"What did you find?"

The prince wore a broad smile. His eyes were soft and spellbinding. They were like deep pools, and she was willing to leap into them.

"For you, my princess," he said and presented her with a red rose. The fragrance was stronger than any Elsta could recall. "Truly the red rose of Kronnoburg's forests, though beautiful, is no match for the loveliness of Kronnoburg's princess." Theodorus bowed and then looked straight into her eyes. Elsta felt her pulse quicken, and she was sure she was blushing the colour of the rose.

Athenian men were known to be romantics. They captivated women with their passionate, mysterious ways. She now understood. The entire forest disappeared around her. Only Theodorus stood before her. She consumed it all—this moment, those words, the flower's fragrance, and the softness of his voice.

"Aw, take a look, boys. Two lovebirds."

Elsta turned to see a group of dishevelled men emerge from the undergrowth. Bandits! They carried an assortment of dangerous weapons.

A fellow with red, straggly hair stepped forwards. "Come on, my pretty. Hand over that necklace and anything else you got tucked away."

"Elsta, my dear, get behind me," said Theodorus. He unsheathed his weapon—a glittering, long sword with a ruby-encrusted handle.

"Careful, Theodorus." Elsta grabbed his hand and pulled him away from the men.

The four bandits closed in.

"Young fellow wants to prove his undying love to his sweetheart," said Redhead, and he spat on the ground. "Let's show him what we think of heroes."

The bandits drew their weapons: rusted blades, curved hunting knives, and a long spear.

"Don't worry, my dear. I'll make short work of these deviants," said Theodorus.

"Get him, boys!" cried Redhead.

Two bandits charged forwards. Theodorus elegantly sidestepped the first and felled the second with his sword. It was as though the man was a mere fly to be swatted from the air. Theodorus then ran his blade through the first, who was just turning around.

Elsta screamed and retreated, pressing her back up against a tree trunk.

Theodorus didn't wait for the next bandit to attack. He leapt forwards and knocked the hunting knife from Redhead's hand. He lifted the fellow and threw him into a bramblebush. The last bandit watched Redhead fall. Theodorus swivelled and smacked him on the forehead with the flat of his sword. The man's legs gave way, and he crumpled to the ground.

Theodorus grabbed Elsta's hand. In a single swift movement, he effortlessly lifted her into the saddle of his black stallion and leapt up behind her. He dug his heels into the steed, and the black beast responded, galloping away from the scene of their attack.

Elsta leant forwards. Her face almost touched the stallion's neck. Theodorus was seated behind as her protector and shield. They rode hard. His hands were on the reins, and hers were gripping his wrists.

"It's okay, my dear. I've got you," Theodorus whispered into her ear.

Elsta smiled and bit her lip. She shut her eyes and again let her mind wander in his protective embrace.

My hero. My king.

17

HUNDERFIN

In Rikard Navrosk's mind, the queen's tournament had been an anticlimax. He'd defeated his opponents only to be beaten by a conspiracy of his superiors. There wasn't a choice after General Ulfheart issued his orders. Losing felt bad, but it wasn't the worst of it. Watching Hakar being awarded first prize by Princess Elsta on the podium was deeply wounding.

Now they were both on the same mission. Their unit consisted of twelve men. Five were from his company—Bolt, Kray, Tristan, Luma, and Nathan. Five were from Hakar's, and the unit marched under Hakar's command. Their mission was to survey the neighbouring villages and assess the threat spilling out of the castle city of Krakonite. They were to reach its borders and, if possible, breach them. Hundreds of distraught villagers arrived daily at the gates of Kronnoburg. They pleaded to be let into the castle city, fearful of the machinations of Krakonite. Rikard had even heard rumours of wild beasts roaming the countryside. Some villagers had mentioned Xettin. He knew there were no such monsters.

Ten days south of Kronnoburg, the company had passed a dozen empty villages along the Merchants' Road. The village of Hunderfin, not the most salubrious of places, was also abandoned. The residents had most likely fled to Kronnoburg. News of what had befallen other villages was enough to empty this hamlet.

"Looks adandoned," said Hakar, crouching by his side.

"Your instructions, sir?" Rikard asked.

"What do you think?" Hakar bounced the question back at him. It was a roundabout way of saying, "I haven't got a clue. Any ideas?"

"In my opinion a standard perimeter approach would be best, sir," Rikard replied. Hakar thought about it. Rikard imagined the cogs grinding in the noble's mind.

Hakar gave the order. "Agreed. Keep it tight, Navrosk."

Rikard issued instructions to the men. They fanned out, forming a crescent at ten paces apart. They inched forwards, nice and slow. There was no point taking risks when it wasn't necessary. "Safety first" was Rikard's motto when it came to men's lives.

Hunderfin was surrounded by a moat. *More a mini fortress than a village*, thought Rikard. He wriggled forwards on his belly. It was unusual to see a moat around a village, unless the residents expected unwelcome visitors. Living so far from Kronnoburg but under its patronage, the villagers couldn't rely on the House of Mik to send protection at a moment's notice.

The drawbridge was down. Wooden gates at the entry were smashed, ripped off their hinges, splintered, and broken. Rikard prayed they weren't going to encounter whoever did this. Hakar exchanged a worried sideways glance with him. *He's nervous. Damn it, so am I.* This was the first dangerous incident they'd encountered on their mission. Until now everything had been a pleasant stroll in the countryside. Hakar's legs and arms were shaking. Rikard guessed only the man's pride kept him from turning around and making a run for his horse and the safety of Kronnoburg's walls.

The men waited for Rikard. Hakar looked at him, making it clear he expected Rikard to go first.

"Draw your swords." Rikard issued the order down the line. He edged forwards into the clearing leading to the drawbridge. There was no sudden movement, so no archers were lying in wait. *Good.* A few more steps, and he would be on the drawbridge.

Squawk. A crow flew over the nearest wooden turret and made him jump. He leapt to one side, rolled, and stood up. Sword ready, he expected an attack. *Nothing.*

False alarm. He felt stupid, but it was better to feel stupid than be dead in one's boots.

Hakar was behind him, though he should have stayed back until Rikard had given the all clear. There was no point in them both being shot by waiting archers, but there was nothing to do but press on. "Looks deserted," said Hakar.

Rikard ignored him. It didn't *feel* deserted. There were people inside. He was sure. He put his hand to his lips and moved along the drawbridge. They were both totally exposed. Rikard was halfway across the drawbridge when he heard a snapping sound from below him in the waterless moat. He peered down. A pack of dogs gnawed at bones. *Ugh, it's a person.* Half eaten, only a head and stump remained. The flesh on the legs and arms had been chewed off.

Another body lay a few feet away, and others were further along the moat. Dozens of bodies had been dumped in the water, and packs of dogs were sharpening their teeth on what remained of the corpses.

Rikard felt his stomach churn. Hakar retched over the side, splattering the dogs below with the remains of his breakfast. Rikard was having trouble steadying his legs. Curiosity trumped discipline, and the other soldiers approached to see what was going on, and they emptied their stomachs. The dogs below weren't pleased by the interruption, and they padded on to find a different body to gnaw at.

Inside the village square, more corpses were scattered about. Some were piled up against the sides of buildings, and some were gruesomely nailed by their wrists against a perimeter wall. The acrid stench of rotting flesh was overwhelming. Rikard held his nerve but could feel the tightening of his throat and stomach.

Even goats and cows were butchered and bleeding on the paths. *Who kills good livestock? It doesn't make sense.* The massacre was absolute. There were no survivors.

"Why do such a thing?" said Hakar. He had composed himself and was by Rikard's side once more. *Xettin. The villagers speak of Xettin scouring the woods. We all know the stories, but they aren't real. Are they?*

It was inhuman to commit such atrocities. Signs of torture, dismemberment, and slow, painful death were everywhere. Whoever did this took sadistic pleasure in it. It was little wonder the villages had emptied. He would have run away if he'd had a family to protect. He'd have sent them inside the impenetrable walls of Kronnoburg.

The remainder of the day was spent collecting the bodies and burying them in a mass grave. It was the best they could do. Piling the bodies was not dignified, but they didn't have time to dig a separate burial mound for each villager.

Rikard knelt down and prayed for the people they'd buried. He was joined by Bolt and Nathan. It was a quiet ceremony but one he felt necessary. It was a final moment of reflection for the poor souls. Hakar looked on with a curious expression. The nobles of Kronnoburg had little time for religious rituals and belief in the unseen. Still, Hakar silently observed as the ceremony took place.

Rikard had permitted the men to start a fire in the village square for the night. The perpetrators, after all, weren't likely to return to the scene. Sentries were posted at the perimeter and entrance to the village, and every soldier, including himself and Hakar, was given a shift to stand guard during the night. Rikard remembered his father saying, "Never give a person a task if you aren't prepared to do it yourself."

"Listen, Navrosk, our orders are clear. We must go to Krakonite," said Hakar. "But when General Ulfheart sent us on this mission, he never imagined we'd encounter such barbarity. I'm going to split up our party. You take your men to Krakonite. It's best you travel with fewer men. Keep a low profile, and stay hidden along the way. In the meantime, I will take my men back to Kronnoburg and report what we've seen to Ulfheart personally."

Hakar's men were his academy buddies. They were all querulous nobles who were idling away a few years in the army before advancing to bigger and brighter things. Clearly there was no point placing their lives in danger. Rikard and his party were dispensable commoners. If he refused Hakar, it would be the end of his military career. He had no other livelihood, and neither did his men. The choice was already made for him, and Hakar knew it.

"You're right, sir. Orders are clear. Krakonite is our destination," replied Rikard.

"There's a good man. I'm sure you understand that without reinforcements, we don't stand a chance, so some of us need to return," said Hakar.

Rikard felt like punching him in his snooty nose, but it wouldn't serve any purpose other than self-satisfaction. "I understand, sir," Rikard replied.

"General Ulfheart will personally hear from my lips the bravery you and your men have shown today, Navrosk," said Hakar.

Sounds like you're already writing my obituary.

His men, seated about him, looked at Rikard and then at Hakar. He could see it in their eyes. Every one of them wanted to go home to the safety of Kronnoburg's great walls. He couldn't blame them. They were scared, and so was he. Soldiering in Kronnoburg involved lots of drills, exercises, and parades but very little real fighting. Most of these soldiers had never seen death in the field before today.

He fixed Bolt, Kray, Tristan, Luma, and Nathan with a deadpan stare. That was it. Rikard's men knew him well enough. He just hoped they trusted him enough and weren't going to disappear during the night.

By the time the sun rose the following day, Hakar and his company were ready to head back down the Merchants' Road to Kronnoburg. Bolt, Kray, Tristan, Luma, and Nathan were packed and ready to move with him towards Krakonite. For now they followed him, but if he were in their boots, he'd have serious doubts about his leadership.

We are marching to our deaths.

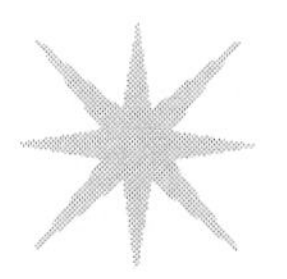

18

PROPOSAL

The request for Elsta to attend the meeting with the minister came as a surprise to her. She had been privy to such gatherings before, as it was her right and duty. The ministers governed in her name after all. It was rare, however, for them to request her presence. It had been apparent from her first cabinet meeting that her suggestions were going to have little impact on these old men.

Elsta took her seat at the head of the table. The old men were few today. She had expected the entire cabinet. Instead, First Minister Karlsen, her father's dear friend Reider, and General Ulfheart received her.

Their looks were grave. It was as though she had walked into a home for the dying rather than the halls of power at Kronnoburg. Karlsen wore the same expression as when he had told her Father had died. Since there were no more family members, it couldn't be a death in the family they were going to tell her about. What else could be so awful?

"Your Majesty," started Karlsen, "these are trying times. We have many enemies bordering our lands. They mistakenly believe that in the absence of a king we are ready to be overrun. This sentiment has even reached the Great Council of Avantolia presided over by Chancellor Sargon himself. Kronnoburg is seen as weak and ailing, and there is talk of Chancellor Sargon spreading the Avanist Revolution to our lands."

Why would he do such a thing? We have always been at peace with them and fought alongside them when the barbarians crossed the Black Sea.

The first minister continued. "We are surrounded by threats to our sovereignty—the Avanist Republic of Krakonite, the outlaw Olaf the Generous, and recent reports of our merchant ships disappearing in the Black Sea. Securing our borders remains a perennial problem. Every king carries this burden. While serving your father, we made efforts to forge alliances. It seems many of those old allegiances died with the people who made them and are no longer honoured by their heirs. New Krakonite rulers no longer regard the old treaties as valid."

The seasoned general shuffled in his chair. He'd led the last defence of Kronnoburg as a young major. *He is a living legend*, she reminded herself. *Men such as Ulfheart don't get nervous.* The prolix Karlsen droned on about politics, playing the game with a weak hand, and making personal sacrifices. Elsta's thoughts, however, were with her fiancé, Theodorus.

"We cannot accept such a marriage proposal..."

Marriage proposal? When had the subject shifted from politics to weddings, and who exactly was getting married?

"First Minister, did you say 'marriage proposal'?" asked Elsta.

"Yes, and it's an absolute disgrace," said Reider.

"Whose wedding?" Elsta asked.

The old men exchanged glances. "Your wedding! Chancellor Sargon has proclaimed that you are to marry General Volek, ruler of Krakonite," replied Karlsen.

"Sir. You are mistaken." *Volek is a butcher. A fiend known for killing his wives once he's had his way. Is he on wife number six or seven?*

"The instructions from Chancellor Sargon are clear," said Reider. "Of course we cannot accept such terms. Your father had already made the arrangement with the father of Prince Theseus."

"However, our safety is dependent on support from the Republic of Avantolia," said Karlsen. "Should they withdraw that support, it poses a threat to our security. I assure you, Krakonite will not wait long before making a play for our resources. Avantolia will do nothing."

"It is marriage or war, Your Majesty," said General Ulfheart.

"Without a strong king, we leave Kronnoburg open to accusations of weakness," said Reider.

"I am ready to marry now," whispered Elsta.

"I beg your pardon, Your Majesty," said Reider. "My hearing is not what it used to be." The crippled old man craned forwards to listen.

Elsta spoke up. "I am ready to marry now. We do not need to delay matters with Prince Theseus. We must herald in a new king who will rule over Kronnoburg and protect its people."

"I am concerned, Your Majesty, that Prince Theseus has not visited us with any members of his extended family," said Reider. He paused to look at the other old men. "His late father passed away soon after the engagement, and his immediate family sadly drowned when their ship capsized in a storm off the Durian coast. This is the first time we have met the prince, and though he is a fine, dashing young man, I am worried about the lack of support from his kin. It is important to know the Athenians are still fully behind this marriage, and we have not been able to correspond with the prince's government," said Reider.

"Come, dear minister. Of course his government will be supportive. He is marrying into the House of Mik and into Kronnoburg—the greatest fortress in the world. I know you are concerned for my welfare, but I assure you Prince Theseus is more than capable of taking care of me. He will make a fine king of Kronnoburg," said Elsta.

"I'm sure he will, Your Majesty, but in the absence of your father, I worry for your welfare as I would for my own daughter. So please forgive me for being overly cautious. It is only because I want the best for you," said Reider.

Elsta loved the crippled old man now more than ever but didn't share his concerns. "I thank the minister for his views, but I am ready to marry Prince Theseus. Our marriage will make the Athenians our allies, and we need to reinforce our borders through new allegiances. The old no longer hold firm."

"I did say that, Your Highness, but the Athenians are not exactly a force to be reckoned with, if I may say so without disrespect to Prince Theseus," said Karlsen.

"That may be true, but the Athenians are cousins of the Durians. Are they not?"

"Yes," said Karlsen.

"And Heraclius, ruler of Duria, is certainly an ally worth having. Is he not?"

"Yes," they all replied.

"So my marriage to Theodorus will ensure the Durians become our allies."

Ulfheart puffed out his cheeks. "The princess has a valid point, gentlemen. The strength of Duria behind us would make Krakonite think twice about threatening us."

"You make a compelling case for the prince, Your Highness," said Reider.

"We will try and reach out to the Athenian government one more time. In the meantime we will try and stall the request from Chancellor Sargon. The chancellor is not known for his patience, and neither is General Volek. We will need to play a very diplomatic hand if we are to ensure the sovereignty of the kingdom," said Karlsen.

"Indeed," said Reider. "I'd hate for the princess to be placed in a situation where marrying Volek was the only alternative to secure the safety of Kronnoburg."

So would I.

19

PROTECTOR

Rikard led his men down the Merchants' Road, but the lingering image of Hunderfin was a constant flicker in his eye. The further south they moved, the more fortified the village compounds became. They saw higher walls, moats in some places, and even the odd murder hole above a drawbridge from which the defenders could pour boiling oil. With every step, Rikard felt a darkness enveloping the landscape. He hadn't seen the sun in days. The heavy clouds threatened rainfall.

They stopped for the night in an old well house. It was a three-storey circular structure constructed from stone with a slate roof. Within was an enormous well for fresh water supplies. The first and second floors contained living quarters. A family had recently resided there. Rikard observed they'd left their kitchen utensils, most of their clothes, and bedding behind.

Luma started a fire, which was a welcome relief. Rikard's bones were frozen from the constant chill. At least tonight he and the men had some heat and a roof over their heads. As the warmth radiated around the walls, the atmosphere relaxed. Bolt roasted the two pheasants he'd caught earlier, and Rikard was ready for a good night's rest. He fell asleep with the fire still burning.

As soon as Rikard heard the movement outside, he knew they should have put the fire out. *Stupid.* They were lit up like a beacon in this grey landscape.

The heavy footsteps outside the well house woke the others. They scrambled for their weapons. Tristan, Nathan, and Luma took up positions at the window. Bolt and Kray covered the stairwell. Rikard could see a dozen men surround their refuge. They were carrying swords and axes. Charcoal-grey body armour covered their fronts and backs. The men, though Rikard wasn't sure he could call them men, had enormous foreheads, deep-set eyes, and wolfish dentition. They were also very big. Their fingers were thick, and their boots curled upwards like talons. *Xettin!*

Stories of half men, half who-knows-what circulated at evening gatherings in Kronnoburg, but these were ghost stories to frighten little children. Rikard had been told these when he was a young boy. Wandering hermits spoke of each Xettin possessing the strength of five men. Their skins were said to be hardened like varnished stones. A blow from a sword merely left a scratch on the brutes, and the Xettin were known for pulling out arrows from their bodies before continuing to fight. The old stories said that when the Magrog army was defeated, the Xettin had disappeared to their mountain caves.

"Xettin! We're surrounded, sir," said Nathan. The men knew the foes, and like Rikard, they stank of fear. The Xettin stood outside waiting and watching.

"Put the lamps out," said Rikard. He knew it was too little too late, but at least it might slow the bloody beasts down. Tristan crouched low, moving swiftly around the room and snuffing out the lamps.

"What now, sir?" asked Bolt.

He wished he knew. "Bolt and Kray, I want you downstairs. Anything that tries to come in, open fire."

"Wargh!" one of the Xettin howled.

Rikard hoped it was hurt but realised it was a sort of battle cry. The others joined in. A moment earlier the silence had been draining his blood. Now ululation of the creatures numbed him with fear.

Tristan and Luma slid down onto their knees and covered their ears. Rikard felt like doing the same. *Whack!* One Xettin slammed into the door below. It rattled violently. Had it come off its hinges? He heard running feet, and then another smashed into the door. He hoped Bolt and Kray held their nerve. Of his men they were the bravest. Rikard was certain one more blow would split the door into a dozen pieces. They'd need as many arrows as possible.

"Luma, take the upper staircase. Keep your aim steady and sure," he said.

Rikard peered over the lower sill of the window frame. Below, two beasts were taking turns battering the front door. Standing behind them in a ragtag formation were the remaining Xettin. If they broke the door down and entered, he'd have to leap from the window and attack them from behind. He might take one down before the others realised what was happening.

Wait. There is someone else. Rikard could see a luminous green light speedily approaching through the forest. The Xettin were oblivious to it. The light was in the form of a long, slender shape. It burst out of the undergrowth and struck the Xettin nearest. The creature crumpled as though a cliff had fallen on it. The light slashed through the air. Two more Xettin went down.

What can be more dangerous than Xettin? Whatever it was, Rikard didn't want to meet it. The other Xettin whirled to face the threat. The luminous weapon swung upwards in a high arc. The Xettin moved together and surrounded its poised gleam. If there was a person in the middle of that group of beasts, Rikard was certain he or she was about to be slaughtered. It was the perfect time for him and his men to escape, but he couldn't bring himself to move away from the window. He was half scared and half eager to see what was going to happen.

The great Xettin broadswords rose and fell. The radiant green weapon blocked, parried, and thrust higher, lower, and faster than the beasts. It looked as though there were three or four weapons dancing around the Xettin. To Rikard's astonishment the Xettin fell one by one until only the wielder of the green weapon remained. Then the weapon was sheathed, and the light went out.

The person, for Rikard could now see it *was* a person, looked straight at him. He froze. Was he next? No. The expression held no malice. His protector walked away as silently as she had approached.

With his back against the wall, Rikard slid down to face his men. "Tasburai," he said as they gathered around.

20

TRUST

When Adan came into Naram-Sin's office, Raven and Fur were already present. The two lapdogs stood on either side of the grandmaster. Naram-Sin didn't offer him a seat, but Adan wasn't expecting one.

"I have an important mission for you, Vega. You are to bring in a high-profile target denounced by the chancellor as a counterrevolutionary. I'm against giving you this assignment, but the chancellor insisted."

Why would Chancellor Sargon choose me to carry out the assignment? I've never met the man.

"Here is the arrest notice." Naram-Sin handed him the document. The person to be incarcerated in the

Oblivion Prison was Minister of Ethics Nezullas. Adan read the accusation of crimes against the Republic of Avantolia. There was no point asking for clarification about the precise nature of the crime.

"When do we arrest the criminal?" asked Adan.

"Tonight," said Naram-Sin.

Adan insisted on Saphira joining him for the mission. He didn't want the heavy-handedness of Raven and Fur when it wasn't necessary. From the research he'd done on Nezullas earlier in the day, she was a robust woman who had suffered early in life after the loss of her husband and family. Suri-Yi once told him, "Tragedy moulds the path for a person's life."

Minister Nezullas lived in a quiet neighbourhood called Wimpot in the suburbs of Avantolia. It was an unusual place to find a government official of such high standing. Most chose to live in official residences in the upper tiers in the heart of the city. Wimpot, on the other hand, was a lush green district entirely at odds with any other location within the city. It was a world away from the Gallows. Adan wondered what residents of that downtrodden place would make of Wimpot with its manicured lawns, prim hedges, and golden flower beds. Cottages built of ancient stone stood at irregular distances from one another. Adan imagined himself settling down in a place like Wimpot one day and maybe having a family. He smiled at Saphira, and she looked back with a quizzical stare.

"You okay?" she asked.

Adan nodded and kept moving. She followed close behind but kept low. In the early evening, moving swiftly between cottages, they were shadows in the shadows. They leapt a green fence and skirted around a neat lawn with inch-high grass. He liked working with Saphira. Their styles were complementary. She possessed strengths in his areas of weakness.

The evening air was still. It was so silent Adan could locate the crickets on the lawn and hear the gentle neighing of a horse in a nearby meadow. These sounds were uncommon to the town dweller. He told himself he should come out to these parts more often. It might help him create the inner stillness necessary to better perform his daily remembrance. It might even help him form the question the Shufi said he was in search of—the question he would one day ask the wise old man in the Tasburai temple.

They could see Nezullas sitting and sipping a drink on the rear porch of her cottage. She was about to receive a nasty surprise, but once they had gagged her, it would be a simple enough procedure. The collection carriage, drawn by four horses, waited on the outskirts of Wimpot and would arrive when summoned. The prison guards terrified people, so Suri-Yi always used to ask them to remain out of sight until the last moment. Public panic before an extraction was never useful.

Adan padded through the undergrowth of the garden. He was silent as a gentle eastern breeze. Saphira approached from the other side. The minister lived alone.

Adan had no reason to expect anyone else was on the property, but there was little point taking a risk either. He was close to her when he paused for a quick glance about. There was a smell in the air. Men were close by. He'd come across that mix of sweat and anxiety on too many occasions to fail to notice it. Where were they? Should he go or stay? His fingers itched as he gripped the hilt of Tizona, and sweat trickled off the bridge of his nose. He couldn't wait any longer. Adan leapt from his hiding place. Nezullas spotted him too late. She couldn't make a run for it.

Adan hit the deck. He rolled and picked himself up off the ground. Two hooded adversaries stood before him and protected Nezullas. They had been on the roof—the one place he hadn't thought to check. *What a foolish, amateur mistake.*

His opponents were dressed in white robes and silver gloves. Their faces were hidden. They were foot soldiers of the Shining Fist. Adan had heard these fighters were trained in many aspects of the martial arts. Some said they even rivalled the abilities of a Tasburai apprentice. *Well, I'm about to find out.* The minister, like Ab Isaac, was involved with the Shining Fist.

Saphira remained hidden, but Adan was certain the Shining Fist had seen her coming. With clinical precision they drew their blades. Adan did the same. Tizona pulsated blue.

"Who sent you, Tasburai?" Nezullas asked him.

"I have instructions to arrest you, Minister, for crimes against the republic."

"Where have I heard that one before?" Nezullas said. "Oh yes. Listening to Chancellor Sargon at the council. At least he could have thought of a more original accusation to hang on me."

"Association with the Shining Fist is a counterrevolutionary act and a crime against the republic," said Adan.

"What's your name, Tasburai?" she asked.

"What does it matter?" Adan lunged at the two guards surrounding her. They blocked his advances with clever swordplay. They conserved their energy by not striking back. They watched him for weakness and kept an eye out for Saphira. They were good. He liked that. It would be a challenge.

The taller guard made his move, aiming his sword at Adan's legs with a powerful swing. Adan leapt clear, but as he did, the second warrior swung his blade at Adan's head. He arched his back and somersaulted. He landed on the flat of his palms and then leapt straight up and over the two guards, avoiding the flashing blades.

Saphira appeared by his side as he landed. The duel was getting serious if she thought he needed her help. "Looked like you were enjoying yourself too much Adan," she said.

He loosened his grip on Tizona and swung the blade at a ferocious speed. The taller guard could only defend on his back foot. With a follow-up thrust, his opponent's blade was shattered, and Adan knocked the Shining Fist warrior into unconsciousness with a blunt blow to the head. Saphira easily despatched the other warrior.

"So you're Adan de la Vega," said Nezullas, "apprentice to Grandmaster Suri-Yi, and this is the legendary blade Tizona. Suri-Yi told me you were the best she'd ever trained, and I can see why. You are a worthy owner of Tizona. The blade does not yield to all who own it."

"Suri-Yi told you about me?" asked Adan.

"Why not? She's proud of you, young man. She thinks of you as a son."

But she is not my mother. If Ab Isaac knew my mother, did Suri-Yi also know her?

"Careful, Adan. She's playing mind games," warned Saphira.

"And you must be Saphira. Your former master, Vink, was a good man. I was sorry to hear of his disappearance as I was of all the good Tasburai masters who've gone missing. It seems only Grandmaster Naram-Sin remains, and we all know he is no stickler for justice."

"This doesn't change anything, Minister. Our orders are clear. You're going to the Oblivion," said Adan.

"You're right, young man. My fate is sealed. It was on the day I went up against Sargon. I just have one request before you take me."

She wasn't in any position to make requests, but Adan was curious what she had to ask. "What is it?"

"When it's all over, come and find me in the Oblivion. If I'm still alive, I'll be waiting for you."

"When what's all over?"

"The war that's coming," said Nezullas.

21

KRAKONITE

Rikard peered down from the mountain pass overlooking Castle Krakonite. He tried to work out a way in. For the past week, it had been all he'd thought about—arrive at Krakonite and discover a passage into the castle city. Now he was there, he didn't know what to do. He kept up appearances, though, in front of his men. Rikard prayed a wave of tactical insight would suddenly overcome him, but nothing was forthcoming—not even after two days of watching troop movements in and out of General Volek's great fortress.

Bolt, his loyal lieutenant, was by his side. The other men camped further back. Bolt was a decent man and also from a lowly background.

Renewed movement at the fortified gates to the south of Krakonite caught Rikard's attention. In the past day, Rikard had seen a number of infantry battalions leave and head north. Armed cavalry had followed, and now the gates opened for the third time in two days. Rikard did a double take.

Dozens of infantry and cavalry brigades marched out in tidy columns. Hundreds of soldiers walked together in precise formations to the drumbeat of war. Each column was identical to the next. *What planning,* Rikard thought, *to organise such a military parade.* Where were they headed? He prayed for the safety of those who'd feel this army's steel.

Rikard felt the hairs on the back of his neck stand as thousands of military boots crushed pebbles in their path at the foot of the mountain. They sent a booming echo up and down the valley. Further back new columns emerged. They were pulling enormous catapults. One look at these machines made Rikard tremble. Even the mighty walls of Kronnoburg might be damaged by an onslaught from such weapons. Where was this army going—Phoenix, Athena, Kronnoburg? No, there were treaties and alliances of mutual protection between the old kings of Krakonite and Kronnoburg. Those old kings were dead, though, he reminded himself. Volek had ended the rule of kings at Krakonite when he swept into power on the tailcoats of Avanism. Krakonite was now a republic with General Volek as its leader, and it was an ideological ally with the Republic of Avantolia.

Hundreds of mercenaries came next. Each was carrying a long sword and a shield with the seal of Krakonite—a white broadsword on a black background.

At the head of each mercenary column marched a warrior Rikard was unfamiliar with. Each wore a lavish black robe with what looked like a bloodred lining. From a distance he wasn't quite sure. If it hadn't been for their attire, Rikard could have sworn they were Tasburai. In every other detail, including their weapons, they looked like them. However, Rikard knew from the storybooks that Tasburai wore simple dark brown cottons and wools. They had humble dispositions. These warriors appeared arrogant. Their strides told him that. Rikard didn't fancy his chances against them.

It was a relief to see the final troops leaving Castle Krakonite. The last line of soldiers marched by below. Rikard noticed one soldier slow as though tying his boots. He looked up and dashed away from the army. The deserter sprinted into the gorge below, which led back into the forest. If he could be caught, Rikard might be able to extract important information.

"Let's go," he instructed Bolt. They gathered their weapons and set off. The deserter moved at speed through the undergrowth. Rikard was finding it difficult to keep pace.

"Look, sir," said Bolt. He pointed to armour shed by the deserter. It was thrown under a bush.

Bolt followed the tracks. They were hardly noticeable, deft marks left in the ground. Rikard had been expecting heavy boot prints. A young girl would have stepped with greater weight. Then the tracks disappeared.

"I don't understand, sir," said Bolt.

Rikard did. A boulder caught his attention, and he imagined leaping onto it. With enough speed and momentum, the runner could scale up the shaft of one of the surrounding pine trees and disappear into the thicket of overhead branches.

Still, moving amongst the trees without being spotted would be difficult, so Rikard kept searching for any sign of movement. He tried to imagine where he'd go if he were escaping.

"Sir!" Bolt pushed Rikard aside and unsheathed his sword. The deserter must have been silently observing them. He had leapt down from an overhanging branch and landed beside him. Bolt didn't hesitate. He lunged forwards for a killing stroke.

"No!" Rikard screamed, but it was too late. The thrust was delivered.

Rikard cursed with frustration. "I wanted to question him!"

At the same moment, he realised the deserter, who should have been skewered by the sword thrust, had stopped the blade in one swift manoeuvre. He had slapped his palms against the blade as if applauding.

He fired a fluid upwards kick at the weapon, and it shot into the air. The deserter caught it and flicked it adroitly so that it buried its point into a nearby tree trunk. Bolt was gaping at having been disarmed with such artistry. Then he received a heavy kick in the stomach, and he was sent cartwheeling back into the undergrowth.

Rikard could only admire the skill of his opponent, and he wished they were on the same side. It dawned on him to unsheathe his weapon. Sensing his intent, the deserter somersaulted at him, whipped his blade from its sheath, and buried it into the same pine trunk that housed Bolt's sword.

"I wouldn't," said the deserter. It was a woman's voice, soft but commanding.

Rikard took a step back as she lowered her hood. She was Tasburai and the one who had saved him and his men from the Xettin. "We are indebted to you, Master Tasburai," said Rikard as Bolt struggled back to his feet.

"What are you doing here, Nostvektian? This land is far from Kronnoburg."

"We're on a reconnaissance mission. We are to survey and report back to my superiors," said Rikard. He wondered why he was telling her this. He should be the one asking the questions. She was, however, a Tasburai warrior, and Tasburai were the stuff of legends, myths, and folklore. Rikard remembered listening as a boy to tales of their valour. At one time all he had wanted was to join their order. He had never seen a Tasburai before this, and he wasn't disappointed. She was as beautiful as she was dangerous. Alone she could outfight an entire regiment of his soldiers.

"And what did you see?" she asked.

"An army like no other. I fear for the city they march against," said Rikard.

"Then fear for your people. Krakonite marches upon Kronnoburg."

"The Council of Avantolia is governed by Chancellor Sargon. They will not allow it. They will order General Volek to move his troops back," said Rikard.

"The council sanctions it," she said.

"But...there are treaties and allegiances. They have stood for years! Such an act of war cannot be approved."

"What is your name, Soldier?"

"Captain Rikard Navrosk. This is Lieutenant Bolt. I have more men camped up on the mountain. And how might we address you?"

"My name is Suri-Yi, and I am a Tasburai grandmaster. I am sorry to be the bearer of this news, but Kronnoburg is without protectors or friends."

"Then come with us to Kronnoburg," Rikard blurted. "Advise us. Counsel our leaders. Tasburai are known throughout the world as protectors and upholders of justice. What can be more just than preventing an unjust war?"

"Your point is moot, Captain."

"Then you will not come with us to Kronnoburg?"

The Tasburai hesitated. Rikard wanted to say more to champion his case, but he knew silence could be the best ally.

"I must travel to Duria and to the coast. There are worrying stories coming from the Black Sea," she said.

"Magrog?" asked Rikard.

"I don't know, but these lands are brimming with Xettin. The chief of the Xettin has ordered his tribes to massacre at will. It is a sign. It has always been this way. Before the arrival of the Magrog, the Xettin come down from the mountains. It happened like this before, but I never thought I would see it again in my lifetime."

22

NEW ORDERS

Adan ran the wooden sword into the practice dummy, directing a killing blow at its imaginary heart. "There," he said to Harold.

"Will it kill?" the doe-eyed boy asked him. The comment drew giggles from the other children standing in line behind Harold with their wooden swords at the ready.

"Yes, it will," Adan said. "Here. You try."

Instead Harold froze and stared at the ground. Adan could see other children were visibly scared. Grandmaster Naram-Sin was striding across the yard. Raven and Fur were by his side. *No wonder they're terrified. I would be too.*

"You have been summoned by Chancellor Sargon. Prepare yourself. I will await you at his offices. Don't be late," said Naram-Sin. He walked past Adan and the children. Raven and Fur stopped.

"Better they learn from a real Tasburai," said Raven, and he shoved Adan away.

Adan hadn't wanted to leave his young wards in the hands of Raven and Fur. With more notice, he would have arranged for Saphira to cover, but he didn't know where she was.

Adan collected Tizona from his chambers and strapped on the belt holding the sheath.

Naram-Sin prowled with impatience at the base of the stairwell that led to the private offices of the chancellor. Adan had never been to the council headquarters. It was simultaneously formal, highbrow, stuffy, and self-indulgent.

"Grandmaster Naram-Sin, have I done something wrong?" Adan asked as they began to ascend the spiral stairs.

"Probably," said Naram-Sin.

"Why would the chancellor want to meet me?" Adan asked. They passed a group of young secretaries coming down the staircase. All were dressed in the crisp white-and-blue uniforms of administrative staff. Adan wondered if one had been the secretary to Minister Nezullas, but that was unlikely. She would have been incarcerated in the Oblivion along with the minister. The prim group of ladies smiled at him as they brushed past.

"You'll find out soon enough," replied Naram-Sin.

They were ushered into the chancellor's office by his private secretary. She was a young, attractive woman with a frigid smile.

The high ceilings and ornate decoration in the chancellor's office were a reflection of the rest of the building. Somehow the decadence around him reminded Adan of the Gallows.

Chancellor Sargon was alone and sweeping the city with a long gaze from his high vantage point in the adjoining balcony to his office. He wore the long white robes and red sash of a council member.

"Chancellor, I introduce the apprentice Adan de la Vega," said Naram-Sin.

In spite of his years, Sargon turned quickly. His blue eyes were full of energy. Adan had never imagined he'd look like this. He'd expected a bearded, old, stooped man with the years showing on his lined face.

"It's an honour, Chancellor," said Adan, slightly bowing. He had no idea of the correct protocol, and Grandmaster Naram-Sin had deliberately omitted the detail.

"Nonsense, young man. It is I who am honoured by meeting you. I have always regarded the Tasburai with the utmost respect. It is good to meet with the next generation of adherents."

The statement caught Adan off guard. It was a fine compliment.

"The Tasburai code and daily remembrance are ideals we should all strive for, Vega. They make a person complete. In the balance of the material and the spiritual lies the golden equilibrium," Sargon continued.

He speaks like a Shufi. "It is good to know you value our beliefs and way of life," said Adan. He wasn't sure what he had expected, but the acuteness of the chancellor's comments made him uneasy.

"How can any sane person not?" Sargon glanced at Naram-Sin when he said it.

Adan began to feel insignificant. He was a mere apprentice standing in the shadow of a great leader. It would be best to only speak when necessary. Suri-Yi had once told him, "Every person appears intelligent until they open their mouth."

"I asked Naram-Sin to bring me the most skilled and capable apprentice from Hamara. I wanted one who had shown great desire and commitment to hard work and who, in his opinion, was destined for great things," said Sargon.

Adan stared at Master Naram-Sin. As usual he ignored Adan.

"Master Naram-Sin has the utmost respect for your abilities and has selected you above all others," said Sargon. "I have a very special and important mission, and since you are the best amongst your peers, the choice was obvious." Sargon swept into his grand armchair, which was more like a throne. "Your former master, Suri-Yi, was a formidable Tasburai. She served Avantolia and its people for more than three decades. She wielded her sword and fine intellect to uphold justice in the name of the republic. She was our foremost weapon...until she was declared a subversive counterrevolutionary. Did it surprise you when you heard the news?"

"Yes."

"Did you believe it?"

"I...not at first. When Grandmaster Naram-Sin told us, though, there was nothing to do but denounce her," said Adan. *Choose your words with care.*

"I appreciate it was difficult for you to believe in her subversion, but we had no choice once we learnt of her involvement with the Shining Fist."

"What will become of her?" Adan asked.

"Once she is captured, we both know there is only one place for criminals and traitors to the cause of Avanism."

"The Oblivion," said Adan. *They're staring at me and studying me. They're observing how I react.* "All criminals must be processed through the Oblivion for crimes against the Avanist Republic."

"Correct," Sargon replied, and he flicked back a tuft of hair from his shoulder.

A raven landed on the balcony and eyed him before flying away. If only he could fly from this place. Master Naram-Sin stood beside him.

"Adan de la Vega, you will accompany Master Naram-Sin to Castle Krakonite. You will receive further instructions there about your involvement in the campaign against Kronnoburg. However, your personal mission is to capture the traitor Suri-Yi," said Sargon.

Adan wanted to unsheathe Tizona and put an end to these lies, but his hand remained still. He calmed himself. “I accept the mission, Chancellor.”

PART II

23

PARTY PLANS

"What would you prefer, my love? Sweet honey or passionate magnolia?" asked Elsta.

"The honey, my dear. It brings out the natural colour of your hair," said Theodorus.

Elsta turned to her royal dresser. "The ribbons for my hair will be the colour of sweet honey."

Theodorus had been so helpful in planning for Kronnoburg's summer solstice ball. He had been content to listen to the painstaking details she'd planned for the grand day. He had heard her describe every element of her dress and go through the finery of the ceremony. Elsta wondered at times if she was imposing too much on him. He did, after all, have his princely duties to perform.

"Your Highness," Karlsen interrupted.

Elsta wondered what he was doing there but remembered she had commandeered the office and meeting quarters where her ministers resided. The summer solstice ball was the most important event on the calendar, though, so it made sense to use her government's offices to organise the great ceremony.

The first minister moved aside a row of silk dresses and pulled out a thick dossier. It was stuffed with important but tedious papers. "We've had further reports of our merchant navy losing ships along the straits of the Black Sea."

"I'm sure they'll turn up," replied Elsta with a nonchalant wave. "What do you think, my love?"

Theodorus leant forwards and took the dossier. He flicked through a few pages before pushing the papers back to Karlsen. "If there was any trouble, Minister Karlsen, my cousin Heraclius would know of it. He'd send a message from Duria. The sailors will show up. They're probably off for a bit of fun on one of our Athenian islands. It gets rather lonely out at sea. Who can blame them?"

"Your Highness, the merchant navy transports vital supplies to the city. It delivers its cargo at the Spice Port before items are moved along the Merchants' Road. With the latest disappearance, the city will start to run short of certain food items," said Karlsen.

"Such as?" asked Elsta.

"I'm not entirely sure which items, but I know at least one of the ships was carrying Eastern spices," said Karlsen.

"What? No garnished chicken? I jest, First Minister. Send out a scouting party along the Merchants' Road. Get a feel for what's happening out there," said Theodorus.

"We did," said Karlsen. "Captain Hakar returned with half the party. They found abandoned villages and signs of a brutal massacre at the hamlet of Hunderfin. The other half of the patrol, under Captain Navrosk, is on its way further up the Merchants' Road towards Krakonite," said Karlsen.

"It is sad to hear about villagers killing one another. However, until Captain Navrosk's party returns, there's no need to fret," said Theodorus.

Elsta's king-to-be was an authoritative presence and put the minister firmly in his place.

"There is also the matter of the steady flow of villagers arriving daily at the gates," said Reider. He had entered and sat listening quietly.

"Why are we letting them in?" asked Theodorus.

"These people are quite distraught," he replied.

"What in the world can be so traumatic? They just need a bit of cheer in their lives. The summer solstice ball will soon make them forget their melancholy." Theodorus turned to the chamberlain and said, "Be sure to give the people three free meals on the day of the ball. Let it not be said the royals did not care." The chamberlain nodded and retreated once more to the room's fringes.

Reider continued. "They relay stories of beasts. Xettin marauding through villages and along the Merchants' Road."

"Xettin? My grandmother used to tell me fairy tales about Xettin, Ifreet, and Tasburai. They are stories to entertain and frighten little children. Come, Minister, we have to live in the real world," said Elsta.

"Did Captain Hakar and his company see any Xettin?" Theodorus asked.

"No," said Karlsen.

"Ifreet?"

"No."

"Tasburai, maybe?"

"No, Your Highness."

"There you have it," said Theodorus. "Now let us return to planning the ball."

"Your Highness—"

"My fiancé is right. Not now, First Minister. Come back tomorrow. We might continue this discussion after lunch. Right now we have to finalise the colour palettes for the royal guests attending the reception. Leave us!" said Elsta.

***

The carriage crawled over the pebblestone path. Elsta felt every bump despite being seated on plush velvet cushions, and it was hotter than she remembered it being recently. The rainy season was approaching, and humidity was increasing. The uneven road was awfully uncomfortable. She made a mental note to speak with her cabinet about improving it. Elsta had no choice but to come down this route and visit the Shrine of the Blessed Saint. It was an integral part of the summer festivities. As royalty, it was expected of her.

The carriage stopped.

"What is it?" Elsta asked her chamberlain.

"Allow me a moment to investigate, Your Highness."

The chamberlain returned with a grim expression. "The road to the shrine is blocked, Your Highness."

"Why?"

"It's the villagers who have been arriving daily in the city. They have no food and have gone to the shrine seeking provisions from the priest," said the chamberlain.

"Feed them then," said Elsta.

"The shrine has no food left. Its stores are depleted. The priest has already distributed what surplus he had to the people."

This was unwelcome news. Elsta hadn't realised the city was running short on supplies. Was that what her ministers had been trying to tell her earlier?

"Remind me to send provisions from the royal store to the shrine. Now clear the road."

The Royal Guard pushed forwards on their steeds and down the narrow alley to the plaza housing the shrine. The buildings along the alley hugged the road, and soon her carriage moved in shadow. It was almost as though dusk had fallen.

Lines of Nostvektians were pinned against the alley walls. Their hungry eyes were on her carriage as it went by. Elsta waved, but no one returned the gesture. *How rude! I am their queen-to-be. They must learn to love me, for I will be like a mother to them.*

The carriage came to a halt outside the shrine. Elsta felt the cold, hard stares of the people.

"Long live the princess." It was a single voice in the crowd. No one joined the chorus.

The sound of hooves pounding cobblestones caught her attention as she alighted. It was Theodorus. He was accompanied by Captain Hakar and a troop of his men.

"Elsta, my love, I hope I did not keep you waiting," Theodorus said. A radiant smile was on his face as he leapt off his black stallion.

"No, my love. We have just arrived. Come, let us complete the ceremony together."

Theodorus took her by the arm, and they approached the shrine.

Hakar addressed his troops. "Get these peasants out of my sight."

Elsta looked back one last time before going in. Her people were hungry and frightened.

24

IFREET

Leaving the best thieving gang in the world was hard. It reminded her of pulling out a splinter from under her fingernail. It hurt. Father had sent them to look after her, and now she'd abandoned them and Kronnoburg. They'd realise it by the time they were up in the morning, but she'd have put plenty of ground between them by then.

It seemed she was the only one going south along the Merchants' Road. All other folk were coming towards Kronnoburg. Most of them weren't in good shape. Their faces were as cold as a morning frost. They were skeletal forms shuffling down the road with their torn and muddied rags hanging on their sorry backs.

"Hey, girl! Where you headed? It's not safe in the south," said a father leading his family of four.

"Why? What will I find?"

"Misery. Death."

"Did you see any tree folk?" asked Ylva.

"No. They're housed up pretty tight in the forest, but Volek will get 'em. He's sending an army out the gates of Krakonite. Nothing is safe outside them walls of Kronnoburg. Come with us, child. The Nostvektians will take you in. The House of Mik has always protected the folk who live off the land."

"I'll be all right. You head on straight up this road. You'll soon see the great walls of Kronnoburg over the next ridge," said Ylva.

"May the spirits of the forest protect you, child," said the father.

The number of folk she saw dwindled. When evening came, there wasn't a soul to be found on the road or in the forest. Everything was dead as ash.

She'd trapped a plump rabbit, skinned it, and cooked it in her mother's old steel pot. Then she hauled herself up a great cedar tree so she wasn't exposed by sleeping on the forest floor. There was no telling what folk or beast might pass by and give her a kick in the night. The cedar had a trunk that ten tree folk could join their arms around. Up she went until she found a branch wide enough to make a bed for the night.

It was a warm evening. She thought about the gang and how far back they were. She was sure they'd be tracking her. In many ways she wanted them to find her. Being on her own had never been to her liking.

She soon settled down and fell asleep. Sometime during the night, the snapping of twigs on the forest floor woke Ylva. She didn't move. She just lay still in the groove she'd settled in on the branch. She stared up at starlight, wishing she could fly and be gone from this place. She heard the sounds of boots marching and crunching twigs and leaves below. Who was it—enemy or friend? For one joyous moment she thought it was Hallbjorn the Bear and she'd hear his voice booming out and calling her name. It didn't come.

She remained still. Finally curiosity got the better of her, and she peered over the branch to look down at the forest floor.

They were soldiers but not the type she'd ever seen before. These were massive brutes with faces like nightmares, jaws of a wolf, and huge foreheads. Xettin! The stories were true. It was no wonder the villages around Kronnoburg had emptied. With such evil monsters swarming through the country, every villager would run for safety behind Kronnoburg's great walls.

Ylva couldn't run. Luckily they hadn't seen her. She could hear her heart pounding. *It will pass.* She was one of the tree folk and bold as the sun. *Nothing scares me.*

The Xettin continued to file by below until the last of their number marched past the cedar. Ylva followed their progress away from her until she couldn't see them.

Ylva rolled back to her lying position, but as she did, a figure caught her eye. She froze. Staring directly at her from the branch of a close-by cedar was a form. Fiery coloured, its shape shifted. With deep eye sockets, the slits were red, and where there should have been the white of the eye, it was orange. It looked like a man, flickering as though he were the flame of a candle in wind.

Ifreet! It was a demon that Ylva had never believed existed. Its face creased in a wicked smile. It leapt through the air and hovered before landing on Ylva's branch.

The hairs on the back of her neck felt as if they were about to jump off her skin. She scrambled back.

The Ifreet came towards her. It was not quite walking and not quite gliding. "Child." Its septic voice crackled.

"I'm no child." Ylva felt as if she'd suddenly woken from a trance.

The Ifreet stretched its arm out, and it reached further than it should have. Like a piece of elastic, it drew closer to her. Ylva could see its black fingernails. They were more like claws. The veins in its arm pulsated as though volcanic lava flowed through them.

Ylva was on all fours and scrambling. The Ifreet had not moved, but its arm kept coming.

"Dear child," said the Ifreet, and an evil smile spread across its face.

She'd backed herself up against the tree trunk but ran out of space. Its arm kept coming. The fingertips now glowed molten orange.

She had no weapons, no space, and no time. *Is this how I die?*

Then she remembered she did have a weapon. It was placed beside her blanket. Ylva sprang forwards and rolled under the outstretched arm. She snatched the sword and raised it. Down it came. The Orlisium blade sliced through the Ifreet's arm.

"Argh!" The Ifreet screamed like the wailing wind. It looked at its arm. Only a stump remained from the elbow downwards. Its face anguished, it stared at the blade and then at Ylva.

"Kill child...next time." The one-armed Ifreet leapt from the cedar, glided through the air, and landed on the next tree. It was soon gone from her view.

"Great Spirit of the Cedar, I thank you."

Ylva dropped the sword. Her hands were trembling. The severed arm of the Ifreet had already turned to ash on the forest floor.

25

FORBIDDEN

The feast General Volek put on for Grandmaster Naram-Sin's arrival at Krakonite was notable. The banqueting hall brimmed with guests—rowdy soldiers, mercenaries, and petrified entertainers thrown into a den of wolves. *They won't last long,* thought Adan.

Drink and food flowed like a gushing fountain. There was enough for everyone to gorge. The mood was merry.

"Allies of the republic but so different," said Saphira.

Adan suggested he and Saphira remain as far from the boisterous guests as possible. They took discreet seats arranged near the rear of the hall. The only fellow diners around them were asleep or in a drunken, somnambulant state.

"I haven't heard anyone mention revolution or subversion since we arrived. It's a different world here, even though they profess to follow the ideals of Avanism," said Saphira.

"Raven and Fur are enjoying themselves," said Adan. The two boys were drunk on wine—an intoxicant forbidden to the Tasburai—and their behaviour grew rowdier by the minute.

"They're going to embarrass themselves," said Saphira.

"Let them make fools of themselves. Look, even Cardaro is smiling watching them try to stand straight with chairs balanced on their shoulders," said Adan.

"Who are they?" Saphira motioned towards a group of warriors seated beside Grandmaster Naram-Sin and General Volek. They weren't military. They were more akin to Tasburai. Adan recognised them. He had fought them in the Temple of Remembrance. The memory of the laughing voice inside his head and his loss of control was still raw.

"They call themselves the Hawarij," said Adan.

"Never heard of them," said Saphira. "What's their role in this?"

"Suri-Yi and I fought them in the temple. They attacked us after the morning remembrance. If they are here, it might mean Naram-Sin knew of the attack. Perhaps he even organised it."

"We are Tasburai. It is against the code," said Saphira.

"We are Tasburai. Is he?"

"You say too much," said Saphira and placed her fingers on his lips.

Moves were afoot, changes were taking place, and the ground was shifting about him. Adan didn't know what to do. He needed Suri-Yi's advice, but he would not see his master until Kronnoburg, and he was sure tough choices would be necessary before then. If he didn't understand the implications of his decisions, how would he know how to choose? *I must keep Naram-Sin's trust, but I must not break my vows to Suri-Yi or the order. Even if we are the last of Tasburai, we are Tasburai, and I will not compromise.*

The Hawarij were cloaked in plush black fabrics. Rich layers of red silk lined their robes. Their ostentatious dress was at odds with his order. Only their magnificent Orlisium swords resembled those of the Tasburai.

"They don't smile very much," said Saphira.

"Some would say the same about us."

Saphira gave him a gorgeous beam.

Bong! A brass gong silenced the guests. General Volek stood up and eyed the room with a commanding glare. He was a tall man with a broad, smooth face and a military haircut shaved close at the sides and back.

"On behalf of all Krakonite, I welcome Grandmaster Naram-Sin," said Volek.

Cheers went up around the hall.

"He's popular here," said Adan.

"Regular guest apparently," said Saphira.

Volek raised his glass. "A toast to the success of Avanism."

The night air after the feast was cold, and it bit deep. Adan wrapped his cloak tight. Castle Krakonite was still, and few ventured out this evening. The merriment of the feast took its toll. Preparing to march the next day, soldiers slept like babies through the night. It was the perfect time for Adan to discover what General Volek and Grandmaster Naram-Sin had planned. Seeing the Hawarij had disturbed him. They had tried to kill him and his master, and he didn't doubt they would try it again. Only this time he would be better prepared. Suri-Yi had said he had great ability but had to learn to check his anger. Without that control he would never attain the rank of master.

Adan had many questions. What would he find at Kronnoburg? What was the looming war Minister Nezullas had spoken of? How did Ab Isaac know his mother? The key was to find Suri-Yi. She knew the answers, and he was now halfway to Kronnoburg.

Perched like a crow on a wall above the battlements, Adan was reminded why he didn't like heights. The main yard in the central castle quadrant was deathly still. The few soldiers on duty lay prostrate from the evening's drink. He moved towards the entrance gate.

General Volek's offices were in the western tower. Armed guards surrounded it, and to Adan's disappointment, they were wide-awake.

Adan glided over the battlements and took up a position hanging upside down over the entrance gate to the western tower. The next patrol should be coming any moment. *There.* Adan dropped and straightened himself. He landed with his feet on the heads of both soldiers. With firm kicks to their foreheads, he knocked them out, tied them up, and locked them in the gatehouse. *Keep moving. I don't have much time.*

Two more soldiers were at the end of the corridor. Adan raised his hood. Face covered, he rounded the corner and stumbled as though drunk.

"Hey, who goes there?"

Adan tripped, stumbled, and caught himself before falling. "Got a drink?"

The soldiers approached him together. *Good. Easier to deal with them.*

One grabbed his arm and yanked him up. "Useless drunk."

Adan disposed of the first soldier with a punch to the face. He jarred the man's nose back into his head, and it cracked and broke. The second fell as Tizona's hilt smashed his forehead. Adan tidied up and entered through the doorway. *Keep moving.*

Adan found a small crack in the wooden boards overlooking Volek's offices. As he peered down, the general and Master Naram-Sin were deep in conversation.

"Once Kronnoburg falls, we will have access to the Forbidden Quarter."

"Do you know what's there?" asked Volek.

"Chancellor Sargon believes it is filled with enough riches and minerals to build an Avanist empire," said Naram-Sin. "The Nostvektians have foolishly protected the sanctity of the place when they should have exploited it. The ancients chose the race with the least ambition to be the custodians of the Forbidden Quarter."

"Maybe that was their purpose," said Volek.

"We cannot live by the wishes of the ancients."

Volek walked over to a map hanging on the western wall of his offices. He drew a line across the name Kronnoburg, and a smile filled his face. "Not long now, Naram-Sin."

"How many men do you have inside?"

"For every twenty villagers entering the city, there are one of my men, so there will be hundreds of mercenaries within Kronnoburg. Its walls will not fall. They will be opened from within."

Naram-Sin nodded and joined him beside the map.

"I'm looking forward to getting married again. I hear Princess Elsta is quite the beauty," said Volek.

"You don't tire of beautiful women."

"A man should have some vices."

Naram-Sin turned away, as though deep in thought.

Seeing the Tasburai master's lack of interest in the subject, the general's mood also turned sombre as he pointed to the Black Sea on his map. "Have you heard the stories about merchant ships disappearing in the Black Sea?"

"They are only stories," said Naram-Sin.

"How can you be so sure? If the Magrog were to return..."

"We defeated them. We destroyed their civilisation and annihilated every single one of them. I was there. I should know," said Naram-Sin.

"And they say I have blood on my hands."

"We did what had to be done," said Naram-Sin.

"And you would do it again? Exterminate an entire race?"

"Of course."

Naram-Sin's reply sent a shudder through Adan. Suri-Yi had told him of the battles she had fought against the Magrog but had never mentioned the annihilation of an entire race. Was she part of what Naram-Sin did?

"You will have your wish at Kronnoburg. The Nostvektians are soft. We will squash them," said Volek.

"Are the Hawarij ready?" asked Naram-Sin.

"They have undergone the physical and mental training as you ordered. They are ready to fight, and they are ready to serve your ideals. They are a band of bloody narrow-minded zealots. These warriors are willing to die for their cause, which, quite frankly, I don't believe in myself. Still, they make very efficient fighters, and that's all I ask of you at this time. Just make sure there is no interference from the Tasburai Order. They have a history of unravelling the best-laid plans, and I don't want them anywhere near mine."

"The Tasburai are no longer a threat now Suri-Yi is out of the picture," said Naram-Sin.

"But she's not. She continues to show up."

"Where?" asked Naram-Sin.

"A few sightings. She's been massacring Xettin as though they were children with wooden swords."

"Xettin?"

"Yes."

"The Xettin went back to their mountain caves after the Magrog were defeated. They haven't been seen in the lowlands since."

"They have been showing up these past few weeks. My men have come across them. There has even been talk of sighting an Ifreet."

"Impossible," sneered Naram-Sin.

"Nothing is impossible. You more than anyone should know that. For now it seems she is wiping out Xettin wherever she finds them. Truly her skill with Shamshir is unparalleled."

Adan stopped breathing and strained to hear what they had to say about his master.

"Always was. The Magrog used to quake with fear when they saw her. Imagine that! Even the Ifreet were terrified of Suri-Yi. She was truly exceptional," said Naram-Sin. He had a smile on his face as he said it.

"You were close?"

"Very."

Adan couldn't reconcile Suri-Yi and Naram-Sin being close. They hated each other and were so different in every conceivable way.

Master Naram-Sin had a faraway look like a man watching sunset on the horizon. "It was a long time ago," said Naram-Sin. "We have to think about tomorrow. I will leave with the Hawarij at dawn."

26

CHOICES

An ominous black mark was etched on the green landscape. It was the army from Krakonite camped on the forest edge. Suri-Yi sat hidden in the undergrowth of a nearby hill with her Nostvektian travel companions.

Captain Navrosk returned from his scouting mission. His face was a mask of worry.

"That bad?" said Suri-Yi.

"Volek's army is thousands strong. It stretches back as far as the eye can see. Regular infantry, mercenaries. They're all heading for Kronnoburg," said Navrosk.

Chancellor Sargon had not wasted time marshalling the Krakonite forces to fight his war by proxy. The old politician was playing a game Suri-Yi did not understand.

Why send an army against Kronnoburg when its walls were impenetrable? She was missing the full picture. Her hand went to the hilt of her sword, Shamshir. The coolness and familiarity of the grip gave her comfort.

"Captain, this land is familiar to you. You know it better than Volek's army. Cut through the hills, and arrive a few days earlier than Volek's forces," said Suri-Yi.

"What then?"

Indeed. Kronnoburg's walls had never been breached. The ancients built impressive defences to protect the gateway to the Forbidden Quarter. If an army did get past the outer and inner walls of Kronnoburg, they would need to pass through the narrow straits of Burg before the gates of the Forbidden Quarter were visible. That was no easy feat. The natural obstacles made marching an army into such an area a fool's errand. She had been there once long ago. King Usk Mik and Major Ulfheart had taken her to gaze upon the magnificent gates to the Forbidden Quarter from across the straits.

"Mobilise the defences, raise the banners, and send birds and riders to Heraclius of Duria and the Maharaja Jagbir Singh of Pathan. Tell them to despatch a regiment each. We must display a united front. We do not need numbers. The walls will hold, but we must have their banners. I fear Avanism has an unquenchable thirst, and it is time we stopped it," said Suri-Yi.

"Why would Heraclius and the maharaja come to our aid?"

"Because Suri-Yi has asked. We stood together many years ago to repel the forces of the Magrog. Lifelong friendships were forged, and those friendships have deep roots."

"Avantolia was still a kingdom back then?" asked Navrosk.

"Yes, the last monarch was King Sanjar from the House of Seljuk. The war with the Magrog destroyed him. He lost many members of his family, Avantolia's finances were depleted, and his will to live and rule ended. A period of instability followed. He kept up the appearance of grandeur only to cause resentment amongst the people. At the time, a group of young, ambitious courtiers seized power in a revolution."

"Sargon?" said Navrosk.

"Yes. King Sanjar was killed along with the last remaining members of his family. The revolutionaries established a republic and carried the support of the people. But then...then they gradually lost sight of the aim of the revolution—justice. Maintaining their power became more important than the Avanist cause they professed to follow. They are now worse than the regime they overthrew," said Suri-Yi.

The young Nostvektians silently observed her. "Is there any way we can convince you to return with us to Kronnoburg?" asked Navrosk.

"My journey must be north to Duria."

The young captain lowered his gaze in disappoint ment.

Suri-Yi reached out and touched his arm. "The people of Kronnoburg will need the strength of you and your men," she said.

Navrosk looked up, and a weak smile formed upon his face. He nodded.

"Grandmaster Suri-Yi, some robed fighters broke off from the main army and went into the forest," said Bolt.

"Like Tasburai?"

"Yes, but also different. More ostentatious," said Bolt.

The Hawarij fighting alongside Volek's forces only added to her list of problems. It meant Naram-Sin was accompanying Volek, but it might also mean Adan was with Naram-Sin. She longed to see her apprentice again. Only she hadn't expected him to arrive so soon. She had wanted to meet Heraclius first and then journey back.

"What lies within that part of the forest?" asked Suri-Yi.

"Nothing but outlaws," said Navrosk.

"Outlaws?"

"Criminals led by a man called Olaf. They call him Olaf the Generous. He is a thief who steals from the rich..." said Navrosk.

"To redistribute to the poor," Suri-Yi finished.

So Olaf did what he threatened those long years ago. She remembered his words in the letter he wrote to her: "What is needed is a redistribution of wealth for the benefit of the needy. If the rich won't willingly do it, I'll force them." Back then Olaf made many bold claims, but he had apparently gone through with this one.

"Sorry?" said Navrosk.

"Olaf the Generous, if that is the name he goes by today, was known to me," said Suri-Yi.

"You know this dangerous outlaw?"

"Years ago he was a flamboyant mercenary who led and won many key battles against the Magrog. His victories prevented the Magrog from reaching the walls of Kronnoburg. Every Nostvektian alive today owes his or her safety to Olaf...the Generous."

The young Nostvektians glanced about. Olaf being a hero didn't fit into their world view. Their puzzled looks brought a wry smile to her face. It was refreshing to see emotion so openly expressed. It was so different from Avantolia. Out here honesty prevailed, and it was worth fighting for.

"What will you do, Grandmaster Suri-Yi?" asked Navrosk.

North. I must head to Duria, meet with Heraclius, and assess the threat across the sea. "If Olaf is in that forest surrounded by Volek's forces, I must help him. The man has a good, sound heart. He is a caring and chivalrous leader of his people."

"And then?"

A smile crossed her face. The Nostvektians did like to ask a lot of questions. At times they resembled excitable children. "If I leave the forest alive, I will head for Duria."

27

THE KEY

The ceremonies for the upcoming summer solstice were endless. Elsta didn't know how other Nostvektian royals put up with it. Earlier in the week she had been kneeling at the Shrine of the Blessed Saint. Today it was the Great Hall of Antiquity. The vast museum was housed within the central plaza of Kronnoburg.

Elsta had managed to keep the priests on time, and things were wrapped up quickly.

"I never imagined there'd be so many ceremonies," said Theodorus.

She had to admit that the priest's voice had a somnolent effect, but they were only performing their ritual function. Many of these men and women she had known from childhood. They had performed ceremonies with her father, mother, and other siblings. Elsta felt a pang of embarrassment at Theodorus's words.

"Come, Theodorus. You must see the key," said Elsta, taking him by the elbow.

"Key for what?"

"The gates to the Forbidden Quarter."

Elsta and Theodorus walked with arms interlocked into the circular map room, where shelves of books and scrolls dating back dozens of generations surrounded them. An oval table in the middle held a brass map of the world with each region etched onto it.

"Look, dear. Here we are," said Elsta, touching the engraving of Kronnoburg.

Theodorus put both her hands in his and leant forwards and whispered, "King Theseus and Queen Mik—the rulers of Kronnoburg. How does that sound?"

She felt a tingle up her spine. "I like it."

Theodorus kissed her forehead. "Me too."

For a moment Elsta was lost in his deep eyes and charming smile. Then when she noticed some of the priests walking by in the connecting hallway, she regained her composure.

Slipping her hands out of his, she turned back to the table. "That table, my dear, is over five hundred years old. One was left in every city by the ancients. There is one in Duria, Avantolia, and Pathan. I'd even hazard a guess there is one at Krakonite, but those brutes have probably destroyed it by now. A map of the world, left for us."

The prince spread his fingers out across the portion indicating the Black Sea. "Here is my home—the islands of Athenia. We're the only thing after Duria and before the straits of the Black Sea from which sailed the Magrog, bringing death and destruction in their wake."

"Scary," said Elsta.

"Don't worry, dear. If they ever showed their ugly faces again, I'd skewer them with my sword." Theodorus unsheathed his weapon, mimicked a defensive posture and a block, and then sprang a counterattack against an imaginary enemy.

What fine swordplay. He was a skilled fighter. She had seen how he'd despatched the bandits. She warranted he could even best Captain Hakar, which would make him the best swordsman in the land—a fine title to bestow upon a king.

"Whoosh...one Magrog battalion falls. Smash...another goes. This is how it's done, my dear."

Theodorus is so dashing. I bet he could teach the commoner Navrosk a thing or two about fencing. Wait, why am I thinking about Rikard Navrosk? She shrugged the thought off.

"The greatest sword in the land defeats the evil Magrog with a single hand," said Theodorus. His blade cut through the air. Then he sheathed it and knelt down before her, taking her hand in his. "And so he saves the beautiful princess from peril...once again." There was a cheeky smile upon his face when he added those last words.

Elsta felt goose pimples up her arms. She was still blushing when she said, "Let's pray I don't have to be saved too often. Come, let me show you the key."

They strolled past a number of artefacts on exhibit. This included a Durian sword said to belong to the great-grandfather of Heraclius, which his son had given as a gift of friendship to the Nostvektians. In another display was a ring said to belong to the family of the last king of Avantolia—the family of Seljuk. It was funny how it always looked like half a ring to Elsta. She wondered where the other piece was. She moved on until she reached the key. It was placed within a glass-framed display case and hung down from the ceiling.

"The key," said Elsta. The dull metallic object was oblong and about the length of a grown man's hand.

"It doesn't even look like a key. More a metal offcut from a scrapyard."

"When the ancients left the miracle of the Forbidden Quarter as a trust to Kronnoburg, they sealed its entrance with two master keys. This piece of scrap you refer to is one. There is one other key in the world. It was entrusted to the Tasburai Order for safekeeping."

"So now you believe in the Tasburai?"

"It's the story I have been told."

"Key or no key, a sturdy battering ram will open any gate."

"Not these ones. I have seen them from afar. Father took me when I was a child. They rise up to the sky and are as wide as an entire fort. No, these gates cannot be opened by force."

"So where is the other key?" asked Theodorus.

"Lost in the world."

"My love, this is beginning to sound like a fairy tale filled with legendary warriors, powerful demons, and sorcerers. Do you believe any of it?" said Theodorus.

He has a point. She didn't really believe in the tales, but they made for exciting bedtime stories. She had enjoyed them as a child when her father and mother narrated them to her. Her parents had explained how the Forbidden Quarter was a blessing for her people. The River of Mercy flowed from it. Passing underground and into Kronnoburg, it irrigated her lands and replenished the bellies of her people and their livestock. The ancients had promised that whoever drank from the river would never go thirsty, and it would cure him or her of all ailments. They also said the river would continue to flow so long as it lay undisturbed. The day humans interfered with it, the flow would stop. It was truly the source of life.

"I'll tell you what, my dear, when I'm king, I'll order an expedition to the Forbidden Quarter for you, me, and a troop of our finest soldiers. Let's go and find out what's really behind those gates."

"No, my love. It must not be tampered with."

"Come, come."

"No!"

Elsta hadn't expected to raise her voice so sharply. The mood between them soured, and Theodorus looked away in a morose and unsociable manner. Elsta stared at the key.

It's a good thing the other key is lost.

28

HAWARIJ

Lined in neat rows, wearing immaculate robes billowing in the breeze, and holding finely polished swords glittering in the sunlight, the Hawarij looked a formidable fighting force. Adan stood amongst them. He was dressed not as Tasburai but as Hawarij. Adan didn't dispute the uniform was impressive. It just wasn't in keeping with Tasburai traditions. *But I must play this game. My master has instructed me to.*

Glancing across at Saphira, he thought she looked beautiful in her new robes. She always did, however, whatever she wore.

Saphira had urged him to wear the robes. It had been a difficult choice. "Fit in, Adan. The time of the Tasburai is over. We have to look forward, and it is now the era of the Hawarij. By being part of this new order, we can still achieve all we dreamt of, peace, justice, and goodwill towards others. Yes, we have to struggle to begin with, but once the fighting is over, there will be a better world for all to enjoy."

Can I hold firm to what I believe in, even when my best friend is headed in the opposite direction?

He had kept secret from Saphira the instructions Suri-Yi had given him. So when Saphira spoke with such enthusiasm about the Hawarij, he could only pretend to agree with her.

Raven and Fur were in their element. The other Hawarij, men and some women, came from diverse kingdoms, though most were inhabitants of Krakonite. Grandmaster Naram-Sin had let the Tasburai fall into disrepair whilst investing his time in creating this extreme order of puritanical warriors.

Grandmaster Naram-Sin and General Volek stepped onto the balcony, glaring down into the courtyard where Adan and the others were assembled. The Hawarij waited, eager for their instructions.

"My fellow Hawarij, rejoice. Today is the dawn of a new age. It is our time, so let us grasp the future with both hands and mould it to our needs. Just as the Tasburai had their moment in history, so will you," said Naram-Sin. The Tasburai elder had assumed Hawarij attire. "Our beliefs take the best from the Tasburai teachings and ignore what was weak. We show no mercy to our enemies. We are pure in our righteousness and uncompromising. The Tasburais' leniency and pluralism caused their downfall. We will not let this happen."

Our kindness didn't cause our downfall. It was our cruelty.

"Our faith is strong. We will reshape the world in the image we choose. Today we are the sword that cuts through Kronnoburg. All hail Avanism!"

"Hail!" The collection of voices sent an earsplitting sound around the fortress walls.

General Volek stepped forwards. "Grandmaster Naram-Sin, I thank you. For too long Kronnoburg has lived off the fat of the Forbidden Quarter. The River of Mercy makes their land green and fertile, whilst we survive in a harsh, barren environment. Why? The House of Mik is weak. It is ruled by a girl with no world experience. Its people are wealthy and ignorant. They live carefree, useless lives. Why? We as Avanists have grown tired of this. We will consume the fat of Kronnoburg and make Avanism stronger. Together Avantolia and Krakonite will consume the kingdoms of the world. To Heraclius in the north and to the maharaja in the south, I send warning. We are coming."

He's even crazier than the grandmaster.

"You, my friends, are the vanguard of revolutionary change. You are the elite foot soldiers that will rip open Kronnoburg's defences." Volek stopped. Looking left and right, he weighed the impact of his words before continuing. "As for the impregnable walls of Kronnoburg, let's just say we've made arrangements. One final item. Loyalty and dedication are vital in any army. Last night some of my best soldiers let me down."

The gates below the balcony opened. Four blinking soldiers emerged into the sunlight. They were armed with swords and shields. *They're the ones I disarmed last night.*

"An intruder entered my private office. It was the role of these four to guard it. They failed."

Volek turned to Naram-Sin. "They are yours," he said and departed.

With a single swift movement, Naram-Sin leapt from the balcony and landed in the midst of the four soldiers. They backed off with shields raised and swords at the ready. Naram-Sin had no weapons.

The Hawarij around Adan remained still. No one moved or uttered a single sentence. Adan could sense the soldiers' fear.

The first soldier brave enough to attack Naram-Sin thrust his sword forwards, hoping to catch the grand-master off guard. Naram-Sin moved to one side, grabbed the soldier's wrist, kicked his shield away, and violently snapped the soldier's arm around in a circle. The soldier flipped over and landed on his back. Naram-Sin's boot rose and fell, breaking the man's windpipe. Adan heard the bones crack in the man's throat, and then the soldier's body went limp. Naram-Sin took the soldier's sword.

The other three backed off. Naram-Sin shrugged and threw the sword away. He stepped towards them. The second soldier had his windpipe pulled out. The third had his head split open, and the fourth had his back broken. All four lay dead. It had only taken a few seconds.

Naram-Sin looked straight at Adan.

29

OLD FRIENDS

As soon as Suri-Yi entered the enclave where the forest folk lived, his imprint was unmistakable. The place had Olaf written all over it. The meticulously prepared defences, the archers overhead in the trees, and the traps lying in wait on the forest floor—she'd seen it all before. She and Olaf had devised the same traps against the Magrog.

Olaf had never served in a conventional army, but one would have never known. He must have been the world's most organised mercenary.

Suri-Yi spotted six archers perched up in the trees. She knew they weren't going to fire. It wasn't Olaf's style. He wasn't one to shoot first and ask questions later—a trait she respected. *If only I had been so charitable over the years.*

"Stop!" It had taken longer than she'd expected, but the instruction finally came. Suri-Yi raised her hands and showed her empty palms.

A young man's voice spoke out. "Who goes there?"

"A friend of Olaf's," said Suri-Yi.

"State your name, and I'll decide whether you be friend or foe."

"Grandmaster Suri-Yi of the Tasburai."

Even though Suri-Yi couldn't see them, she could discern the whispers and flurry of tiny movements in the trees.

"Wait...Don't move."

Suri-Yi waited. Soon there was another voice. It was older and more mature. "What did Suri-Yi tell Olaf when they watched the Magrog retreat across the Black Sea?"

She remembered it well. "Olaf, you are a courageous but self-interested man. In bad times such as these, that makes you a good man. But to be a great man, you must learn to be generous," said Suri-Yi.

The leaves of a hedge parted ten yards ahead, and Olaf the Generous emerged grinning. "I took your advice."

The cheeky, boyish smile and ruffled hair were still there. Though he was quite grey from the years. He'd grown a beard, and it made him look mature and wise—important traits for one who leads many.

"Suri-Yi, you haven't changed. An orchid frozen in ice." He embraced her.

"And you..."

"Yes, yes. You can say it openly. I've aged. What do you think about the beard? Nice touch, eh? My late wife, bless her, convinced me to grow it when this lot made me headman. She said folk would take me seriously if I looked the part."

"A wise woman. I'm sorry to hear about your loss."

"Thank you. She was the joy of my life and a fine lady. So what brings the world's greatest warrior to our humble wood?"

Others started emerging from their hiding places. A ragtag bunch of old, young, men, and women. Some even looked like young children.

"Volek's army surrounds this wood," said Suri-Yi.

"I know."

"And?"

"They won't come in 'ere. Not if they know what's best for 'em," said Olaf. He adjusted his sword belt and looked around at the motley crew as if to seek their approval. The forest folk nodded and seconded his comments.

"Aye," a young lad said.

"That be right," offered a woman with a bow strapped across her back.

Turning back to her, Olaf asked, "What's Volek brewing anyway?"

"He wants Kronnoburg. We both know why."

"The cheek of it," said Olaf, puffing out his cheeks and scratching his head. "After all we did to retake Krakonite from the Magrog."

"Men have short memories. Especially ambitious ones."

"What about Avantolia?"

"Revolutionary zeal runs deep. Sargon and Volek plan to shape the world in a new Avanist order," said Suri-Yi. Something caught her attention, and she looked over her shoulder.

"Madness. Why fight one another? The real enemy's the Magrog. We all know it," said Olaf.

Still turned the other way and squinting into the distance, Suri-Yi said in a soft, hushed tone, "If only everyone shared your feelings, Olaf, they would all be generous."

The tree leaves rustled above them. The archers were restless. They'd seen what she had sensed and released a volley of arrows.

"Soldiers," one of the archers shouted down.

"How many?" Olaf asked.

There was a brief silence. "Fifty. Maybe more. Difficult to say."

Olaf ushered the folk deeper into the forest.

"Do you still have it?" Suri-Yi asked Olaf.

"Of course. If Volek wants it, he's going to have to come and get it," said Olaf.

"If I'm not mistaken, that's exactly what he's trying to do," said Suri-Yi.

"You always were so direct."

"Brevity is a virtue," said Suri-Yi.

They fell back deep into the forest where the redolent pine trees were so dense they prevented any light from entering. The air was still, and the temperature rose in the clamminess of the woodland.

Suri-Yi was concerned the community of forest dwellers was larger than she'd expected—five hundred at least. Many families stood amongst them.

"I was expecting a hardened bunch of men. Not children and infants," she said.

"Even tough men have families," replied Olaf.

The expressions around her were fearful. She had seen it too many times in the past not to recognise it. *Olaf will need to move them to Kronnoburg.* An army wasn't going to be slowed by archers in trees, and she didn't think the forest folk would be able to hold them off for long.

"You have to get them behind Kronnoburg's walls," said Suri-Yi.

"Is it already time for the retreat?" said the young man who had first spoken to her when she entered Olaf's territory.

"My son, Torvin. He's a brave lad," Olaf said. He spoke to his son. "If Suri-Yi says we ought to fall back, then we do. She's the only person whose military advice I accept without question. She's never been wrong, lad. Not in my experience."

He says too much. I have made terrible mistakes.

"We have a safe corridor through the hills. We can arrive before the army lays siege to the city," said Olaf.

"Then go at once," said Suri-Yi.

"You're not coming with us?"

"No."

"Still the loner," said Olaf.

"Unfortunately," said Suri-Yi. Her attention was distracted. The archers released a fresh volley of arrows, which whistled through the air. "I will buy you some time. Now go."

Suri-Yi turned. Her robes fluttered in a gust of wind, and she headed into the path of the oncoming army. Olaf grabbed her by the elbow and drew her close so none could hear them.

"Are the Xettin coming down the mountain?"

"Yes."

"Then the Magrog will soon appear on the Black Sea. You must warn Heraclius."

"Yes, if it is not too late already."

Olaf let go of her arm and brushed the side of her cheek with a kiss. "Suri-Yi, thank you."

She looked at him one last time. *My dear old friend, if only you knew the things I had done.* Suri-Yi smiled, unsheathed Shamshir, and left Olaf the Generous and his people behind. She was alone once more. It was a familiar but uncomfortable path.

30

NO ONE AT HOME

Tangling with the Ifreet had made her jumpy. It made Ylva look over her shoulder once, twice, or three times a minute. She ended up with a pain in her neck from all the looking. She clasped and unclasped the hilt of the Orlisium sword. It had saved her from the Ifreet, and she didn't want to lose it. She was edgy, and sleep was nearly impossible. She didn't want to die dreaming. That was a pitiful way to go. If she was going to snuff it out here, it would be better with her sword swinging. She might even take a limb or two off the next Ifreet that decided to poke its fiery nose her way.

Bands of fighters coursed through the forest, but they didn't see her. She was small, and they weren't looking for a girl. Once or twice she'd raised her head over the heather to see the Merchants' Road. It had been completely backed up. The army from Krakonite had spilled across the road and stretched back for miles. The numbers didn't matter. They wouldn't get into Kronnoburg. Those ancients built that castle's walls strong. She reckoned even if the sea made its way to Kronnoburg, it couldn't pass.

Ylva desperately missed the gang's banter. With no one to talk to for days, she felt as if she was condemned to walk through a field of the dead. She couldn't shrug off the sensation the Ifreet stalked her. She felt its fiery red eyes watching her every movement.

On the second full day after the encounter with the demon, she reached her home in the forest. She knew something was wrong as soon as she arrived. The archers weren't on guard in the silver birch trees.

The dwellings were empty. Pots and pans lay about, children's wooden toys were abandoned, and even workable weapons were left behind. They'd left in a rush, but at least they'd left. No bodies were scattered about. *Thank the Great Spirit, but where have they gone?* The cooking fires were still warm.

Ylva heard a jingling sound like coins in a purse. She listened for where it was coming from. Moving in its direction, she realised it was swords clashing together. A vicious fight raged close by.

She crept forwards and emerged into the spot where folk had gathered on moonless nights to gaze up at the stars. The spot was a wide piece of earth in a clearing. She froze when she saw the fight before her.

A woman in dark brown robes wielded a sword. It pulsated green. Tasburai! It was just like Father had told her in the old stories. He had said a Tasburai moved with grace like a butterfly, flitting with ease between the currents of the wind. Only she was jumping, diving, and rising to avoid deathly blades trying to cut her down. Her own blade penetrated the enemy around her.

Ylva couldn't count the number of soldiers around the Tasburai, but it seemed to be at least fifty. Another fifty or so lay bleeding to death about the clearing. The fight must have been raging for a while.

The Tasburai was calm. Her well-practised movements flowed. The soldiers fell around her like leaves from an autumn tree. It was a massacre. The soldiers had no chance, and Ylva felt a tremendous amount of envy. *I want to be able to wield a sword like that.*

The Tasburai blade flicked out with the venom of a serpent's tongue. It was too fast for the soldiers, who continued to go down before it. It was as though the Tasburai was casually shearing the wool off a sheep's back.

As they fell, Ylva noticed the fighting kept shifting towards a large sycamore tree. It was a steady but constant movement. Ylva looked up and saw a black-robed figure perched in the tree. It was a trap. The Tasburai wasn't aware of it. Ylva had to do something, but what?

The last soldier was felled. The Tasburai stood motionless with her sword still raised. She was listening. Was there someone else coming? From the opposite side of the forest, six new adversaries emerged. They were dressed like Tasburai, but in many ways they were different. Their clothing was similar, but the black robes were much richer with red silk linings. They moved in unison towards her. They were identically dressed to the person in the tree.

"Who do you serve?" asked the Tasburai.

"Grandmaster Naram-Sin."

The person in the tree sat motionless. Watching the spectacle, the Tasburai still didn't notice the would-be assassin. Ylva needed to help her. She edged forwards but didn't dare to breathe aloud.

"Suri-Yi, Tasburai are the past." They rushed at her like a charcoal cloud.

Suri-Yi! She is the one in the stories. Father had spoken of her grace and beauty, and even after so many years, she still shone like a jewel. Ylva was frightened by her, but she also knew her to be Father's friend. *I must help her.*

The warriors moved with finesse. Ylva wondered if they had been Tasburai at some point. They were much younger and stronger than Suri-Yi. *Watch the one in the tree.*

Ylva scrambled through the undergrowth and came up against the trunk of the tree with the hidden adversary. He was still perched motionless like a statue. Suri-Yi had her back to him. The others cleverly moved her towards the assassin. They blocked her movement in all other directions and forced her back.

Ylva kept watching the person in the tree.

The Tasburai had the better of the six opponents, but Ylva could see she was tiring. Her defensive blocks were not as firm. Her leaps and skips through the air were a bit slower than before.

An opponent momentarily lost his footing. Suri-Yi saw the opportunity. Knocking the weapon from his grasp, she placed her blade upon his neck. Shamshir was just as Ylva's father had described it.

The others stopped.

"I will..." warned Suri-Yi.

"We know you will," said one of her opponents. The unarmed warrior plunged forwards and sliced his throat upon her blade. Shamshir severed his windpipe. Suri-Yi staggered back and away from her opponents. She walked straight into the path of the hidden assassin.

Ylva looked up. The person in the tree was no longer there. He was leaping downwards. A spear clasped between his hands, he aimed directly at Suri-Yi's neck.

"No!" Ylva cried out.

She dashed out from hiding and jumped onto an old tree stump. She flung herself through the air. Suri-Yi spun around. *I'm too late*, thought Ylva. The enemy's spear was going to impale Suri-Yi. Ylva swung her sword. Slicing through the air, it caught the man in the back. The blade went cleanly through.

Ylva crashed to the ground, rolled, and picked herself up. The other Hawarij exchanged glances before melting back into the forest.

"Are you hurt, child?" said Suri-Yi. She helped Ylva up.

"No. I'm okay...I think." Ylva still tightly gripped the sword.

"Thank you, child. It's fine now. Let go of the blade. Look." Suri-Yi pointed at the fallen Hawarij. "He is no threat. What are you doing wandering around in the forest with an Orlisium sword?"

"I live here. This is my home. My father sent me to Kronnoburg for my safety. That's where I found the sword," said Ylva.

The Tasburai asked for the sword. She held it up to look at it closely in the light. "Where exactly did you get this sword?"

"In Kronnoburg. In one of the basement vaults."

"This sword is called Curtana—the sword of mercy. She used to belong to a great Tasburai. Idealistic, strong, and true to our cause. That man is...dead now."

She handed the weapon back to Ylva. "Where did you encounter the Ifreet?"

Ylva was shocked she knew, but her father had said the Tasburai were a mysterious bunch. They could see things others couldn't. "A few days ago. In the forest not far from here. It was with a pack of Xettin."

The Tasburai seemed to mull over the information. "What is your father's name?"

"Olaf the Generous."

The Tasburai took a deep breath and shook her head. When she looked up, there was a smile upon her face. "Looks like I'll be going to Kronnoburg after all," said Suri-Yi.

31

THE RECEPTION

"The door to the outer gatehouse on the southern perimeter wall is open, sir," Bolt remarked as soon as Rikard and his men had crossed over the ridge looking out towards Kronnoburg.

Unusual. Could General Volek's forces have arrived? Rikard didn't think so. There were no signs from the terrain of an army having crossed it, unless they came from the west. No, south was the direction of approach. He had to assume he and his men were first back.

He was exhausted, and his nerves were torn to shreds by the events of the past few days. The nightmare starting at Hunderfin had progressively worsened. The only bright spark amongst the melancholy was meeting the

Tasburai grandmaster Suri-Yi, and he'd probably never see her again. If he had been able to spend some time with such a great warrior, he could have at least learnt something.

They passed through the gatehouse. The soldier on duty lay sprawled across a bench.

"He's drunk," said Luma.

"Shut the gate. Scan the perimeter for any breaches," said Rikard.

Where is everyone?

The narrow tunnel leading from the outer gatehouse into the outer walls of the southern battlements was unguarded. Upon arriving they found the inner gate also open. *Unbelievable. There is an army heading to Kronnoburg, and our defences have gone to sleep.* The pain in his neck flared. His head throbbed worse than ever. The noble buffoon Hakar should have reinforced the defensive positions. Instead he stood them down.

"Do you hear that, sir? Sounds like music," said Bolt.

Rikard and his men crossed the open land to reach the inner defence walls. They entered through the gatehouse and battlements and came into the city in the Konno Quarter. There was an enormous party in progress.

Young girls ran by, sprinkling Rikard and his men with confetti as they passed. He caught the last one by the wrist. "What are you celebrating?"

"The solstice! The solstice!" she sang and skipped away.

Of course! It was the summer solstice. He had totally forgotten.

The next quarter they passed into was even more raucous and full of revellers. There were long tables flowing with food and drink. Everyone looked happy. They had full bellies and tankards of ale to wash down the good food. Many had drunk too much and were staggering in gleeful bliss about the place.

"We should look for Major Ulrik," said Bolt.

It was sound advice. It had been his plan all along to seek out his superior officer and brief him immediately. This unforeseen turn of events had temporarily disturbed him.

The central army garrison was empty but for a scattering of soldiers. Rikard left his men after instructing them to gather those few present and start to reinforce every gatehouse across the city's defences. The walls would hold, but they had to ensure the enemy didn't enter through a weakened side door.

The duty sergeant had informed him the upper echelons of the military command were at the royal palace enjoying the summer solstice ball called for by the princess. Rikard made his way there. His anger and frustration grew with every step. It was madness the military was celebrating at this time. Rikard was rough and unclean from the road. He smelt bad, and his clothes were soiled with dirt and specks of blood. There was no time to return home to make himself presentable. The advanced guard of Volek's army might be upon them before sunset tomorrow.

The Royal Guard waved him in. His friendship with the late Prince Tromor made him a familiar and friendly face. As he walked through the plush surroundings of the palace, Rikard became conscious of his awful smell, scruffy looks, and haggard appearance. He felt even worse inside. He had an anxious stomach cramp. Servants he passed gave him odd stares.

Rikard entered the great banqueting hall of the royal palace. It was packed with finely dressed guests, and they were not just Nostvektians. He could see well-tanned Durians and dark-skinned Pathans. *Perfect. Our allies are here. They all need to know.*

Couples danced elegantly in the centre of the hall. The princess was present. She was dancing with General Ulfheart. For a moment Rikard felt as though he should go directly up to the general, interrupt him, and communicate the urgency of the situation, but he refrained.

Major Ulrik was also within the dancing circle. He was hand in hand with a beautiful Durian. Rikard didn't have the gall to step in and call an end to their dance either. The longer he dithered, the more the pain in his forehead flared.

Rikard spotted the useless scoundrel Captain Klas Hakar. He was surrounded by his usual coterie of fickle noble officers. Approaching Hakar was the least preferred option, but time was not on their side. It was better to start the mobilisation and spread the message. The army needed to make arrangements, and if it meant ordering these useless nobles into action, he felt sure Ulrik would support him later.

Hakar saw him coming and nudged a noble standing beside him. There was also someone new with them. The visitor was not Nostvektian but was dressed as regally as a prince. By the time he reached them, the entire group was staring at him disparagingly.

"Captain Navrosk, good to see you, but you don't look entirely presentable," said Hakar.

"Listen here, Hakar. There's no time to stand on formality," said Rikard.

"Come—" Hakar started.

Rikard, however, cut him off. Maybe it was the betrayal of being abandoned at a dangerous time by Hakar and his buddies. Maybe it was the tiring journey back and the awful things he'd witnessed. Regardless, Rikard snapped.

"You useless piece of noble skin. Listen to me," he shouted.

Those around them fell silent. They gaped at him with open mouths.

Good. They might as well all hear what I have to say. "After you and your silver-spoon chums abandoned us for dead, we actually made it to Krakonite. General Volek has sent the biggest army since the last Magrog invasion to attack Kronnoburg. They'll be here tomorrow.

You should have mobilised the defences as we discussed and raised the banners. Instead you are here prancing around. Come on. We have to leave and get things ready."

The entire hall went quiet. Rikard suddenly noticed Elsta standing beside them. She looked stunningly beautiful. His face flushed red with embarrassment.

Elsta moved over to the new fellow and wrapped her arms around him. "What is the problem, my love?" she asked.

Who is he?

"Captain Navrosk," said Hakar. "Poor fellow has had one too many drinks celebrating the solstice, Your Highness. Don't worry. We'll take him away. A night in a cell with a bucket of cold water over his head will do him a world of good."

The newcomer spoke for the first time. "Very well, Major Hakar. As you say."

Hakar has been promoted to major? He's my superior? What is the world coming to? The enemy would be at the gates, and Kronnoburg had become an alien place.

"Yes, Your Highness," said Hakar.

"No, wait..." Rikard tried to protest, but they weren't having any of it.

He was dragged away in front of the royal guests—the very people whose support he needed.

32

DAYDREAM'S OVER

The past few days had been the most joyous Elsta had ever experienced. She had finally convinced her cabinet that her marriage to Theodorus should go ahead. Since then she and her fiancé had begun to actively plan the grand wedding, which would take place sooner rather than later. As each day progressed, Theodorus was more charming and chivalrous than she'd dared imagine. She didn't know why she'd doubted he would be. Marriage, her late father had said, was something she would only do once, so she best get it right.

Upon Theodorus's advice, one of her first actions was to change her old ministers and advisers. "Out with the old, in with the new," thundered Theodorus. "A new king and queen need a fresh set of ideas which will restore Kronnoburg's glory."

She liked the sound of that, and she was sure her father and mother would have agreed with his counsel. He might not be a native of these lands, but in her eyes, he was even better.

The new cabinet of senior ministers and advisers was in session. Theodorus had said it would be a supportive gesture if they both showed up for the inaugural meeting. The most difficult aspect of attending for Elsta had been deciding what to wear on such a formal governmental occasion. She'd gone with a sombre cream-coloured gown with her hair braided and tied up. Fortunately there weren't any ladies from court present, so there'd be no idle gossip about what she wore.

Theodorus had suggested to her that Major Klas Hakar should be the new first minister. He was a gallant choice firmly backed by Elsta. Hakar chose a number of his closest advisers who'd been with him during their military campaigns. Elsta didn't know any of them, but they all looked the part, smartly dressed and turned out.

"Food shortages are very severe in many parts of the city, particularly in the Southern Quarter," said Reider. Elsta had insisted on retaining her father's dear minister as a special adviser to this youthful cabinet. Theodorus had been against it, but when he saw she wasn't going to budge, he'd consented. She'd rather hoped Reider would remain on the periphery. She wanted him to coach and mentor the new ministers outside the cabinet rooms.

She didn't necessarily want him speaking at the meeting itself. He was droning on about food supplies and general provisions running out.

"How low?" Theodorus asked.

"Very low, Your Highness. Perhaps they will last another two weeks. With the Merchants' Road seemingly impassable and our navy either lost at sea or under repairs, we are rather at the mercy of chance," said Reider.

"We shouldn't be in this situation. This was poor management by the previous administration, of which you were a part," said Theodorus.

Elsta felt sad for her father's friend. He was the only survivor of the previous cabinet, and throughout the day, blame for any previous administrative shortcoming was laid squarely upon Reider's shoulders.

"Can't you send word to your cousin Heraclius in Duria? Surely he can help," said Elsta. She realised she'd said something wrong as soon as she saw Reider's expression.

"Of course, my dear," said Theodorus. "But Heraclius is a man who respects strength. It is better not to go to him in a weakened position."

"The prince is right, Your Highness," added Reider. "Your late father used to say a fellow king would only respect him if approached as an equal."

"Thank you, Reider. I can see why the princess values your judgement," said Theodorus.

"Your Highnesses, there is also the matter of sporadic food riots breaking out. These are primarily in the Southern

Quarter, where most of the villagers have been housed. The riots just flare up. One minute the villagers are in an orderly queue and collecting their rations. The next, fights break out, municipality officials are attacked, and we end up having to withdraw from the area," said Reider.

"Why would people deliberately start a food riot when they are going to receive the food?" asked Elsta.

"Quite, Your Highness. More to the point, who would do it?" said Reider.

"Some nut kicked off a plague rumour in the Eastern Quarter yesterday. Took the army nearly the whole day to restore order," said First Minister Major Hakar.

"Was there a plague?" asked Theodorus.

"Of course not," said Hakar.

"It would appear certain agents provocateurs are currently at work within the city. We need to stop them, or we could have full-scale civil unrest on our hands," said Reider.

"No need to be a scaremonger, Reider," said Hakar.

"I am merely making observations on known facts and planning for eventualities. As you will know from your military training, this is what leaders must do," said Reider.

"It is, but you are now an adviser, and we thank you for your advice, *former* Minister Reider. Please leave us now whilst I discuss the remainder of our business with the ministers," said Theodorus.

Reider was quite taken aback. These meetings were about making bold decisions to bring joy to the people and restore glory to Kronnoburg, so Elsta remained quiet while Reider dislodged himself from his seat, collected his walking stick, and left the room.

His departure created a momentary lull in the proceedings. Then Hakar blurted out, "I thought the silly old fool would never stop moaning. No wonder they never got anything done before."

His minions burst out laughing. Even Theodorus had a smile upon his face. Elsta felt the comment was unfair. There was little point in denigrating the old man. She adjusted her dress and laid her palms upon her lap. She looked affectionately at Theodorus.

"What's next on the agenda, First Minister?" Theodorus asked.

"This next item is quite a peculiar request, Your Highness. Someone claiming to be a Tasburai grandmaster seeks audience with the princess. She says she knew your father, Your Highness," said Hakar.

"She?" said Elsta.

"Tasburai?" said Theodorus.

"It's bizarre, if you ask me," said Hakar.

"What name did she give?" asked Elsta.

"Oh come, dear," said Theodorus.

"No harm in asking, my love."

Hakar shuffled the piece of paper with the message. "I have it here. Grandmaster Suri-Yi of the Tasburai Order signed it. Does that mean anything to you?"

"No. What do you think, my love?" Elsta asked Theodorus.

"Sounds like some opportunist looking to cash in on the general mood in the city. Tell the woman to come back tomorrow. If she is who she says she is, she will come. Tasburai, from the stories I heard as a young boy, were known for their patience. If she is an impostor, why should we waste our precious time?" said Theodorus.

Spoken like a king. Deep inside, however, Elsta wished it was true. She wished there were Tasburai in the world and one was currently within her city.

"I like the sound of that, Your Highness," said Hakar.

Someone knocked three times at the ministerial meeting room door and then entered without waiting for a response. It was a lieutenant, and he looked terrified.

"Yes?" barked Hakar.

Hands trembling, the ashen-faced lieutenant silently passed Hakar a piece of paper.

The blood seemed to drain from the first minister's face. "You sure about this?" said Hakar.

"Yes, sir," said the lieutenant.

"What is it? Speak up," demanded Theodorus.

Hakar's voice was suddenly shrill and high-pitched. "The report...it would seem our perimeter outpost on the southern side of the River Sjorn has sighted an army approaching. From the direction of Krakonite."

"Ridiculous. They wouldn't dare," said Theodorus.

33

DEAD BRASS

It wasn't the perfect beginning to his first ministry. Major Klas Hakar had been hoping for a pedestrian start to the inauguration of his time in office. He imagined it would consist of signing papers in the morning, talking to a few chaps over lunch, seeing the odd commoner with some unjustified complaint in the afternoon, and rounding the day off with a game of cards. He imagined the first few months would be peppered with trips to foreign lands and sampling delectable cuisines at state banquets. Plus he'd fit in the odd fencing session or two. War hadn't been on the menu, but now it was the only dish being served.

"Blast Volek. Damn commoner," said Hakar. He scowled as he took his seat at the emergency meeting of the ministers and the military. He'd had to cancel a haircut, wash, and manicure. "Who does the scoundrel think he is?" Hakar muttered. The meeting's remaining attendees shuffled into the dark oak-panelled room with its polished lacquer floor.

"Dastardly fellow," said one of Hakar's old chums.

"Rogue," added another.

Finally everyone was seated, and the hall went quiet. They all stared at Hakar. *Flaming daggers!* He'd forgotten he was first minister, and he was to chair the meeting.

"Gentlemen, thank you for coming on such short notice," he said.

To his left sat General Ulfheart. He looked awful. He'd come down with a terrible bout of food poisoning. Anyone else his age would have keeled over, but Ulfheart had a stomach like lead. Beside Ulfheart sat Major Ulrik. He'd also fallen foul of food poisoning. He'd have to ask the government secretary to look into what they'd been serving at the officers' mess. He'd only been away a week, and the bloody standards had already dropped. *I'll have the cook locked up in the dungeons for this.*

His appointed ministers filled up the remaining seats at the table. The fogey Reider had tried to get in, but he hadn't let the old cripple be present. The very sight of him was enough to put a man off his breakfast.

Prince Theseus had said the princess was rather distressed by the news of Volek's approaching army, and he would be accompanying her back to her chambers. *All right for some. The rest of us have to put in a hard day's work*. Being first minister was fine, but being king—that was an idea he could really take to.

"General Volek, that blighter and miscreant, had the audacity to muster up a brigade of fools which he calls an army. Then he decided to march on Kronnoburg," said Hakar.

Those present stirred, and conversations broke out around the room. This was news for most around the table. Hakar beamed as he said it. He loved to break shocking news to people and watch their faces contort. Then his own mood became pensive as he wished this particular news didn't carry such deep ramifications for his first ministry.

He raised his hand to restore silence. Only nobody was looking at him. So he banged his fist on the table. *Ouch*. It silenced the room.

"Volek will be at the outer defence wall by tomorrow," said Hakar.

"Let him rot there," added one his buddies.

"Fools," said another of his appointees.

"I agree. He has no way of breaching our impenetrable walls. So let him start his ill-fated siege. After a few days, when his supplies run low, he'll be gone," said Hakar.

"First Minister," started General Ulfheart. He paused to cough violently and hold the pit of his stomach. "It is my understanding food supplies within the city are running low. Only two weeks of stock are left."

Damn Reider. He's been feeding the general. "Not at all, General. You know the old saying—Kronnoburg's never short," said Hakar.

"I suspect Volek has deliberately shut the supply lines and artificially created this food shortage," said Ulfheart. "This presents a material risk to our position. He will be taking *our* supplies to maintain his army, whilst we run short within Kronnoburg. He's planning to starve us out."

"There is no shortage," said Hakar firmly. "Now I suggest we focus on the matter at hand. We must respond with a show of strength. Send a clear message to Volek that we will not be trodden on, we do not fear him, and in the end, he will be defeated."

From around him where his buddies sat, they trumped up with plenty of comments supporting him. "Hear, hear, too right, I second that," they said.

Ulfheart began to cough violently and then took several deep breaths.

"First Minister, I remind you that words are easy. Action is a lot harder," said Major Ulrik.

"Lost your spine, Ulrik?" said Hakar. A few weeks ago, he would never have spoken to his superior officer in such blunt terms. Now he could do what he liked. Being first minister was almost as good as being king. Only he didn't have the comfort of the princess's shoulder to rest his tired head.

"No..." Ulrik began to say, and then he started to cough uncontrollably in an awful spasm. A globule of saliva came out of his mouth.

Disgusting fellow. No manners. It was red. The man was spitting blood. *Have they been poisoned?* Hakar pushed away the mug of water before him and looked around the room.

Crash! The meeting room door flew open. *Now what?*

Hakar's jaw dropped. A troop of six men wearing long black robes marched in. The soldiers guarding the meeting room leapt forwards with their weapons ready, but each was almost severed in two with consummate ease. Blood flowed across the lacquered floor.

One amongst the six strode up to General Ulfheart. "General, it's been a long time."

"Too short, Naram-Sin," said Ulfheart.

Major Ulrik was now on his knees and clutching his throat.

"Looks like the man has been poisoned," said Naram-Sin.

Major Ulrik collapsed. Blood trickled out of his ears, eyes, and nose.

"I demand to know the meaning of this!" said Hakar while thumping his fist on the table.

"Who's the new noble?" Naram-Sin asked Ulfheart.

"First Minister Klas Hakar," said Ulfheart.

"Well, First Minister Klas Hakar, you've just lost a major. Now you're going to lose a general," said Naram-Sin.

Before Ulfheart's hand had even begun to move towards his weapon, the man called Naram-Sin had driven his sword straight through the general's heart.

Everyone else leapt up and drew their weapons. Hakar jumped out of his seat but bashed his knees into the table rim. He fumbled for his sword. The edge of the ornamental handle was stuck to his frock coat.

Hakar was suddenly aware of another sword. It came into and out of him three times. It was as though the sword-bearer was slicing cheese. It was Naram-Sin's blade, and it had such a wondrous sheen to it. The Orlisium steel was so sharp and light. It even seemed to glow as it passed in and out of his chest.

34

NIGHTMARE

The sound of her bedroom door being kicked in woke Elsta before the angry voice of the intruder. "Get up now!"

"What?" she mumbled.

Elsta rubbed her eyes and pushed back the soft locks of hair from her forehead to see six ghastly men standing in her bedroom. They were dressed in long black robes with red silk lining. She screamed.

"Never fear, my dear. I am at your side," said Theodorus, taking hold of her. He had been standing behind the row of men and pushed his way forwards.

A cold-eyed older man in the group approached. "Your Highness, we are very sorry for this rather brusque awakening. It is, I admit, most undignified and not befitting a person of your station. Please accept my apologies. Having said that, I want you dressed and ready to travel in two minutes."

"Guard!" shouted Elsta.

The older man smiled. "They can't hear you. The next thing they will hear will be the horns of Ujithana."

Elsta cried out.

"I will ask politely only one more time. Then my rather less respectful comrades will drag you out of bed and dress you."

"Do as he says, my love," said Theodorus.

"Sirs, if you would be so kind as to avert your gaze," said Elsta, and she walked behind her clothes dresser. A fresh set of hunting clothes was laid out. She'd been planning to go on a ride with Theodorus before news of the invading army. She quickly changed.

"Hurry up, Your Highness. We need to go now," said the older man.

Who are these men, and what are they doing?

"Now," the cold-eyed man shouted, and the clothes dresser was yanked away. Elsta was just pulling on her boots.

The entire group of men had blank expressions—no malice but certainly no warmth. When they emerged into the corridor, she saw her Royal Guard. They were dead, and blood was filling the corridor. Many of these portly old men had guarded her throughout her life. She began to cry.

"I'm sorry, my love," said Theodorus, and he took her by the hand.

The men led them out of the royal palace on a route littered with dead soldiers, guards, and servants. Elsta counted at least thirty bodies along the way. Eventually they ended up beside the great banqueting hall. Only recently they'd held a feast there to mark the end of the queen's tournament. She longed to return to that moment and cocoon herself within it.

The older man led them down a stairwell and underground. They emerged into a semilit tunnel. The lanterns cast long, flickering shadows across pale plastered walls.

"There will be two guards at the end of this corridor," the older man said to one of his clandestine comrades. He then passed his hand across his throat.

"Where are you taking us?" said Elsta. Whoever these people were, they'd taken great care in planning this bold move.

Their captor glanced at Theodorus. "Your Highness, I'm taking you to see your future husband."

"What is he saying, my love?" Elsta gripped Theodorus by the arm.

Her prince held her close and turned to the older man. "I am her fiancé."

"Shut up!" said the cold-eyed man, and he slapped Theodorus upon the cheek. The weight of the blow threw him and Elsta to the floor.

"Get up," barked the older man.

Soon enough they passed two more dead soldiers, and they entered an enormous armoury with weapons made of a peculiar sort of steel.

"What is this place?" said Elsta.

"A very special armoury. It contains weapons made from Orlisium steel. We keep them just in case you-know-who"—he pointed at an enormous oil painting hanging at one end of the room—"should return with their demons."

"Magrog..." Elsta's voice trailed off in fear of the word.

The cold-eyed man led them down the steps towards the painting. It illustrated a battle. Elsta could clearly see Castle Kronnoburg in the background and legions of brave Nostvektian troops protecting its walls against an army of enormous men wearing black armour—the Magrog. Before the Magrog were beasts with wolfish looks, the Xettin, and beside them wispy forms. These were the demons the stories told of—the Ifreet. Elsta felt a great weight crush her shoulders. The stories she'd dismissed as fairy tales might actually be true. Then she saw the small group of men and women dressed in flowing dark brown robes on the side of her people. Their swords glowed in their hands—Tasburai.

"Just stories," said Elsta, trying to convince herself of it. She wanted Theodorus to agree, but he remained silent. He was staring at the painting, then at the older man.

"Yes, I can confirm that is exactly what it was like," said the cold-eyed man.

“How do you know?” said Elsta, eyeing him up and down.

“Because he’s in the painting,” said Theodorus.

Their captor grinned. It was his first show of emotion she’d seen. He marched around the back of the painting and moved aside a velvet curtain to reveal a tiny round door. It was about shoulder height.

The man inserted a key and unlocked the door. “Still works after all these years,” he said. “Come, Your Highness.”

Elsta clutched her prince’s hand and then followed their captor through the door into a narrow, dark tunnel. Only the blue light pulsating from the man’s sword guided them.

35

RELEASE

"Guard!" shouted Rikard. His voice was hoarse with the effort.

No one had listened to him for days. Meals were presented three times a day. His treatment had been fair, but those who'd sent him down here had largely forgotten about him.

It must be deliberate. Now that Hakar has power, I'm really done for. "Guard!"

Rikard kept himself busy by exercising regularly in his cell. By prison standards it was more of a luxurious room. There was a bed, chair, desk, and separate toilet. The cell was reserved for enemy dignitaries who had been made prisoners of war. The prison warden, whom he'd only seen upon arrival, had suggested he take this cell to make his stay more comfortable.

His was the only occupied cell in the western wing of the prison. The southern wing was awash with inmates, judging by the volume of noise coming from it. Pickpockets, vagrants, and other petty criminals were usually incarcerated there. The summer solstice must have led to a spike in these petty crimes.

"Guard!"

He discerned footsteps. Rikard waited eagerly. *Are they going to finally release me?* It was about time. He'd only expected an overnighter at most.

When he looked up, he saw Lieutenant Bolt. "Bolt!"

"Sir."

It felt good to be addressed as "sir" again. "It's good to see you, Bolt."

The lieutenant had a bunch of keys and was clutching one, which he inserted into the lock of Rikard's cell.

"What's going on, Bolt?"

"Mayhem, sir."

The cell door swung open, Rikard stepped out, and he hugged his lieutenant. Freedom felt good. "Tell me."

Bolt's face drained of colour. "Volek's forces have laid siege to the outer perimeter wall," he said.

"As expected."

"But he also sent some type of advanced unit. The survivors said they dressed like Tasburai. They penetrated the royal palace. They massacred everyone at the emergency meeting. Everyone. They then broke into the princess's chambers and left the city with her and her fiancé."

"The princess has been taken hostage?"

"Yes, sir."

The memories of Elsta as a young girl watching him and Tromor practise with their swords flashed before his eyes. The sense of loss was immense, as was the guilt of not protecting his friend's younger sister.

"Elsta."

"Sir?"

"Sorry, I have known the princess since she was a young girl."

"I know, sir. You were close to the family."

"As close as a commoner is entitled to be, I suppose."

"Sir, when I said the military leaders were all killed, I meant *all* of them—General Ulfheart and Majors Ulrik, Code, and Nurthwa. Even Major Hakar. All put to the sword. The city is awash with rumour of invasion and plague. Riots have broken out, and there is lawlessness in the streets. The military is doing its best, but we're not anywhere near controlling the panic. I've never seen anything like it, sir. You are the most senior military officer alive. No ministers were left alive either. The city, sir, is in your hands."

Bolt placed the keys in his hand. Rikard shut his fingers around them. "We'd better get to work, Lieutenant."

36

PLANS

This is what it were like the last time, Ylva thought. *Before I was born.* Her father and the Tasburai were gabbing away and scheming with Uncle Albertus and Hallbjorn the Bear. They were joined by Eydis the Green, Brynjar the Blade, Sigrun the Hidden, and herself. They hadn't named her yet, but it would be soon. She'd get her title, and she'd be called Ylva the something. She hoped it was a good title because it was going to stick. Folk often forgot a person's actual name and just called him or her out by title. She'd heard folk yell for the Bear more than they ever called for Hallbjorn.

Ylva wasn't quite sure of the names and places being discussed by her father and the Tasburai, but if she knew one thing, it was how to spot trouble, and a whole heap of it was heading their way.

Ylva figured her luck must be in to have met Tasburai Grandmaster Suri-Yi when she did. Otherwise there was no telling what misery and mayhem she would have ended up in. There were crazy folk out there on the Merchants' Road, and demonic spirits were floating around the forest. The Tasburai had listened to her tale of the Ifreet, but she'd not said a word during or after it. It had seemed as if she was lost in another time. By the look on the Tasburai's face, Ylva reckoned Suri-Yi had plenty of experience with Ifreet and their sort.

The only good thing to come out of the mess was they'd caught up with her father just as he and the forest folk reached Kronnoburg. Uncle Albertus knew some guards, and they had looked the other way as more than a hundred forest folk came through the southern gates of Kronnoburg. The Nostvektian citizens had been too busy celebrating the summer solstice to notice. Ylva reckoned most had been on the drink longer than they should have.

Now she was hearing about the princess's abduction from the city, and the news spread through the city like fire in a dry forest.

"All dead. Every single one of 'em. Even the old warhorse General Ulfheart," said Hallbjorn.

"Ministers as well," said Uncle Albertus.

"Who's running the city?" asked Ylva's father.

"Some young captain named Navrosk," said Hallbjorn.

"A good man," said Suri-Yi.

"You know him?" asked Ylva's father.

"We met on the road. His heart is in the right place, but he will need your experience, Olaf," said Suri-Yi.

The Tasburai master always spoke with such softness. One would never think she had a bad bone in her body or a bad thought in her heart. Ylva, however, had seen the Tasburai fight. *She is a demon. No one who fights like her can be safe to be around.* The Tasburai scared her. She was dangerous and attracted dangerous sort of folk.

"My dear brother's reputation amongst this young generation of Nostvektians isn't going to open any doors or win him any favours in Kronnoburg," said Uncle Albertus.

"Tell the captain you are a friend of Grandmaster Suri-Yi," said Suri-Yi.

"Still works. The ultimate calling card to open every door, even after all these years," said Ylva's father with a cheeky grin.

Ylva hadn't seen him so alive for a long time. He almost looked to be enjoying the action and attention he was getting. He'd told her he was in the military in the last war with the Magrog. *I suppose things have been quiet since then.*

"He knows the truth of what you did for his people. He will listen to you, Olaf...the Generous," said Suri-Yi.

"Ha! She jests with me, Brother, but we still love her all the same," said Olaf. He got up from his chair and walked over to give the Tasburai a great big hug. Suri-Yi patted him on the shoulder and encouraged him to sit back down. As Olaf returned to his seat, Ylva could see the Tasburai's cheeks had gone pink. It was the first time she'd seen any emotion register on her face. *She's an ice warrior. A bit of Father's love and affection will thaw her a little. Can't be a bad thing.*

Ylva reckoned the folk seated before her in Uncle Albertus's cellar were the only ones left in the city who'd kept their heads.

"I hope you're right about this lad Navrosk," said Hallbjorn.

Navrosk. Where have I heard that name before? How can I possibly know him? Then it came to her—Golden Hair. The good-looking fellow from the great banqueting hall.

"She's right 'bout the captain," Ylva blurted.

All heads turned in her direction. She'd been sitting quietly beside Hallbjorn and suddenly wished she'd remained so.

"Ylva, you know him too?" asked her father.

"Sort of. I saw him once in the great banqueting hall. Heard him called to by name. Know his face. Wouldn't forget it."

"Unforgettable, was he?" said Eydis with a wry smile.

"Oh leave off. You're making the child blush," said Hallbjorn, and he gave Ylva a great slap on the back.

"Take Ylva with you when you go to see Navrosk," said Suri-Yi to Olaf.

"All right, but I'll be keeping my eyes on the captain as well," said Olaf.

Now she'd done it—created a rumour when there was nothing to base it on.

"What do we do about the princess?" asked Uncle Albertus.

They all looked at the Tasburai. She remained silent. It was as if she was already thinking about something else entirely.

"Suri-Yi, what do you say?" said Olaf.

"Sorry?"

"The princess," said Olaf.

"Leave them to their fate," said Suri-Yi.

"What good is a kingdom without royalty?" said Hallbjorn.

"If Volek has them, he will soon send an envoy. That envoy will order the gates of Kronnoburg to be opened lest the princess be put to the sword. Volek cannot breach the walls. This is his only way, but we cannot allow the city to fall," said Suri-Yi.

"And the royals?" asked Olaf.

"The lives of the citizens of Kronnoburg and guarding the entrance to the Forbidden Quarter are of greater importance than two royals," said Suri-Yi.

"The Nostvektians may not agree," said Olaf.

"It is for you to convince them, Olaf," said Suri-Yi.

"What will you do?" asked Olaf.

"Volek's army, I leave to you—the defenders of the city. So long as you keep him outside the walls, you will be safe. I must watch for the Xettin. I feel they too are coming, and I fear they will bring Ifreet with them. The mayhem outside the walls will only embolden the Xettin, and they have always craved the Forbidden Quarter's treasures. There are hidden ways into Kronnoburg through abandoned tunnels. The Ifreet will know these ways," said Suri-Yi.

"Where will you go?" said Olaf.

"Deep below the city. The Ifreet will use the tunnels below Kronnoburg to breach its walls."

37

GUILT

Pathview Inn, high on a hill, was the last resting place before Kronnoburg's outer perimeter wall loomed up on the horizon. Travellers would stop for a drink and take in the view before venturing the remaining distance down the Merchants' Road to the city's outer gatehouse. Elsta gazed across at the walls her ancestors had built and felt tears welling up. *I must not show weakness. I have to be strong.*

The inn had long been cleared of guests. Its proprietor had been told his dwelling was to become the property of General Volek. The innkeeper had been a Nostvektian loyalist and refused. They'd put him to the sword. Elsta had seen his body dumped in the grounds behind the building. The staff were too scared to refuse any further demands and moved like apparitions between the men occupying the main hall of the inn. The central dining table contained a large map and several scrolls and dockets littered around it.

Theodorus sat at the table beside her. Holding her hand, he was protecting her from these wretched men. She felt comforted by his presence. Volek sat on the other side of the table, and his men ringed it. They were heavily armed and wore ominous scowls. Elsta dared not meet the gaze of any of them, so she just stared down at the table and fiddled with the cup of water they'd put before her.

"You are more beautiful in person than I'd imagined. The stories of your elegance do you no favours. Ours will be a happy marriage—for me at least," Volek declared. "You will bear my children. Strong sons who will be heirs of Kronnoburg, Krakonite, and the Forbidden Quarter. Our united kingdom will be feared for its strength and envied for its wealth."

Elsta felt a tear roll down her cheek. She quickly wiped it with her thumb.

Seated beside Volek in a high-back chair was the man called Naram-Sin who had led them out of Kronnoburg. Standing in the shadows of the room behind him were the dark-robed warriors who had accompanied him. Others in similar attire were dotted about the inn. There were also a half-dozen soldiers who Elsta took to be Volek's subordinates.

There were even two warriors who looked about her age. One was a young, handsome man, and close to him was a young woman, also dressed in black.

"We will be married in the morning, and then we will enter Kronnoburg as man and wife," Volek continued.

"I am already engaged to Prince Theodorus Theseus of Athenia. He is to be my king and protector," said Elsta.

Now was the time for Theodorus to speak up. He stirred beside her, and when she gazed into his face, he was smiling. So were Volek and a number of others in the inn. For a brief moment, she hoped the whole scene was some kind of grand jest—cruel but just a bit of fun.

"Prince Theodorus Theseus," said Volek, rubbing his chin and gazing over at Naram-Sin. "Will Theodorus Theseus please stand up?"

Elsta looked at her fiancé. He did not move.

"I said, will Theodorus Theseus please stand up," repeated Volek. This time he began to chuckle aloud.

Nothing happened. Elsta stared long and hard at Theodorus. The wicked look upon her fiancé's face made her flinch.

"He doesn't seem to be here, Your Majesty," said Volek. "Now, will Toni Bezodilidis, small-time actor and conjuror, please stand up?"

The man Elsta had taken to be her fiancé stood. He crossed to where Volek was seated, standing between the general and Naram-Sin.

"General," he said, his once-sweet voice pinching her nerves.

"Toni," said Volek.

Elsta tried to hold her tears back, but now they openly poured down her cheeks.

"Someone give my bride a clean handkerchief," said Volek.

A man with shaggy red hair stepped out from the shadows. It was the same bandit who had attacked her and Theodorus when they'd been on the hunt.

The redheaded bandit grinned at her with his broken teeth. Having given her a clean handkerchief, he went back to stand beside a group of other men, whom she now recognised as the rest of the bandit gang.

"Oh, the perils of true love, Your Highness. Always dashed by politics," said Volek. "The walls of Kronnoburg are impregnable, so why lose time and men trying to breach them? My dear friend Naram-Sin said that. So when he presented me with a plan based on winning the heart of a beautiful princess, I thought, who better to pull off the deceit than an actor? Someone who could play the part for a fee and then walk away with his head held high, knowing he'd starred in the role of his life? Cue Toni Bezodilidis—famous amongst theatregoers who frequent those distant Athenian islands on the easterly coasts of Duria, where every pleasure is accessible to those who can pay."

Elsta's sobs became stronger. She felt as though her heart was on fire.

"The people of Kronnoburg are soft and love the House of Mik. When I tell them to open the gates of the city to spare your life, they will comply," said Volek.

She knew it was true.

With increasing discomfort, Adan de la Vega watched the fate of Princess Elsta Mik unfold. He had not been privy to the scheme Naram-Sin masterminded. He felt a hot rush of blood to the head and tried to regulate his breathing to calm his anger. Adan glanced across at Saphira. She returned his look with a deadpan stare. It was as though she was looking through him. *She's changed. Am I the last Tasburai? No, there is Suri-Yi. But where is my master? Is she already at Kronnoburg?*

The princess finally stopped crying and looked up at Volek with watery eyes. "What did you do with the real Theodorus, my fiancé and true prince of Athenia?" she asked.

Volek turned to Naram-Sin, who pointed at Adan.

"Thanks to this young man," Naram-Sin said, "the real Theseus was incarcerated in the deepest pit of the Oblivion Prison below Avantolia. Whether he still lives is anyone's guess."

The princess stared at Adan. Her eyes were like daggers.

"Don't look so surprised, Vega. Don't you remember the man in the iron mask?" said Naram-Sin.

How could he forget? Suri-Yi had wanted to question that prisoner. Adan felt as though he was going to be sick.

The other men in the room were openly sniggering. Only the princess didn't smile at his expense.

38

SEEKING AN AUDIENCE

When Rikard thought about making a name in Kronnoburg, he imagined some daring act on the battlefield or deep behind enemy lines. He'd never considered being housed in a command-and-control centre, surrounded by paperwork, transcribers, messengers, runners, and other soldiers who looked as baffled as he felt. The problem was everyone expected him to know everything. He was officially in command, so he tried to appear as if he knew what he was talking about. At least this appearance of decisiveness would give the troops some confidence. It was a weak thought to console himself with, but it was the only one he could cling to.

He was reliant on the royal scribe. He was one of the few survivors from the old guard, and seemed to have some inkling about the machinery of government. He kept suggesting to Rikard that if General Ulfheart had been alive, he'd have done so and so, only because he'd read about it in previous governmental records. That was bad luck for Rikard. The decorated general was dead, and Rikard sat in his place feeling grossly inadequate and not up to the task at hand. As time ticked on, he felt someone would turn up sooner or later and kick him out as commander of the united defence force. He was hoping it would be sooner, but so far no one had come.

Rikard was leaning on clenched fists over a table with maps on it. He was trying to memorise the information, but his mind wasn't responding.

A beleaguered messenger approached him. "Captain, sir, permission to report."

"Go ahead," said Lieutenant Bolt, who stood beside Rikard.

Rikard's knuckles were sore from being clenched too long. *Damn, this map isn't making any sense to me.* Maybe the messenger had some information that would help him concentrate. He looked up.

"General Volek's army has moved closer to the outer perimeter wall, sir," said the messenger.

"How close are they now?" asked Rikard.

"Closer." The soldier stared at them as if expecting to be congratulated.

"Thank you, Soldier," said Bolt.

"Sir." The messenger clicked his heels and left.

Rikard shook his head in dismay. What a waste of time. His men were bringing him information he could do nothing with.

The next haggard messenger stepped forwards. "Captain, sir, permission to report."

"Go ahead," said Bolt.

"Fourth Infantry of the Queen's Own is posted at the outer defence walls on the southern perimeter. They have sent word that General Volek's army has made camp outside the perimeter and is building a series of catapults, sir."

"Did you say catapults?" snapped Rikard.

"They said it, sir."

Bolt saw Rikard's frustration and dismissed the messenger. Rikard's head had been throbbing since morning with all the detail he was taking in. All the plans, scenarios, and eventualities had been written years ago when the army was a proper fighting force. The soldiers then had been educated, trained, and combat ready. The plans he looked at were for an army that knew how to fight a battle. The men he now commanded could not. *I have ceremonial soldiers and sons of nobles. The army is just a pastime to them—an opportunity to impress young ladies who like the look of men in uniform.*

The gate guard approached. Rikard's heart sank. Already he'd dealt with an odd assortment of distressed citizens presented by this fellow.

"Captain, sir, there's a motley crew of forest folk outside the building. They are led by some fool claiming to be Olaf the Generous. I've ordered them to be arrested."

"No," cried Rikard.

It was too late. He could hear the clash of swords outside and the piercing crack of a spear striking the marble floor. *Whack!* The door to the war room smashed open. The soldier stationed beside it was sent sprawling across the floor.

"Weapons!" Bolt shouted.

An enormous fellow with a beard down to his large belly filled the doorway. He gripped both ends of an axe casually resting across his shoulders.

"Who's next?" he said and strolled into the room. The soldiers backed off.

"Enough, Hallbjorn. Let's not scare the blighters," said another man. The new fellow swaggered in as though quite familiar with his surroundings.

"You're too generous, Olaf," said Hallbjorn.

Olaf the Generous. Friend to Suri-Yi! Rikard stepped forwards. "My name is Captain—"

"Rikard Navrosk. A wise Tasburai grandmaster named Suri-Yi said you'd need a helping hand, son. So here we are," said Olaf.

"Suri-Yi is here?" said Rikard. His face lit up.

Olaf studied him for a moment. "She has that effect on men. To answer your question, lad, yes. She was here, but no, she's not with us any longer. She is somewhere within Kronnoburg. I couldn't quite be sure where. She's a difficult one to pin down."

Rikard realised his men still had their weapons drawn. "Stand down. They're friends," he said.

"I'd hate to be their enemies," quipped Bolt.

"Ha! That you would, laddie," boomed the giant Hallbjorn.

Amongst this group of forest folk, Rikard saw a pretty young woman slender as a sword blade. She ambled over to Olaf and casually entwined her arm with his.

"He be the good 'un," she said.

"I am terribly sorry, but do I know you from somewhere?" Rikard asked.

39

SEED OF HOPE

Her captors had left Elsta imprisoned in the inn's attic room. The roof slanted downwards, so she was only able to pace half the room. She spent most of the time curled up in bed and comforted by the blankets she'd rolled herself in. Tight as a ball, she tried to convince herself they would protect her from the dangerous men downstairs.

She knew they could come into the room at any moment. It prevented her from sleeping. She had tried to move a chest of drawers in front of the door. It had been too heavy, and she gave up. Instead she wedged a blanket at the foot of the door. It might slow them down and give her a moment to get ready.

The room had no windows. There was only one skylight. The full moon blazed a cold silver slither of light into the attic. Tears soaked the sleeve of Elsta's gown. She wept like a newborn, and every time her gaze fell upon the wedding dress they expected her to wear in the morning, she cried further.

Volek's name filled her with fear. He'd said they would take their wedding vows in the inn after dawn. They would then enter Kronnoburg together as man and wife. The general was sure her people would see reason and open the city gates. If they didn't, she'd be put to the sword.

The House of Mik was crumbling, and soon it would be under the shadow of Krakonite. It felt like a spear through her heart.

Her father once shared with her the words of a wise man, "If the world around you is ending, and you have a seed in your hand, plant it. In that seed there is hope for the future, and in hope you will find strength for the present."

She needed hope.

Tap, tap, tap.

She looked up. A dark hooded form hovered on the other side of the skylight. It obscured the moon from her view.

"No," she whimpered and retreated further into the recesses of the room.

Tap, tap, tap.

She screwed up her eyes. She didn't want to look at this wretched chimera. When she opened them, the thing outside the skylight had not moved. *Be gone, demon!*

She forced herself to be brave and look. When she did, she realised the demon had two hands and a face.

Tap, tap, tap.

It was the face of the young man from the inn. How could she forget such an evil, vile individual? He had incarcerated her fiancé—her prince, her king, and the real Theodorus Theseus of Athenia. Elsta turned away from him. Fear had left her. Hate filled her heart.

Tap, tap, tap.

"Enough!" Elsta threw off her blankets and marched over to the spot below the skylight. "Go away!" she cried.

He removed his hood. His face was solemn and empty of anger or pride. He almost looked hurt. He placed his hand upon his heart and mouthed words she could not hear, but there was no mistaking their meaning. He then indicated he wanted to come inside. *Don't trust him.*

"Please," he mouthed.

Elsta was curious but fearful. Maybe it was another trap set by the beastly Naram-Sin.

"How much worse can it get?" Elsta muttered under her breath. She pulled up a chair and reached up to unlatch the skylight.

"Thank you," he said. He lifted up the skylight and dropped down to the floor beside her. He unsheathed his sword.

40

FEAR

The princess retreated. Adan realised he had scared her. He went down on one knee before her. Placing Tizona on the palms of his hands, he bowed his head and outstretched his arms.

"My sword arm belongs to Your Majesty, for I have wronged you. I did not know what I was doing," said Adan.

"What?"

"Naram-Sin was correct. We did arrest a man in an iron mask, but his identity was not known to me."

The princess stared at him with a sterile curiosity. "Tell me more."

"My master and I were told to apprehend three Athenian sailors wanted for crimes against the Republic of Avantolia. Our intention was to bring them to the

Oblivion for questioning, but Grandmaster Naram-Sin intercepted us. He took the man in the iron mask away, saying he was acting on the instructions of Chancellor Sargon. The prisoner was incarcerated in the Pit—the lowest level of the Oblivion."

"Is my fiancé alive?" said the princess.

As Adan stared into her clear blue eyes, he realised why it was said her presence at the front of any army would spur its soldiers to fight beyond their abilities. Adan lowered his gaze. "He was when I last saw him."

"And now?"

"I don't know, Your Majesty. The Pit contains a ruthless collection of the most hardened criminals."

"He is no criminal."

Adan remained silent.

"What is your name?" asked the princess.

"I am Adan de la Vega. Apprentice to Grandmaster Suri-Yi of the Tasburai Order."

"Suri-Yi?"

"Yes. Do you know her?"

"She is at Kronnoburg. She sought an audience, but we ignored her request."

Suri-Yi had told him to meet her at Kronnoburg, but he never believed she'd already be there. "Then we must leave at once. When we find her, she will know what must be done," said Adan.

"You will help me escape?"

"Yes, Your Majesty. The Tasburai have always served the royals of Kronnoburg, and I mean to carry on that tradition. I will not fail you. Come."

Adan climbed back up to the skylight and then stretched down with his hand. The princess hesitantly reached across. Her soft fingers slipped into his, and he gripped her firmly. He lifted her up and out through the skylight. Her gold Nostvektian ring bore the seal of the House of Mik. It rubbed against the ordinary half ring on his finger which his mother had left him.

Elsta couldn't believe they'd be able to evade the guards with such deftness, but the Tasburai moved like a shadow. He told her to step where he stepped, and he held her hand, firmly guiding her between the encampments. He had given her a man's riding cloak to camouflage her features.

She wasn't sure he could be trusted, but what choice did she have? She'd rather die than marry Volek. Knowing her fiancé might still be alive, however, filled her with hope. If she found him, they could wed after all, and if the young Tasburai was a means to achieving that, then she would trust him.

The horse the Tasburai had left stood silent. Its head down, it chewed the grass below a cedar tree. They mounted the beast, and he rode it away from camp slowly and quietly. They were like ghosts tracing a path back to Kronnoburg and her people. Kronnoburg's walls disappeared as they dipped into the valley. The Tasburai suddenly reined in the horse. Hundreds of Volek's troops were encamped in the valley before them. Campfires lit up the valley floor like firecrackers across a lawn.

The Tasburai exhaled loudly. "We need to go around," he said.

They moved sideways and upwards. Even though backtracking at times, she was glad he was being cautious. She had no intention of getting caught again. The heavy sound of the horse's breath filled her ears as they ascended the mountain pass under nightfall. The full moon blazed a path for them. Eventually the Tasburai dismounted. He took the animal's reins in his hands and walked alongside it, and they crept up the mountainside higher and higher. The firm tracks disappeared and turned into pebble-filled pathways. The horse's hooves began to slip.

"Your Majesty, I think it wise if you dismount. We should make our way on foot."

She had to agree. It was a precipitous ascent, and she was beginning to lose her nerve upon the steed. She let herself be gently lifted off the saddle and brought down in the Tasburai's arms.

"Thank you," she whispered and smiled at him.

He returned her smile but then looked away. With the horse trailing behind them, they followed the ridge upwards. The campfires in the valley became less bright the higher they went. She could see Kronnoburg once more. Her sprawling dominion was a city of spires, towers, battalions, and imposing walls. To its north, wild dark peaks dominated a craggy mountain range. Further north, she knew, was the Forbidden Quarter. Over to the east was a sea of wild grass into which an entire army could disappear. It was wave upon wave of green and yellow. To the west the River Sjorn flowed and formed a serpentine line that sparkled in the moonlight. Behind them the route south led to Krakonite and trouble.

"Am I correct in assuming you are familiar with the way?" asked Elsta.

"I studied maps of the terrain. There is a plateau that leads to a path down the cliff, and we need to follow this."

"So you've never actually been this way before."

"No, but..." The Tasburai froze and pressed his fingers to his lips. Elsta couldn't hear anything. "Yah." The Tasburai released the horse. He pulled Elsta away, moving fast up the trail and towards the plateau.

"What is it?" asked Elsta.

"We're being followed. Soldiers. Lots of them."

"Who?"

"Volek's men."

Elsta quickened the pace. She could hear them now—a jangle of armour and voices crying out after them. Elsta and the Tasburai ran up the steep path. The muscles in her calves ached, but she flashed a glance back and saw a party of thirty or forty soldiers pointing at them with their weapons. They were gaining fast.

They reached the plateau, a vast expanse of rock. It was interspersed with patches of wild grass, bony trees, and potholes. The moon's white light lit it up like a frozen wasteland.

"Where now?" said Elsta.

"Across the plateau. On the other side is a bridge which will take us across the gorge and down to the river. Come on!"

Elsta gripped the Tasburai's hand and ran. The hems of her garments ripped on thorns as she passed. She looked down to avoid falling into a pothole.

"Faster!" said the Tasburai.

She shot a look back. The soldiers were closer than they had been. If she fell now, they'd reach her within moments. Their voices grew louder, and the plateau seemed to stretch on and on. Her lungs gasped for air, and her legs began to tire.

"Don't give up, Your Majesty. We can make it."

He is right. I will be the queen of Kronnoburg and am daughter of the House of Mik. I will not let these vandals get the better of me.

When she glanced back, she saw the soldiers were also tired. The obstacles on the plateau were unforgiving on the legs. They kept moving and avoided the gullies scored into the rock surface over hundreds of years.

At the other side, the plateau abruptly ended. The mountain sloped dangerously downwards. Close to where the sloping edge ended, Elsta saw the bridge. It was a flimsy crossing. Rope, hemp, and wood, many pieces of which were missing, strung the bridge together. A few hundred feet below the bridge, the white waters of the River Sjorn rushed.

Elsta froze. "I can't go down there. The cliff edge makes me dizzy."

The Tasburai's expression was sympathetic but firm. "Your Majesty, I have the same problem. I don't like heights. Unfortunately we don't have a choice."

The soldiers were almost on their heels when the Tasburai yanked her by the arm and urged her down the slope in the direction of the rickety bridge. Elsta instinctively froze and dug her heels in. Her hand slipped out of his, and she fell back. Adan plunged onwards down the steep gradient. The movement caused Elsta to fall on all fours.

As the Tasburai turned around to come back for her, Elsta felt someone crash into her back. She and her assailant tumbled over and over. Down the slope they went, speeding towards the cliff edge and the gaping ravine.

Elsta clawed at the smooth rock face but was unable to obtain any purchase. Twisting like a corkscrew, she spun with her assailant up and around.

The drop approached. They weren't slowing. Then everything seemed to slow down around her. The Tasburai leapt and stretched out his hand to catch Elsta, but a pack of soldiers rammed into him, and they all went tumbling down the slope.

The soldier who had attacked her began poking the serrated edge of his knife into the ground and scratching the rock. Elsta thought he was attempting to inscribe his name, but why would he do such a strange thing?

She rolled onwards. Then all the bumps and crashing ended, and she felt weightless. *I am flying.* Elsta saw the soldier flying beside her. He was upside down and screaming at the top of his voice. *Whack!* She landed. The soldier did not, and he continued his descent down the sheer cliff wall.

I'm saved! Elsta was on all fours on the rope bridge. She glanced downwards and saw the white waters of the River Sjorn rushing past. She pushed herself up. She heard the wooden slats under her feet crack. Then she fell.

41

RAGE

Everything happened in slow motion. Adan reached out to the queen as she headed towards the cliff edge, but his arms and legs were knocked away. Adan was tumbling down the smooth rock face, and some of Volek's soldiers barged into him.

From the corner of his eye, he saw two people go over the cliff edge. Others around him yelled. He was rolling over and over, so he unsheathed his hunting knife and jammed it into the ground. It snagged a groove on the rock face, and he held it firm. His arms ached from the effort. His descent stopped, and he could draw breath. As he got up, another soldier rammed into him, grabbed Adan by the waist, and sent him backwards and careering towards the cliff edge once more. Adan slammed the hilt of his hunting knife into the soldier's nose and snapped his head backwards. The soldier released his grip, but it was too late. They went over the edge.

Adan's robes snagged on a thornbush growing on the cliff edge. This momentarily slowed his fall. He was desperately trying to stab at the rock face with his hunting knife. It stuck. There was a tiny fissure. He hung there. Perilously swinging, his body strained.

The soldier who had knocked into him screamed as he fell towards the river. Two other soldiers also swung from the cliff edge. They were gripping the wild grass growing on its edge. The grass ripped, however, sending them downwards and crashing into the cliff face.

With his free hand, he removed Tizona and rammed the Orlisium steel into another crevice. The blade went through it. He planted his feet against the cliff wall and took a deep breath. Glancing down made him dizzy. He'd never be able to shake off his fear of heights now.

Removing the hunting knife from the fissure, Adan wedged it into another crack further up. He repeated the process with Tizona. The white water rushed below him. He gazed down again and shut his eyes. *I didn't come here to die. My master is at Kronnoburg. I must reach her. I must know who I am.*

Adan could hear a group of soldiers making their way down the cliff towards him. Dangling in his precarious position, he was an easy target for an archer. Even a soldier with a spear could take a shot at him. He didn't have long to react. Adan started to scramble upwards, but he could only go as fast as he found cracks to bury his blades. It was painful. His arms felt exhausted, and he had to rush. Adan reached the top and hauled himself up and over. He was back on the precarious slope at the cliff edge.

"Kill him!"

Adan turned to see near to thirty soldiers rushing towards him. It was too many to fight alone, but there was nowhere to go. The first soldier to reach him underestimated the gradient and wasn't able to stop. Adan dodged the man as the soldier swung his sword and missed. His screams echoed as he fell.

The next group slowed and circled him with cautious aggression.

"Careful. He's Tasburai," said one.

They glared menacingly as he twirled Tizona in his hand. Trying to look calm, he felt as though a dog was chewing his insides. *Should I just jump into the Sjorn and take my chances?*

Two soldiers split from the troop and swung their weapons at him. Down came their murderous blades, aiming to slice him in half. Adan deflected the first blow and blocked the second. A flat kick into the first soldier's stomach put him on his back. Adan reversed his sword swing and took the legs out from underneath the second soldier, and Adan rolled him off the cliff. The next two soldiers attacked. The first also went over the cliff, and the second lost his sword arm as Tizona flicked out like a tongue of blue flame.

If the soldiers kept coming down in twos, it would be like a practice drill. It might be some time before a soldier got lucky and took him out. His arms ached. It was as though they were encased in lead. He shot a glance back over his shoulder. Where was the princess?

"He's a tricky one, but he can't fight us all at once. March forward, and we'll push him off the cliff," said one of the soldiers who'd been observing Adan despatch his fellow fighters. He marshalled the remainder of the men to form a line, steady their weapons, and close in on Adan.

"Over the edge." The soldier grinned and spat at him.

Time and options were running out. He took his chances and leapt into their midst. Tizona blazed away at all angles, forming a strip of blue light that moved quicker than soldiers could parry with their swords. Like a scythe cutting hay in the harvest, he was slicing soldiers down as he edged back up the slope.

Then he collapsed. Someone smashed the back of his head with a weapon. Adan fell to his knees but rolled instinctively, hearing a spear tip crack the rock where he'd been a moment before. His head was groggy, and his left knee buckled as he tried to stand. A soldier planted a kick in his face. He saw the boot coming, grabbed it, and twisted the soldier's ankle, causing the soldier to spin around and land on his back.

"Jump him!"

Two soldiers seized his arms. Another grappled him around the neck, and someone stepped down hard on his wrist. Tizona fell from his grip. Fists, elbows, and knees battered him as he rolled about on the ground, trying to protect his head and face. The blows rained down too fast to count. Adan wasn't sure which part of his body was most in pain. One soldier kicked his chest and knocked the wind out of him. Another struck him in the pit of his stomach, causing Adan to double over and retch.

Battered, he lost all sense of direction. All feeling left his body. *Is this the end?* He had failed. Suri-Yi would be so disappointed. She would be the last Tasburai, because he'd be lying at the bottom of the Sjorn. Consciousness crept away over the horizon of his mind.

Then Adan suddenly felt a burning heat and a freezing cold. An ice storm raged in his head, and his blood felt as if it was pumped full of ice and snow. Yet his limbs burnt like a sunspot, and his eyes were hot coals in a furnace. There was no more pain—only rage. Adan heard the cruel laughter echoing once more from the pit of his stomach.

"Why's he laughing?"

"He's crying."

"Who cares? Kill him."

Vega had always been inside Adan but chained down and hidden. He was now resplendent and free. He smiled and wiped his bloody lips with the back of his hand. His laugh had an edge of insanity. It was enough to stop his enemies in their tracks. *Tizona will burn crimson.*

Vega leapt up and landed firmly on his feet. He grabbed hold of the nearest soldier. *Crack.* Vega headbutted him so hard he split the man's nose. The next soldier's windpipe was crushed, and the next lost his eyes. The eyeless man had been holding Tizona, and when he let go, Vega swept up the Tasburai blade. He had seen Adan, the other one inside this body, use it to good effect. Adan was skilled with it, and so would Vega be—a brutal, merciless killer. Tizona pulsated red. He was sure it had been blue when Adan had last used it. What did it matter? Red or blue, it was just as effective in cutting down anyone who stood before him.

A relentless fury of arms and legs, Vega hacked down the soldiers. Indiscriminate blows rained down on those before him. Vega was wounded, but he did not register the pain. The only colour he saw was red, and it attracted him like a bee to honey. Two more soldiers fell as a single blow from Tizona decapitated the first and opened up the neck of the second.

The remaining soldiers backed away. *Cravens.* They were spineless, but that made his work—killing—easier. Vega roared and charged at the pack of soldiers. After fighting his way uphill, no one was left alive.

PART III

42

THE WALL

News came of a breach on the outer walls of Kronnoburg. Saboteurs had lowered the drawbridges from within, allowing Volek's army to spill in through to the inner defence walls. Then word came of a hooded group of warriors infiltrating the city's armoury. Finally strange stories circulated of a mist leaking out from an old, abandoned passage below the city, spreading through some of the oldest quarters close to the Hall of Records.

Rikard had so few battle-ready soldiers. The choice was simple when Olaf the Generous presented him with an offer of help. The man had years of field experience, and he was a friend of Suri-Yi. That alone was enough for Rikard. Gruelling times required hard decisions, and even adversaries could become friends.

Rikard went to the inner defence wall with Lieutenant Bolt and a contingent of the best hand-to-hand fighters he could find. To their number he willingly added Hallbjorn the Bear and Brynjar the Blade. One glance at Hallbjorn, with his enormous size and great battleaxe, or Brynjar, with his knives and dexterity, would give any man a clear idea they were not to be fooled with. Rikard believed them lining up alongside his own men would strengthen their resolve.

To the armoury went a group led by Olaf the Generous and his daughter, Ylva. *Now there is a feisty girl. In better times I might have wanted to get to know her.*

When news of the mist in the old city quarter reached him, Rikard wanted to dismiss it. It was only because Suri-Yi had already departed for the old city that he took a peculiar interest in the report and realised it was serious. The dark labyrinth of disused tunnels below the city's Old Quarter wasn't a location anyone wanted to visit. Suri-Yi was already long gone when Olaf told Rikard of her intentions, so he couldn't assign any soldiers to her. Rikard had felt guilty letting her go alone, but he guessed she was used to it. It didn't make him feel any better, though.

At the inner wall, Rikard and his contingent of men moved along on horseback. They hugged the great defensive structure. The stone-and-steel facade rose up too high for anyone to comfortably stand on. Yet there were sentries posted and watching the horizon. These small specks of men peered down at him. No doubt they were wondering who would join them on the front line. Noble or commoner, any reinforcements would be welcome.

The wall curved, and from around the other corner came a group of soldiers on horseback. Wearing stained, bloodied uniforms, they were decked out with a glittering assortment of weapons. These were a hardened bunch of men. As they went by, they saluted him.

"Whose company are they in?" Rikard asked Bolt.

"I don't know, sir."

"At least you've got some lads out 'ere who've seen action," mumbled Hallbjorn, lifting his thumb in the direction of the hardened soldiers.

Rikard and Bolt led their own little company's horses at a steady trot until they came upon a turret jutting out from the wall. Bolt dismounted and beckoned for Rikard, his other soldiers, and the tree folk to follow.

"We need to ascend the wall from this inner staircase," said the lieutenant.

The spiral staircase wound itself around the turret, so Rikard couldn't see how high up it went. If it went to the top, it would be a long walk.

"Lad, tree folk are born for climbing trees. Not stairs," Hallbjorn huffed.

Rikard felt sorry for the Bear. He almost filled the entire width of the staircase. Evidently the man was not suited to a closed, claustrophobic stairwell. Rikard didn't fancy being the soldier rushing down the staircase and meeting the Bear coming up.

"If you ate less, it wouldn't be such a problem," said Brynjar, and he squeezed past Hallbjorn, taking the steps two at a time.

"Then I wouldn't be called the Bear, would I, lad," said Hallbjorn, but the Blade was nearly out of earshot. He just waved his hand.

Progress was slow and tiring. Rikard had to listen to the Bear panting as he ascended higher and higher. The party eventually emerged on the upper battlements. All the men looked weary. The wind blew in fierce gusts. He shivered as it cut to his bones. He couldn't quite remember the last time he had been here. Then it came to him. It had been with Tromor. In their youthful hubris, they had decided to race to the top on a cold winter's night. The moon had filled the evening sky, and the steps had been slippery from rain. They had nearly broken their necks racing back down. Those were happy but long-gone days. The House of Mik was nearly extinguished. All were dead, maybe even the princess.

The soldiers on patrol were dressed for the elements. He should have brought a riding cloak.

"Status," said Bolt to a sergeant who appeared from a group of soldiers.

All were surprised by their sudden appearance. When the sergeant saw the seal of command pinned to Rikard's uniform, he saluted. "Sir, the enemy has breached the outer walls. They're making camp in the area beyond the inner walls." The sergeant reminded Rikard of the local butcher. He had the gait of a man who enjoyed his meals.

"Let's take a look," said Rikard.

The sergeant led them to a viewing station—vertical slits the defenders could peer through. Here they could assess the approaching enemy within a relatively safe area. When Rikard gazed out at the open land between the outer and inner walls, it looked dire. General Volek's army assumed well-structured formations. Company after company, and still more soldiers, entered through the breach in the outer walls. Their ordered manner led Rikard to one conclusion. *They intend to occupy the city. Not sack it.*

"How did they gain entry? The wall shows no damage," asked Rikard.

The sergeant blushed. "The gate was opened from within," he said.

"I see," said Rikard.

"Our security has been compromised. We have infiltrators. Part of Volek's army is in our midst. We're not sure who can be trusted any longer, sir," said the sergeant.

"So it would seem," said Rikard.

The sergeant seemed to have something interesting on the tip of his boot, and he gazed at it with concentration.

"Captain, you have a leak in your boat. It'll be the death of us all if you don't fix it," said Hallbjorn.

Rikard turned away and cast his eye over the glittering towers of the inner city. How long until they fell to the forces of General Volek? Peering downwards, he noticed the troop of soldiers who'd ridden past him earlier; even at this distance they had a dangerous swagger. They were waiting at the inner gatehouse. One amongst them exchanged words with the guard. It must have been amusing because they were laughing. It was nice to see camaraderie at such a time.

Then the guard toppled over. As he fell, Rikard saw a flurry of knives and daggers fly from the hands of the hardened soldiers. They leapt off their mounts and made for the gatehouse.

"Stop them! They're going to open the gates!" shouted Rikard. He had made his voice as loud as he could muster, hoping everyone up and down the wall had heard.

A storm of Nostvektian soldiers raced towards the gatehouse, but one of the infiltrators fired a flaming arrow high into the sky. It sailed over the inner wall and over their heads and landed in the field occupied by Volek's soldiers. When Rikard heard the battle cry from Volek's men, his blood turned cold. He didn't need to see what was happening. He knew Volek's army would be racing towards the gate.

Rikard led his men down the stairs. Slipping and stumbling, it reminded him of the night he'd pelted down the stairwell with Tromor. Back then he had been carefree. Today he felt the weight of responsibility on his shoulders.

"Stairs. I hate stairs. Whether going up or down. Bad for old knees," grumbled Hallbjorn.

Rikard and his men burst out of the stairwell and headed towards the gatehouse, but the infiltrators had gained entry and locked his soldiers out. His men were trying to batter through the reinforced wooden door. Three, four, and then five soldiers put their shoulders into it. Rikard saw the reinforced gate of the inner defence wall start to rise and the drawbridge on the other side start to lower.

"Coming through!" roared Hallbjorn.

The sight of the Bear charging at the wooden gatehouse door was enough to move his men out of the way. *Whack!* Hallbjorn went straight through, taking the door off its hinges. Rikard and Bolt were first through after him. General Volek's spies spun around with their swords at the ready. Two men wound back the pulley mechanism that raised the gate and lowered the drawbridge. The others formed a defensive line before them.

"No you don't," said Hallbjorn. He swung his great axe, knocking two of the soldiers aside.

Rikard was so busy admiring the way the Bear fought he forgot to draw his sword. One of Volek's spies came for him, swinging his steel. Rikard fumbled for his weapon. The maladroit movement of his hand caused the thing to clatter on the floor. Rikard leapt out of the way as the blade flashed by.

Bolt covered for him and parried the attacker's next thrust. One of the other spies wrestled Bolt to the floor, and they tumbled over a chair, which lifted off the ground and smacked Rikard flush on his nose. He squeezed his eyes shut from the pain and tasted blood on his lips. He stared up from his lowly position. The fight was in full swing.

Hallbjorn's mighty frame moved with remarkable ease. His axe jumped from one hand to the other and cut down the enemy. Brynjar's quick fingers let fly daggers and knives, impaling his opponents. Bolt and the others were holding the line, not letting any other spies out of the gatehouse. Hallbjorn reached for the pulley. Rikard shot a glance at the gate and drawbridge. He could now see Volek's army getting close. The dust from their approach kicked up into the air.

"Cut the rope!" shouted Rikard.

Brynjar threw a dagger. It partially severed the rope, but the men kept heaving it. The remaining spies put their bodies between Brynjar and the pulley, blocking any knife-throwing heroics.

"Argh!" yelled Hallbjorn. His axe split a sword in half, and he lifted a soldier and threw him across the room. The flying soldier smacked into the men protecting the pulley. Brynjar had a clean shot. He threw his knife, and it severed the rope.

Done, Rikard thought. *A reprieve at last.*

Rikard stared at the gate. It was still open. Why hadn't it shut? The rope had severed. The pulley should have simultaneously released the gate and raised the drawbridge. Rikard saw Volek's soldiers propping up the gate with a wooden support beam. Then another beam was put in place. This was followed by two, three, and four more. Soldiers poured across the drawbridge and the open gate. The inner walls were breached.

"Spirits protect us," said Hallbjorn, and he and Brynjar stepped out of the gatehouse to face the oncoming horde.

Rikard wanted to run away, but there was nowhere safe left within the city. He rose, wiped his bloody nose, and went out to join Hallbjorn and Brynjar. If he was going to die, let it be with his sword swinging in defence of Kronnoburg.

43

ARMOURY

It was odd how things turned out. When Ylva came to Kronnoburg, she was as excited as if Blind Belinda were going to cut her toenails. Spending time in the city, however, made it different. She was fighting with the Nostvektians—for them. Father was supporting Captain Navrosk and his weak-kneed soldiers.

The captain said there had been some dodgy types who had invaded the armoury and spooked the regular soldiers. *Nostvektian soldiers are a right iffy bunch. Can't even nock their arrows the right way in a bowstring. Bloody useless.* Ylva considered them only good for one thing—prancing around in their bright uniforms and polished shoes, which looked more like mirrors, and marching up and down the parade ground. *Fat load of good that would do in a real fight.* They talked as though they were itching for a fight, but when one came along, there were none to be seen.

"Armoury looks deserted," said Sigrun.

"Aye, but it should be the busiest place in the city at a time like this," said Olaf. "Only the ghosts of old generals are haunting this place today."

"Aye, Father," said Ylva. *Ghosts are better than Ifreet.*

The men Navrosk sent with them looked as if they might weep at any moment. Their hands shook and knees rattled. Their eyes darted about like terrified rabbits. Ylva was worried about having these men behind her. In their current state, they'd let arrows fly in panic when sighting the enemy. She moved to the side of them. There was no point in being snuffed in the back by some idiot and dying from the wound.

The twelve soldiers in their company followed Olaf. They were glad to obey his orders.

"Sigrun, Ylva, I need eagle eyes," said Olaf, pointing upwards.

Ylva and Sigrun peeled away from the group. They ascended the eastern staircase, which led to the battlements surrounding the armoury. Quick as a wolf, she bounded up the steps two at a time. Sigrun tucked in behind her like her shadow.

Ylva watched her father and the soldiers creep through the main entrance to the fort. It was flung wide open as if it were the summer solstice banquet and the hosts were expecting them. But the solstice was over. It was an invasion, and this place was dead as a graveyard.

The armoury was a tight square stone building with four turrets at each end. In the middle was an empty square. It was gravelled and wrought with smooth stone paths for ammunition to be moved around. Plenty of murder holes were built into entrances, but none had been used recently.

"Did ya see that?" whispered Sigrun.

"What?"

"It was like a fluttering black flag. Around that corner. Gone before I could get a proper look," he answered. "Nice and slow."

"Okay."

Ylva glanced down. Her father and the soldiers shimmied forwards on the ground. Ylva had passed halfway across the battlements when she noticed large barrels placed along the perimeter wall. They were filled with a black powder, and she bent over and smelt it. It was like burnt coal. She had no idea what it was and moved on. Still there was nothing—no sound or people. She looked back over her shoulder, but Sigrun wasn't there. He hadn't moved from the spot where they last spoke. Sigrun was looking up at her. His hands were planted firmly on the stone, crouching and ready to move forward. She beckoned him to follow. He didn't. Sigrun had been thieving with her often and had never behaved like this before. What was he up to?

There was nothing for it but to scramble back. Olaf and the soldiers moved into the western quarter of the armoury. They disappeared within the rooms in that part of the building.

She saw Sigrun's mouth was wide open. He was drooling. *No. Not drooling.*

Tap, tap, tap.

His blood splattered on the stone, and she saw the spear impaling him. It ran through his neck and down his back. *No!*

Ylva screamed as loudly as she could. It wasn't from the fear of dying but anger. The image of Sigrun's wife, his two boys, and the rest of his family flashed across her mind. Then her hand instinctively released the Orlisium blade. The steel swished out from its scabbard. The light caught the end, sparkling like a star on fire. As she straightened her sword, a hooded adversary dressed in long black robes stepped out from behind the turret.

She blocked the killing stroke and rolled forwards and past Sigrun. The spear impaling him was dug deep into the groove between the stone slabs. It held him there like a rag doll. She felt the presence of another hooded warrior behind her and ducked. The blade missed her and split the spear holding Sigrun. Her old friend toppled down and over the battlements. Sigrun had told her he'd probably die one day doing something stupid whilst eagling. Neither of them imagined it would be this.

Ylva spun around and saw a third hooded opponent appear from behind a wall. Only one thing for it—run.

She raced back down the way she'd come, hugging the walls. *Snap.* A dagger hit the wall close to her.

Focus on running. Fast as you can. She couldn't hear them, but she was sure the silent, deadly warriors were right behind her.

As she reached ground level, Ylva headed for the entrance she'd seen her father and the soldiers go through. *Crash.* The window to her left shattered. Glass flew in all directions. The body of a Nostvektian soldier was propelled through the air. Another hooded opponent stood on the other side of the window frame.

Ylva raced through what was left of the doorway to see enemies encircling her father. Most of the Nostvektian soldiers lay dead or dying on the ground. Blood had splattered everywhere.

The Orlisium blade felt part of her now, and she drove it hard through the back of one of the hooded opponents surrounding her father. Two of them spun around to face her. Her father cut the first and second down.

"Run, Ylva!" cried Olaf.

Grabbing each other's hands, they dashed deeper into the armoury, and more hooded adversaries burst through the doorway. They ran. They figured any direction would do just so long as it was away from those swords. The corridor narrowed. Ylva bounced off the walls. Her sword clattered against the rock and chipped the stone.

"Faster, Ylva!"

The hooded adversaries were gaining ground. She came to a junction. Right or left? She went right. *Don't get everyone killed by making the wrong decision.* The corridor sloped downwards into a tunnel. It was dark, and she couldn't see well. Light crept through small openings near the ceiling. They turned a corner and saw a door. She tried the handle. It was open, and they went through and bolted it from within.

They were in a storeroom strewn with weapons and barrels of the black powder she'd seen on the battlements. Ylva went over to take another look at the black powder.

"Smells awful. What type of crop is it, Father?" said Ylva.

"Not something we wanna be next to, my girl. Suri-Yi called it the black fire. It was forged by pyromancers to fend off the Magrog when they came too close to a city's outer walls. Wasn't supposed to be any left. Too dangerous. The Tasburai took it all back to Avantolia and out of harm's way. We don't want to be in this room if that goes off. Look for a way out—a drain, trapdoor, or anything."

Olaf turned over crates and boxes. She joined him in searching for a way out. Minutes passed as they waited for the hooded adversaries to ram down the door. It didn't happen.

"You hear that, Ylva?"

"No."

"They ain't trying to get in."

He was right. The thumping on the door never came, and when she put her ear to the wooden panel, she could hear footsteps retreating. They waited. Not moving, they strained their ears for any sound. It was silent in the corridor. Olaf opened the door. The place was as empty as a rat's nest after a blaze. They crept out and back up the corridor slowly. Olaf cautiously shut the storeroom door as if afraid to disturb the very air around the black fire.

They returned to the room where Ylva had found her father surrounded. Apart from the dead Nostvektians scattered on the floor, it was deserted. Everywhere was a bloody mess. Ylva suddenly noticed the same barrels as in the storeroom. They were placed in the corners of this room.

"Father?"

"Yes?"

"Look. Up in the sky!"

A dozen flaming arrows were heading straight towards the armoury.

"Spirits protect us!" shouted Olaf.

Ylva raced with him back down the corridor. This time they turned left at the fork. She heard an almighty bang, everything went black as coal, and the roof came crashing down.

44

MIST

It was the fiery orange colour of the mist that worried Suri-Yi. An Ifreet emitted smoke from its body when underground. It was a type of internal combustion, and it was orange. She never understood why, but she always heeded the signs. Experience had taught her to be cautious.

The Old Quarter of the city was deserted. Only a few inhabitants of Kronnoburg remained. These people were either too stubborn or frail to leave. She passed an elderly couple sitting on their balcony.

"It's that way. What you've come for," said the old woman, gesturing straight ahead. "Same as last time."

"Thank you," said Suri-Yi. She recognised the woman from the previous time she had visited the Old Quarter all those years ago.

"You haven't aged very much, my dear," the old woman said.

But I feel it. I'm not as fast as I was, and after every encounter with an opponent, my bones ache.

"We all get older. May your path be filled with light," Suri-Yi answered.

The street narrowed further. The ancient stone along the ground was uneven and slippery. She remembered the last time she'd been down this way. Naram-Sin had accompanied her then. They had made a fine pairing in those days. It had been a hopeful time filled with the promise of a better future. The region had been united against a common enemy—the Magrog. The Tasburai had been respected wherever they went. People had felt safe when they saw her. Today they shrank away in fear.

The mist bled out from the sewers. It was fiery orange. *Do I still have what it takes to defeat an Ifreet?* The Ifreet was close. No doubt it was accompanied by a troop of Xettin. Fending off Volek's army was already straining every resource within Kronnoburg. The city really didn't need an Ifreet and band of Xettin to turn up.

She recalled the old saying "When the Xettin come down the mountain the Magrog follow across the Black Sea." It had always been this way. She said a small prayer for Heraclius and Duria—the first port of call should the Magrog appear upon the coast.

When Suri-Yi had last visited this quarter of the city, she'd gained entry to the crisscrossing subterranean tunnels through a drain cover. It had been adjacent to an ironmonger's shop. The shop was still there, albeit empty. The drain cover was also still there. She ripped open the cover with a crowbar she found in the ironmonger's shop.

Whoosh. The air rushed out, and with it came wisps of orange smoke. She let the draught settle into a steady stream before climbing down the ladder and into the tunnel. Faint light illuminated the way ahead and behind. She followed the fiery puffs of orange smoke. The Ifreet wouldn't be too far ahead.

It frustrated her not knowing why the Ifreet and Xettin had come to Kronnoburg and not having someone more knowledgeable to consult with. *So few Shufis to take your worries to these days.*

She soon came upon tracks left by clumsy Xettin. The tunnel split in four directions, but the tracks and puffs of orange only went down one, so she followed it. These tunnels were very old. They were perhaps built at the very inception of the city. Sealed stairways led up to the museum, treasury, and royal courts of justice.

Suri-Yi imagined when government officials had filled these tunnels, moving between locations and avoiding the bustle of the streets above. The trail led to a passageway. Its door was smashed off its hinges, and its notice said the staircase led to the Hall of Antiquity.

Suri-Yi heard the Xettin grunt as it leapt at her. The beast came at a pace, having vaulted from near the middle of the staircase. It had hoped to catch her off guard. If it hadn't grunted like a wild boar, it might have. The Xettin was the height of a doorframe and just as wide. It was also stupid. Suri-Yi stepped out of its path. Her hand flicked Shamshir from its scabbard, slicing the creature's back as it went past. It didn't get up from that blow.

Another Xettin appeared at the top of the staircase, blocking the backlight. Suri-Yi sprinted up the steps three at a time. The Xettin watched her, its face slanted sideways in a dumb expression. The fiend struck out with its blade. She dodged the attack, leapt against the sidewall, and catapulted herself around and behind its weapon. Shamshir removed the Xettin's sword arm, and she kicked the beast down the stairs. She passed through the doorway. There was another narrow corridor. At the end was another door and a third Xettin. This one was smart. It ran when it saw her. She gave chase, and they entered the Hall of Antiquity. A mesmerising black-and-white tiled floor and crystal chandeliers dominated the entrance hall. Two curved staircases joined together on the first floor. The Xettin crossed the lobby and ran up the staircase. She was right behind it and caught up as they reached the top. Two more Xettin joined, and their broadswords rose and fell. She rolled and twisted away from the murderous blades. Suri-Yi could sense the Ifreet was close.

Three more Xettin came from behind. It was now six against one. The familiar sense of calm settled over her, and Shamshir pulsated green. She and the blade were one. It was done in mere seconds. She didn't give the felled Xettin another look before moving on. They were dead. It was time for the Ifreet.

She found the demon crouching over a stone sarcophagus. It had removed the heavy lid, and it lay cracked to one side. It put its hand inside, and when it came away from the sarcophagus, she saw it gripping a smooth oval orange stone the size of her fist. The Ifreet snapped its head up. Its eyes blazed with cruel intent, and it wore a twisted grin.

"Tasburai," its voice rasped.

Am I strong enough?

The Ifreet ripped out a cat-o'-nine-tails from its stomach. She'd seen this manoeuvre before. Every weapon the Ifreet produced was from its own fiery body. Once it let go of the weapon, the weapon simply disappeared. While in its hands, however, it was as real as any killing tool. The strands of fire rushed at her. She ducked and rolled away. As the Ifreet circled the cat-o'-nine-tails in an arc, its free hand flicked darts. Suri-Yi knew these were its fingernails, which would regrow in a few moments. She used Shamshir to deflect the darts. The coolness of the Orlisium steel diffused the fire.

She leapt over the cat-o'-nine-tails as it whipped by. The most effective way to fight an Ifreet was to get as near as possible. The demon arched its weapon back for a third strike, and it simultaneously threw its arm at her. The limb came like a fiery spear. By the time she sliced through it, the limb had been replaced by a new one, and the demon spun the cat-o'-nine-tails at her at an awkward angle.

The Ifreet had whatever it had come for, and it fled. Taking giant strides up and away, it headed for the floor-to-ceiling stained glass window. Suri-Yi quickened her pace, but the demon was too swift. It smashed through the glass image of the gardens of Ujithana. The demon plummeted, and fragments of glass flew before it in a shimmering orange blaze of lights.

By the time she reached the broken window, the demon was leaping over rooftops in the distance. When an Ifreet was in full motion, there were few who could keep pace with it. She wasn't one of them. She waited a moment and gazed out across the horizon as the Ifreet disappeared from view. *I survived, but there was only one to fight.*

She returned to the sarcophagus. Inside was the skeleton of a man who'd been clutching the orange rock the Ifreet took. The bones of his fingers lay shattered. There was an inscription written on the side of the sarcophagus in an old, largely forgotten language. The Tasburai, however, still comprehended. The words in ancient Akkadi said, "Rise from Fire." Few could read the words. Fewer could understand the meaning. She was not one who understood what these words meant. *The Shufi will know*, she told herself. She remembered the library within Kronnoburg had some very old Akkadi books. Finding the right manuscript could shed some light on the meaning. She had no doubt it was vital to the future of the world around her.

Why else would an Ifreet be sent to Kronnoburg with a troop of Xettin when the city was already under siege? Suri-Yi realised that dealing with that orange rock's theft was more important than defending the city. A city could be rebuilt, but what would happen to the world if some unknown thing should rise from fire? She shuddered, standing and staring at the skeleton of the dead man. *If only you could speak.*

45

LOYALTY

The searing pain in her neck woke Elsta. She lay sprawled upon a mossy bank, and the River Sjorn pounded a few feet from her head. The early morning sun cast weak rays through a thicket of conifers. She rose onto her elbows. A bolt of pain went down her back. She felt it at the tips of her toes. Elsta winced, and tears filled her eyes. She remembered where she was, and she remembered what had happened—the fall from the cliff into the river and the raging white water carrying her. She recalled coming up for air and then being pushed down again. Somehow she had survived, and the river had spat her out onto the bank. Elsta wondered what had come of the Tasburai who'd saved her; he said his name was Adan. Volek's soldiers had surrounded him. Had he lived or perished?

He had given his life to protect her, unless he also leapt from the cliff into the torrents of the water. She struggled to her feet and looked about. She was desperate to catch sight of him. The white water of the Sjorn foamed and raced downstream. She had been washed ashore at a bend in the river, and the bank was full of other debris the river had rejected.

Enormous peaks bordered one side of the river. She'd fallen from one of those cliffs, but she had no idea how far the current had carried her before abandoning her to one side.

To her right was a forest choked with tall pine trees. Looming in the distance behind her was her city, Kronnoburg. Its pinnacles dazzled in the early morning sunlight. It was a city under siege but a city that would not fall. Its walls were unbreachable. Her people would remain safe, and the invaders' supplies would run low, forcing them to leave. She was no longer General Volek's hostage, and he had no hand to play.

She brushed down her clothes and set off in the direction of Kronnoburg. The Nostvektians were her people, and she was the rightful queen and last of the House of Mik. She had narrowly escaped death, and now she would serve her people, as a just ruler should. She had so much to look forward to as queen of Kronnoburg.

In spite of her hopes, tears rolled down her cheeks. *I've made such a mess of things. How can I go back and face my people?* She had nearly married an impostor, removed her father's trusted advisers from her inner circle, and neglected the plight of her people when their suffering had been in plain sight. The more she considered it, the more it dawned on her. There was no reason whatsoever for the people of Kronnoburg to want her back.

Where then? Elsta pursed her lips and tied her hair back in a tight bun. *Downriver perhaps.* The route would take her into the vast valleys of rich Nostvektian landowners. Many of these were families she socialised with. Once she'd crossed the valleys, there was the range of snowcapped Blue Mountains to traverse. She couldn't quite remember her geography, but if she maintained her direction west, she'd eventually arrive at the greatest city ever built—Avantolia.

The Tasburai had said her fiancé, the real Prince Theodorus Theseus, was imprisoned in the Republic of Avantolia. She would appeal to the wise Chancellor Sargon to show clemency for her betrothed. Once Theodorus was freed, they'd travel to Athenia to be married. Only then would she return home to Kronnoburg, with her husband, triumphant as the king and queen of their realm. She took one last long look back at the city of her ancestors. *I will return in better times. This is a promise I make on this day. For now, my people, forgive my absence, but you're safe behind our walls.*

As she set off downriver, she removed the ring with her royal seal embedded within it. She threaded it through the gold necklace around her neck. She then tucked this neatly under her tunic shirt. She felt the ring on her chest and patted it. *When the time is right.*

She would reveal her true identity when presented before Chancellor Sargon. Until then she'd pretend to be a commoner. She thought of what she might pass as and settled on a handmaiden. She'd been surrounded by them all her life. It was going to be fun playing a role. It was just like a game, and she was sure she'd enjoy it.

46

HEDGING

"Any ideas?" said Rikard.

Smoke, dust, noise, and clamouring voices rose. Rikard could think of a dozen other places he'd prefer to be. Instead he was holding the single line alongside a colourful band of forest folk whose names were as strange as their behaviour.

"Roar with all the breath you got, Captain. It'll scare 'em off," said Hallbjorn.

The Bear and Brynjar the Blade let off a series of loud gurgling sounds. It was part spitting and part shouting. Rikard joined in but soon felt his throat dry up and voice crack.

These men would be remembered by their names for their achievements. What would he be remembered as?

Captain Rikard Navrosk the Loser or maybe the Foolish? Whatever they called him, he'd be the man who didn't hold Kronnoburg's walls. History was going to ridicule him. Mothers would curse him for destroying their children's futures. The young would spit on his grave, and no one would ever be named Rikard in Kronnoburg ever again. It would be bad luck.

"Come on, ya lazy toerags!" screamed Brynjar.

"I'll have ya for breakfast!" shouted Hallbjorn.

"I don't think that's making much difference other than giving us frightfully sore throats," said Rikard.

"Right you are, Captain," said Hallbjorn.

"Any other suggestions?" asked Rikard.

Hallbjorn gazed out at the approaching horde and rubbed his chin with his enormous hand. The oncoming army, having breached the inner gate, was charging down the high-walled street. "I'll take the fifty soldiers on the left. Brynjar, you take the fifty on the right. Anything left in the middle is yours, Captain."

"What about the fifty in the second row?" said Rikard.

"Don't be rushing me, Captain. Let's get through the first row. Then we'll think about the next lot," said Hallbjorn.

"If we live that long," mumbled Rikard.

"There is that small matter, Captain. I'll warrant you that much," said Hallbjorn.

"So glad we agree on—"

Boom. A deafening explosion filled the air around them with black smoke and flying debris. The approaching army was thrown to the ground. Disappearing from view, they were engulfed in dust and rubble. Visibility dropped to a few yards. Rikard coughed, his stomach twisted in pain, and he retched. The smoke filled his lungs, and his eyes watered. He choked and fell to one knee. A strong arm yanked him up.

"Best make a run for it whilst we can," said Hallbjorn.

The Bear turned him in the right direction, and together they sprinted as fast as their legs would take them. Rikard's bearings came back to him as they retreated. He glanced back over his shoulder. The street brimming with the invading army was still filled with smoke. He didn't think it would slow them for long, but it gave him enough time to live a little longer. He wanted to find a good woman and settle down. He wanted to repay his parents' trust in him and rebuild their old cottage by the lake with his earnings from the army.

"What the dog droppings was that all 'bout?" said Brynjar.

"The explosion came from the direction of the armoury," said Rikard.

"Olaf, Ylva, and Sigrun are there," said Brynjar. "What kind of weapons you got locked away, Captain?"

"I know of none that could cause damage like that."

"I've seen the black smoke before. It be the work of the pyromancers—a most dark and deathly profession," said Hallbjorn.

"Pyromancers? We don't have any at Kronnoburg," said Rikard.

"But you did, Captain. Olaf and I saw 'em. The pyromancers built firestorms to ward off the Magrog from getting too close to 'em great walls of Kronnoburg."

"Magrog. Nasty bunch to come sniffing around your home," said Brynjar.

"Suri-Yi mentioned the Magrog," said Rikard.

"Aye, she was there the last time. Like a pillar of rock. Nothing was going to get past her. I'm a big lad, but I'd be afraid to be left in a room alone with her. No, sir. Better to be her friend than get on the wrong side," said Hallbjorn.

He turned into the main city square with the forest folk running by his side. He could see the royal palace looming up ahead. Fortified like a keep, it was the last defence in case any enemy ever breached the walls. The drawbridge could be raised, and the moat was filled with crocodiles that could bite a man in half.

The city square was empty. Rikard was glad none of the residents were foolish enough to remain. Most of the population had been sent to the Fortress of Eternal Light. This was where the narrow straits to the Forbidden Quarter began. It was a journey through deep, dark mountain tunnels. The passing through of an army en masse was nearly impossible. It was the only way to arrive on the other side. The ancients had designed the route so an army could never approach as a block, and the location could be defended with far fewer soldiers than the invaders brought. Other Nostvektians were put on boats which had set sail for Duria and Pathan along the River Sjorn. The remainder of the population was locked down within the keeps and existing underground strongholds within the city. There were hidden chambers, tunnels, and vaults, but if the city fell, all these hiding places would eventually be discovered. People would need to come out for food and provisions. It would only be a matter of time, and the underground strongholds were temporary safe houses. Those closest to the royal family were housed within palace grounds.

He began to ascend the hill leading to the drawbridge of the royal palace. Movement caught his eye behind him. Volek's army had entered the city square and was stamping across finely tended lawns and flower beds, despoiling fountains, and smashing shop fronts.

Rikard avoided looking down. It always made him wobble when he saw the enormous tails of the crocodiles swishing about in the murky waters. Once he and the forest folk were across the drawbridge and the moat, he barked orders to the gate guard.

"Raise the drawbridge. Position the archers. Boil the oil for the murder holes!"

"I'm gonna see if Olaf made it back," said Hallbjorn.

"Brynjar, I could use your aim to ready the archers on the battlements," said Rikard.

"Aye. By the looks of 'em, they need a steady hand. I'll gladly take care of it, Captain."

Rikard knew their time was limited. They couldn't hold out in the royal palace for more than a few days, and that was if Volek's army merely continued the siege. The invaders hadn't bloodied their swords yet, so they'd be itching to do so soon.

47

HEIR

"Master, I'm here."

Suri-Yi spun round. It was so good to hear the voice of her most accomplished apprentice, Adan de la Vega. Yet it was so unexpected it made her jump. Why was she surprised at the resourcefulness of the young man? She'd told him to meet her at Kronnoburg, and here he was. Then she recalled why she'd sent for him. *This is going to be difficult.* She remembered once more the pain in the face of Adan's mother as Shamshir went through her. The image flickered in her mind momentarily, but she pushed it back into a locked black box.

"Adan!"

He looks awful. There was blood on his hands and smeared across his face. She couldn't tell if it was his. His black Hawarij robes were ripped in the centre and frayed at the edges. He'd been in quite a fight. She forced a smile, trying to disguise her surprise. She had told him to get close to Naram-Sin, and the boy must have had to endure a difficult time fulfilling this mission.

"How are you? How did you get through the siege?"

"The princess..."

"You were with her?"

"Yes. Then an accident. My mistake."

Silence followed. Adan had a distant stare. It was as though she wasn't even in the Hall of Antiquity beside him. She'd never seen him like this.

"Mistake?"

He gave no response.

"Adan, what mistake?"

"The man in the iron mask..." He petered out again.

"What about him, Adan? Tell me about the man in the iron mask."

"He's the prince, the one she should have married..."

Suri-Yi put one hand on his shoulder and gently shook him. "Adan, I don't understand. Tell me once more."

His eyes regained their focus.

"He's the heir to the Kingdom of Athenia, Prince Theodorus Theseus. The man who Princess Elsta thought to be her fiancé was an impostor planted by General Volek, Naram-Sin, and Chancellor Sargon. They wanted him to deliver the princess into the hands of the general so he could secure Kronnoburg through marriage and avoid a siege. It's my fault. I'm to blame."

"It's okay, Adan. It will be all right. Come. I promised I'd tell you who you are at Kronnoburg. Come with me now, and we'll see together."

"Here? How could I have anything to do with this place?"

She smiled. "Quickly. We don't have much time."

The exhibition was how she remembered it. It contained the history of the old Kingdom of Avantolia illustrated through ancient maps, clothing, tools, artwork, poetry, jewellery, and weapons. She crossed to a glass-covered table. An intricate carving ran down its side.

Brooches and necklaces of former queens and crowns that had sat upon the heads of kings were on display in glass cabinets. What Suri-Yi was looking for, however, was right in front of her on a teak, narrow-legged table with gold trimmings. Inside the glass dome, on a purple velvet cushion, was the ring of Noor. The ring had been passed down from one generation of Avantolian royals to the next. The case contained its upper part, for the ring came in two halves.

"Adan, this is your destiny."

The boy walked over to stand beside her. He didn't look right. Something had changed. *Do I need to give him more time? Am I rushing him?* She cursed herself for leaving him alone.

Suri-Yi picked the lock, lifted the glass cover, and removed the ring of Noor. She placed it in her palm.

"This is the ring of Noor. It has been handed down for more than five hundred years amongst the royal families of Avantolia. The ring belongs to the rightful heir of the House of Seljuk, and it comes in two parts. This is the upper portion. I...took this ring from the daughter of King Sanjar. He was the last royal to rule Avantolia before it became a republic. King Sanjar's daughter was killed by...she was killed, and so I brought the ring here for safekeeping. Until today the rightful heir to the House of Seljuk has never stood before it."

She watched his expression change from shock to disbelief. Then it hardened as though he knew this had been his destiny. *Could he have known?* Now she looked surprised, but she tried to hide it.

Adan removed his mother's old ring from the silver necklace around his neck. His hands shook. Adan placed his part of the ring over the one in Suri-Yi's hand. Aligning the threads, he turned them together. The fit was perfect. The two halves were a whole once more.

"Adan, you are the son of Nysa of the House of Seljuk and Antonio de la Vega, and you are the heir to the Kingdom of Avantolia. You are its rightful king and ruler," said Suri-Yi.

The boy sank to his knees, clasping the ring in his hands. Suri-Yi heard shouts and weapons clash outside the Hall of Antiquity. When she peered down from the first-floor balcony, she could see Volek's soldiers streaming through the city and filling the streets. They were headed for the royal palace. It was the last stronghold for the Nostvektians—a place she and Adan needed to reach.

"We have to leave now." Suri-Yi pulled the boy up.

He didn't respond. What had happened to her apprentice? She sensed a shift in his personality. He was edgier and grittier, but there wasn't enough time to explore this. She dragged him from the hall, descended the stairs, and escaped into the underground tunnels. They'd have to get to the royal palace. The others would be there.

48

FLOW

"By the blessings of the Great Spirit. Look, Ylva. Look!" cried Olaf.

Olaf pointed down the tunnel. A solitary beam of light crept through a circular steel gate at the far end. It illuminated the darkness around them. *Good thing Father has his wits about him.* When they'd seen the flaming arrows heading their way, he knew the place was going to blow. Once the black powder ignited, there was nothing to keep it contained. The whole armoury went up like a cooking pot filled with firecrackers.

He'd led Ylva down the left corridor. The passageway went down into a basement that connected to a tunnel. Olaf said this would lead them to another part of the city.

He explained that the Nostvektians had nous for digging below their city and then connecting the whole place up. The tunnels spanned the width and breadth of the city, and you could get around the place without poking your head into the sunlight.

The tunnels below the armoury connected to key military posts that could be restocked with munitions without having to expose any of the arms to folk above ground. She had to admit, it was clever.

"Very smart, those architects. Eh, Ylva?"

"Aye."

Olaf led the way down the narrow tunnel and arrived at the circular steel grate on the wall where the beam of light entered. They wedged their swords under it and yanked the steel grate open.

"Flaming egg yolks. Who are that lot?' said Ylva. Loads of people ran by on the road across the way.

"Soldiers. Hundreds, maybe thousands of 'em. Could only be General Volek's soldiers and mercenaries. They got through the walls, but how? Those walls were meant to be unbreachable."

"What do we do?" Ylva asked.

Olaf stared at her a moment, and then a grin appeared on his face. "We join 'em, my girl."

"What?"

"Aye. The best way not to be noticed is to move with the crowd. Come on. Let's not dilly-dally."

"Won't they see us?"

"Right they will, but Volek's army is made up of a ragtag crew of mercenaries. They have no allegiances, uniforms, or flag they march behind. Two more strangely dressed folk won't turn any heads."

Father slithered through the opening, and they were soon on the street as two more hands joining the army for some booty.

"Just be yourself, my girl, and we'll be fine and dandy."

She found herself walking beside a sordid bunch of mean-looking men and one woman. Ylva didn't know if the woman was a mercenary or had tagged along for another purpose. She looked as filthy as the men, so it was easy to tell they were together. This group was dressed in rags, and they could have been mistaken for beggars. Ylva reckoned they'd nick the first shiny pots and pans their eyes fell upon before turning around and hightailing it. Every one of them had what could be called a weapon. The lucky ones had swords, but most were getting by with a shield, hammer, or pickaxe. She'd wager her Orlisium steel sword would cut through anything they put in front of her, but she hoped she wouldn't need it.

There was plenty of looting by the mercenaries. She watched them fill their grubby hands with anything from abandoned shops. The regular soldiers kept marching in tidy formations.

"Should we pretend to be nicking any gear to fit in?" Ylva asked.

"No time for it, my girl. We need to get back to the royal palace. It's where this lot are going."

"How we gonna get in?"

"Still working on that part, but something will turn up. Always does."

49

THE LADY LIGONIER

The flow of the River Sjorn eased the further downstream she went. The gentle lapping of the waves on the banks was soothing, though it didn't take Elsta's mind away from the sore state of her feet or the rumbling of her stomach. *How can anybody function without a proper means of transport? Having to walk everywhere is most unsatisfactory.* She'd stopped only once to eat some berries she found in the forest, and scooping a handful of water from a stream.

The fatigue preyed on her mind, so when she saw the riverboat moored on the bank ahead, she perked up. It was a large vessel for the Sjorn, and an enormous wheel was attached to its stern. She had heard about boats like this. The wheel would turn and propel the vessel forwards. Burning coal or wood in the engine room powered it. These vessels were the rage in Avantolia, but she'd never heard of one venturing so far south down the Sjorn.

If the crew were headed back up towards Avantolia, they might even offer to drop her off nearer to her destination. It would save her an incredible amount of time and effort. At this rate her shoes would be worn through in a matter of weeks. She could even help the crew keep the boat in order. She was happy to pay her way by doing some work. It couldn't be that hard. After all, she'd seen her handmaidens mopping and cleaning around her all her life. *And they aren't the shiniest pieces of cutlery in the dinner set.* If they could do it, she was certainly more than capable.

Elsta had even been out on the high seas on a few occasions and understood well the workings of a ship. She'd need to be careful, though. Seafaring men were known to be coarse and rude. They might not take well to having a woman on board. She'd heard some sailors say it was bad luck to have a female on a ship. It brought out the worst ocean storms. It all sounded like hokum to her.

Elsta veered off into the nearby forest to remain hidden from those on the ship. She found an opening between a pair of pine trees. This offered a clear view of the comings and goings on the boat. She knew it would be unwise to allow them to see her before she had decided whether she wanted to board the vessel or not.

The deck was empty but for one solitary figure. It was a woman. Round, leathery, and middle-aged going on old, her hair was greasy, she had thick eyebrows, and her skin was sunburnt and wrinkled. She sat upon a chair and fed birds that had gathered around her—a kind act from a vile-looking woman. Elsta reprimanded herself. Looks could be deceiving. *I should know.* The memory of the impostor Toni Bezodilidis was still raw.

An equally wrinkled, sunburnt man, her companion perhaps, emerged from a cabin. He was scratching his head and puffing on a pipe. He began to pull a rope out of the water. It must hold the anchor, she thought. *They are about to set off.* It could be her only opportunity to travel to Avantolia with such ease.

The boat had a name painted on it: *The Lady Ligonier*. It was a pleasant name. Perhaps it was the name of some royal from Avantolia. *What shall I do?* Her feet were sore, and her stomach growled as if it had a life of its own. At least on the riverboat they could catch fish from the Sjorn. At this time of year, it was full of trout. One only needed to cast a net to fill it.

The woman got up off the chair and scratched her backside. *A most rude and undignified sort of behaviour*, thought Elsta. Then she reprimanded herself once more. Not everyone had lived a privileged life where manners and decorum were drilled from an early age.

Elsta broke from the trees and strolled towards *The Lady Ligonier*. She reminded herself not to rush or seem too desperate. They saw her and froze in their tracks.

Looks of total surprise were on their faces. *Have they recognised me?* Elsta waved. Their mouths fell open, and eventually they waved back. As she approached them, she tried to recall the last occasion when she'd actually spoken to a commoner apart from those in the royal household. Then she remembered. It had been with Captain Rikard Navrosk. She would appreciate having Navrosk by her side just now. He'd know the colour of these folk and whether they were trustworthy. There was a lump in her throat at the memory of him. *How silly.*

"Hello," Elsta called out.

"Ahoy," replied the man. He gave the woman a sideways glance. "How can we be helping you, missy?"

"I'm making my way downriver."

"How far down?"

"To where the Sjorn meets the Trike."

"If you don't mind me asking, missy, where will you be heading to after that?"

"Avantolia."

The woman smiled. "By the look on your face, missy, I'd say you're off to meet your sweetheart," she said.

"Well..."

"Grorge, we've a soft spot for young lovers. Don't we? We were young once," said the woman.

"Aye, we were, Mildew."

Elsta heard a thumping sound from the ship's hull. All the portholes were covered up, so she couldn't see inside. "What's that noise?"

"Oh nothing, missy. We keep...uh..."

"Dogs. They be our dogs. Good for hunting, but they get cranky belowdecks. We're about to set off, missy. Why don't you come on board? We can take you down as far as the Trike," said Grorge.

Thump. Thump. This time Elsta thought she heard a muffled cry. She didn't like the sound of this.

"It's okay. Thank you very much. I'll just walk on," she said.

The couple smiled at her, baring rotten yellow teeth. Elsta turned only to crash into the chest of a huge man. He was a giant by her reckoning. Before she could even say, "Excuse me," the giant had lifted her up off the ground and flung her onto his shoulder like a sack of potatoes.

The giant marched towards the boat. Elsta screamed and hit him as hard as she could with her clenched fists. He didn't even twitch at the attack. He just carried on plodding towards the boat. When he stepped onto the vessel, it tilted to one side.

"Welcome to *The Lady Ligonier*, missy." Midlew grinned.

"Throw her in the brig, Clamper," said Grorge.

The giant knelt down, undid a bolt, and flicked open a trapdoor. With it wide open, he dropped her into a dark hole.

"No!"

She hit the deck, landing on her backside. She felt the pain go up her spine. She still managed to jump up and shout, but the trapdoor was shut and bolted. She heard the giant pass to the other end of the boat as Grorge and Mildew sniggered.

There was a dull glow belowdecks. It came from a lone candle flickering on a stand in the corner. The room she'd been most unceremoniously thrown into was full of other girls and young women.

A scrawny woman with mousy yellow hair shuffled up to her. "We tried to warn you by banging on the hull. We tried, but you didn't run. You didn't get away from 'em."

"Get away from whom?" asked Elsta.

"Grorge, Mildew, and Clamper. He's the giant mute."

"Who are they?"

"They be slavers. *The Lady Ligonier* is a slave ship, and they be taking us to the Pearl City to be sold."

50

LADY LUCK

In the end it was close, and they were fortunate to escape with their lives. As far as Rikard was concerned, it was about time Lady Luck smiled on him. He'd been forced to lose the queen's tournament at the request of his superiors and narrowly escaped death after being surrounded by Xettin. He had been unfairly imprisoned in the dungeons when his intentions had been to help his own people, only to be released and put in charge to defend the city against a formidable army the likes of which had not been seen in a generation. If that wasn't bad luck, then he didn't know what was.

So when he'd stared at the front line of General Volek's army and seen them stampeding in his direction, he had truly believed his time was up. He thought he was going to die and join his ancestors in the gardens of Ujithana. It would have been a lot earlier than he had hoped, though at least it would have been a soldier's death. Whoever had blown up the armoury had inadvertently saved him, and he could only be grateful.

"What's it gonna be, Captain?" Hallbjorn asked him.

The Bear was right. A decision had to be made—fight or flight? The enemy was camped outside the palace and would begin the final assault at any moment. If they were going to flee the city, the time was now. It was his decision, and his head swam at the responsibility of having to decide. The eastern tunnels leading out of Kronnoburg and heading towards Pathan hadn't been fully occupied by Volek's men. They could escape, regroup at Pathan, and return with the forces of the maharaja to take back Kronnoburg. The final recourse was to fall back to the Forbidden Quarter. That would mean, however, accepting total defeat and abandoning all possibility of recapturing Kronnoburg

Still there was no news from Suri-Yi. She had ventured underground into the darkness of the eastern tunnels in the Old Quarter of the city and had not returned. If she'd been defeated by whatever lay hidden down there, what chance did they have?

Rikard surveyed the faces in the room. He saw only inexperienced officers. They were fresh young men with no fighting experience beyond the gentle jousting and war-gaming they'd done at barracks. Hallbjorn and Brynjar had more years of real fighting than everyone else in the room put together.

"Gentlemen, we have a kingdom but no royal upon the throne. No one within these walls knows of Princess Elsta's whereabouts, or whether she is even alive. If you want to flee now and save yourself, then do so. Neither I nor anyone else who hears about this day will hold it against you. A part of me wants to do that very thing. Yet another voice within me quells that fear. It reminds me I am a Nostvektian, and for hundreds of years, our people have ruled these lands and been good and just to those who have lived under its protection.

"The Sjorn, the green meadows, the mountains, and the spirits of our ancestors watch over Kronnoburg. They are part of its very essence. So if you choose to leave, do so with your heads held high. If you choose to stay and fight as I do, then be prepared to spill your blood for Kronnoburg. Today our steel will clash upon the enemy's steel, and they will find our grip firm and sure. My brothers, if we return to the soil of Kronnoburg today, there can be no more honourable death than this—the death of a soldier."

That was about as much as he could say. He expected them to wish him well and leave, but not a single one did.

"We fight," said Lieutenant Bolt.

"We stay. We fight."

"Long live the princess!"

"For Kronnoburg!"

Hallbjorn wore a smile as wide as a crescent moon. "Yes!" he shouted and banged his fists against his chest.

"Nice," said Brynjar and burnished one of his knives.

Well, Lady Luck, this is a real test of your abilities. Show me how you are going to get us out of this mess.

Rikard heard footsteps. Someone came running into the room. Heads turned and saw it was a corporal. He was out of breath with a desperate look upon his face.

"Sir." He saluted Rikard.

"At ease."

"Captain, sir, they've sent word. General Volek is outside the palace. He says he's come to negotiate the surrender of the rest of the city."

Keep shining, Lady Luck.

"Won't do any harm to hear him out," said Bolt.

"Hallbjorn, what do you say?" said Rikard.

"If Olaf were here, he'd talk first. If talking didn't get him anywhere, he'd fight. I do the same as my chief."

"I'm with you," said Rikard. "Tell Volek we're on our way."

51

CLOSE ATTENTION

Father was right, Ylva thought. When the army charged like there was no tomorrow, no one paid attention to her. She could have been dolled up like a clown, and it wouldn't have distracted them. This greedy bunch of mercenaries was only interested in getting their grubby hands on the booty.

It was different now. Odd stares were flicking her way. She'd kept her hood on over her riding cloak, but there was no mistaking her frame. It was too small for a man and too fragile for a grown lad.

She marched down familiar streets containing the blacksmith, the tinker, and the baker. She'd only seen them at night, however, when she'd been scouting with

Sigrun. Remembering the Hidden sent a stab of pain through her heart. After the awful way they'd killed him, what was she going to say to his family? Olaf had told her to focus on the now. They'd have time to mourn for their friend later, as long as they didn't get themselves killed. She wanted to find the hooded murderers, shove her sword into them, and see what they thought of it.

"Stay close," whispered Olaf.

They were now stationary amongst a mob of soldiers and mercenaries. She was a good head shorter than everyone about her, and faces kept turning in her direction. Some were trying to catch a glimpse of her face. They'd been marching towards the palace when they'd suddenly run into this crowd, and everything came to a standstill.

"Oy, you a girl?"

Ylva ignored the man, and Olaf didn't hear him. The mercenary put his hand on her shoulder. "I said, you a—"

The flat of her sword smashed into the man's groin. She followed with a kick to his head.

"What happened?" said Olaf when he heard the man collapse on the floor.

"Unwanted attention."

"Let's move over there by them fancy tents they're putting up."

Olaf led the way. Ylva was tucked in close behind him. She felt hands touching her as she walked through the throng of men. A few even tried to pull her hood off, but she shrugged them off.

"Lads, it's a girl!"

"Girl?"

"Where?"

"I want one."

"There!"

"Run, Ylva," said Olaf.

They fled towards a warehouse on the far side of the square. She could hear the dirty old men behind her. She needed to get away and get safe. They stormed through the warehouse door. There was no one inside, and Olaf bolted the door. The warehouse was a carpenter's store for long pieces of wood and logs on two floors. Sawdust and wooden shavings littered the floor. The men rammed into the door, but it held. A rat scurried by and down a hole. *If only it was that easy to get away.*

"I'm scared," said Ylva.

"So am I, my girl." Olaf held her by the shoulders and smiled. "We'll get out of this. Just you see."

Crash. The door burst open off its hinges. The mercenaries poured in. Filthy, ragged men, she could smell their stink from where she stood. Ylva counted twenty with evil grins. She gripped the Orlisium blade and swung it in an arc. She planted her feet in a wide stance and threw off her hood to reveal her features.

"Oh look. She knows how to use it," said a man with a boil growing on his nose.

Laughter spread amongst the men.

"Back to back, Ylva. Don't let anyone separate us, my girl," said Olaf.

"Yes, Father."

Some of the men made kissing noises at her. Giggling and pointing, they lurched like drunkards in her direction. They came for Olaf first. Two scrawny men, all arms and legs, in ill-fitting, torn clothes led the attack. Olaf drew the twin curved swords on his back. Unsheathing them with a practiced flourish, he cut both men down with one stroke.

Two came for her—one fat and one thin. They both wore chain mail and held daggers. *They'll have to do better 'an that.* Her Orlisium blade severed the dagger hand of the fat man, and she stabbed the thin one through the heart.

"My hand!" the fat man shrieked.

Ylva spat on him. "Come on. Who's next?" she shouted.

The men now approached with a degree of caution. They'd stopped laughing and were now scowling. They drew their swords, raised their shields, and closed in. They formed a tight circle to trap her and Olaf.

"Give it up, old man. The girl's ours."

"Mine first."

"No. Mine."

"Shut it. Kill him first."

Olaf turned to her and whispered, "I love you, Ylva." He then sprang forwards. Both his curved swords crisscrossed up, down, forwards, and backwards. They tore and ripped the flesh around him. Two more mercenaries fell.

Ylva struck sideways, splintering the shield of the nearest mercenary and bloodying his hand. The man dropped his shield. Ylva thrust her blade through his waist. Another man grabbed her shoulder. She dug her knife through his wrist and stabbed her sword through his foot.

Two men charged into her with shields before them. They threw her onto the ground. Her sword and knife fell from her grip. Another man kicked her in the face, and the back of her head hit the floor. Everything went dark for a moment.

"Nice sword."

"Good knife. Man can always do with a good knife."

They grabbed her by the shoulders and hauled her up.

"Ylva!" Olaf leapt towards the men who'd seized her, but one of the mercenaries threw a net over him, and he collapsed in a heap on the ground. Other mercenaries surrounded him and kicked him. He rolled around in the netting, trying to avoid their blows.

The two men holding Ylva flung her to the ground.

"Enough!" The deep voice boomed around the warehouse. It was like a shock wave from an exploding volcano.

The man who'd spoken was dressed in commanding black. His long cloak had a red lining, and his magnificent sword rested in a fine leather embroidered sheath. Six hooded warriors, all in black, flanked him.

"Who the hell are you?" said one of the mercenaries who'd thrown Ylva to the ground.

"Get lost," shouted another mercenary who was holding the net tight over Olaf.

"I said *enough*."

"Clear off," said the mercenary with the net.

Even Brynjar would have been impressed with the speed and accuracy the daggers flew from hidden places within the folds of the hooded warriors' robes. Each blade found its target. Twelve blades pierced the hearts of the twelve remaining mercenaries. Each man dropped dead.

The man in black fixed her with a grim stare. "Where did you get that sword, girl?"

Ylva cautiously rose to her feet. "Kronnoburg. I found it there deep in one of 'em basements."

The man swept forwards. Light as a feather, he picked the sword up. He treated it as though the blade were the most fragile piece of jewellery. His eyes lit up, and he smiled fleetingly.

"This is Curtana, the sword of mercy. Many years ago, she was my sword."

"I'm sorry, sir. I didn't know it was your sword. Please take it back. It's the least I can do to thank you."

She heard Olaf rolling free of the netting and getting to his feet. "Grandmaster Naram-Sin."

"Olaf?"

"Right you are," said Ylva's father.

"You look old."

"Precisely what...someone else recently told me," said Olaf.

"Really?" Naram-Sin's eyes narrowed. With a softer expression, he turned back to Ylva. "Curtana does not allow herself to be wielded by just anyone. I sense she and you have already had some encounters with..." He looked with a new intensity at the blade. "A series of interesting encounters. Where did you meet the Ifreet?"

Ylva turned to her father. He nodded. "In the forest a few days ago. It was passing through with a battalion of Xettin."

"Xettin? In the lowlands?"

"We've been in a number of skirmishes with them these past few weeks. Entire villages have been razed," said Olaf.

Naram-Sin rubbed his chin. "If the Xettin have come down from the mountains, we know what follows next."

He returned Curtana to Ylva. "Olaf, this is your daughter?"

"Yes."

"And your name, my dear?"

"Ylva."

"A she-wolf. The irony that a she-wolf is now the owner of the sword of mercy. I suggest, Olaf, you and Ylva leave Kronnoburg. Flee to the hills. Matters are going to get a lot worse," said Naram-Sin.

The grandmaster and his hooded warriors turned and left. Once they were alone, Olaf said, "Naram-Sin and his lot have taken a darker turn since I saw 'em last.

Still, he saved our lives, and we got to thank him for that."

Her father embraced her, and she felt warm tears roll down her cheeks. She'd now met two Tasburai grand-masters, and she wasn't quite sure which one she trusted more. *Neither, if truth be told.*

52

HERITAGE

The presence casting a brooding shadow over Adan was ominous. Every glance at it within his mind's eye left him scared of this malevolent thing. It laughed somewhere inside him like a cackling hyena. It rumbled just below his consciousness and pressed upon him to be released back into the world. He would not. He would keep the demon bottled up inside him. A thing of such barbarity must not be let loose in the world.

The image of what the thing had done upon the mountain burned bright in his mind. It was a beautiful slaughter—an act of violence the thing had enjoyed. It had relished every moment and had not wanted to stop.

"The tunnel narrows here, Adan. Watch your head," said Suri-Yi.

He reminded himself he was apprentice to the most accomplished Tasburai and the best fighter in the world. He had followed her without question his whole life, and now he followed her blindly through the labyrinth of tunnels. He didn't know what else to do. He had lost all sense of direction, and his thoughts pulled him in a hundred different directions at once. As his mind settled, Adan felt his throbbing cuts and open wounds. They needed attention, but they would have to wait for now.

"Where are we going, Master?"

"The palace, but the underground gates have been sealed. If we can get to the moat by the drawbridge, we might be able to get the attention of the royal guards and gain entry."

The word *palace* made his head spin. He was part of a kingdom and a royal lineage—the House of Seljuk. The story of King Sanjar, his grandfather, was tragic. Adan was his heir, but the revelation hadn't sunk in, and it probably never would. *How can it? One day I am told by the person I most trust in the world that I am not who I thought I was.*

The mention of his mother had left him confused. He had never known her, but he had many questions about her. What was she like? How had she died, and who had killed her? If there was one thing for certain, he had been trained by the best, and he would use his training and skills to hunt down and execute his mother's killer.

Whoever that person was, the killer had deprived him of a mother's love, and the only maternal figure in his life was the woman he now followed. If it hadn't been for Suri-Yi's compassion and nurturing, he would never have known what love and trust actually meant.

"Master, please tell me again my mother's name."

"Nysa."

"Tell me about her."

"She was the youngest daughter of King Sanjar. She met your father, Antonio de la Vega, when she was travelling as part of her royal duties in the province of Ibethia, and they fell in love. Your grandfather, the king, did not approve of Antonio, as he had no royal bloodlines, and his ancestry was not clear. Antonio was a simple man from a family of farmers. Your mother married him secretly, and they disappeared to Ibethia to live in anonymity on a remote countryside farm. It was the place where you were born, Adan."

He concentrated as hard as he could to come up with a memory of that time. There was nothing. So he imagined a farmhouse set against a green landscape and baked in warm sunshine. He pictured his parents walking hand in hand through golden meadows and taking turns carrying him. He imagined them giggling, enjoying life, and watching him grow day by day. He tried very hard, but the image was merely a ripple. The picture was from books he'd read on Ibethia. They weren't his memories.

"How did my parents die?"

Suri-Yi seemed to hesitate. Then she walked on. "After the Avanist Revolution, the leaders of the new republic wanted to eliminate every trace of the House of Seljuk. They didn't want any future heir challenging the legitimacy of the republic. King Sanjar and his family were executed. Others close to them were incarcerated in the Oblivion. Assassins were sent out to hunt down any other members of the royal family, including your mother."

"But she revoked her claim when she married my father. What threat did she pose?"

"The republic didn't see it that way. They were very thorough."

Damn the republic. He clenched his fists. "Who killed my parents?"

"They...it was the republic."

What kind of answer is that? Does she know, or doesn't she know? "Master, who was it?"

She remained silent. "Look, Adan. We're here."

Suri-Yi peered through a metal grating fixed into a concrete wall. Below them lay the moat waters outside the royal palace. Above them was the drawbridge. It was lowered. Suri-Yi kicked the grate clear and stepped out onto the edge. As the grate splashed into the water, Adan saw large reptiles swimming below them.

She is hiding the truth from me, but I will learn it. She taught me patience, and I will show it now. The truth always comes to the surface.

"We need to get closer," said Suri-Yi. "Something important is happening, or the drawbridge wouldn't be down. Maybe they are discussing terms."

She swung out. Climbing up the brickwork, she used her fingertips and knife to provide stability. Adan followed. The voices became clearer as they took up a position underneath the drawbridge. Adan knew one of those voices. He'd heard it before in Krakonite.

53

TERMS

General Volek was a formidable opponent. His iron gaze from under heavy brows sent a shudder down Rikard's spine. *Negotiate? More like capitulate.* He knew there would be little chance of coming to terms with this man, but he still had to try.

"Steady, Captain," murmured Hallbjorn.

Rikard was glad the mettlesome Bear had come along with Lieutenant Bolt. Having the Bear by his side on the palace's drawbridge gave him some comfort. The man had physical presence, which meant more than rank or lineage at a time like this.

A man in dark robes accompanied the general. This stranger had a muscular, lean face despite his obvious years. Where the drawbridge met the ground upon which Volek's army was camped was a troop of black-hooded warriors. For all Rikard knew, they could be tall young men or wiry old men.

"That there is Grandmaster Naram-Sin, and we don't wanna annoy him. If he gets angry, there's no one in all of Kronnoburg gonna stand in his way," said Hallbjorn.

Rikard gulped. He'd seen what Suri-Yi could do, and if this fellow was anything like her, they would be in line for a whole heap of trouble.

"There is one person," Rikard said.

"Aye." Hallbjorn grinned.

Only no one knows where Suri-Yi is.

The general and the grandmaster waited for Rikard in the centre of the drawbridge. The general hadn't taken a step further.

"General Volek," said Rikard.

"And you are?"

"Captain Rikard Navrosk."

"Navrosk, eh? A commoner. How amusing one of your kind should be standing here at the gates of the royal palace of this proud city and discussing terms."

"If I recall correctly, General, your troops wiped out the top military brass and most of the nobles when you undertook the massacre in the cabinet war rooms."

"Yes, we have Grandmaster Naram-Sin here to thank for that little piece of theatre. I must say, I felt rather sentimental when I heard of Ulfheart's demise," said Volek.

"What are you here for, General?"

"Come, Captain, don't insult my intelligence. Surrender the city to me, and I will spare you and your people. Defy me, and everyone will be put to the sword. You will be last after I've made you watch every Nostvektian man, woman, and child being executed. You strike me as a decent sort of fellow, Captain. Not the sort who'd want all those deaths on his conscience," said Volek.

"You overestimate your strength," said Rikard. "You hold much but not all of the city. Your supply lines are stretched, but we have enough in our stores to last years." *I wish.* "Our allies, the Pathans and Durians, send reinforcements as we speak." *I wish.* "They will arrive within days and cut through your lines like a knife through butter. As you know, General, the rainy season will be upon us any day. Already the clouds grow heavy in anticipation. Your army will not hold long in these conditions. You should have waited 'til after the rains."

"Captain Navrosk, this is not a war of attrition, and I am not one for waiting," said Volek. He clapped his hands. The sound echoed across the drawbridge to his troops assembled on the other side. There was movement as the flaps of a richly embroidered tent were thrown open. A regal couple emerged. Their garments dazzled amongst the blacks and greys of the army. "I present to you Prince Theodorus Theseus and Princess Elsta Mik," said Volek.

"The princess," whispered Rikard. The blood rushed to his head, and his heart quickened.

The royal couple made their way through the ranks of the army. They respectfully parted and let them pass.

The prince strode confidently forwards. A beaming smile was upon his face, and his finely embroidered gold-and-blue cloak flapped in the breeze. The princess wore an embroidered cloak dress in shimmering white. Her face was veiled. *Not a surprise. She wants to avoid the leering looks of the soldiers.* Still, it troubled him not to be able to look into the face he had known so well since she was a child. He hadn't seen her since he'd embarrassed himself before the royal court at the summer solstice ball.

The royal couple walked hand in hand to the drawbridge and then halted beside the hooded black warriors. They formed a circle around them and unsheathed their swords. The prince's face contorted with fear.

"Wait a minute," the prince said.

Naram-Sin's voice drowned him out. "Silence!"

The general turned back to Rikard. "My dear captain, I really don't have time to wait for the rainy season to begin or the appetite for engaging with the Pathans and Durians in the field of battle. I will make this very simple. Surrender the city, or I will have the prince and princess executed in full sight of all. What do you say?"

Rikard turned to Bolt and Hallbjorn. Both were lost for words. "If I surrender the city, you will spare them?" he asked.

"Of course. I am a man of my word," said Volek.

Hallbjorn put a hand on his shoulder and whispered, "It's your choice, lad. We're with you either way."

Rikard nodded. "All right, General. I—"

"No!" It was a man's voice that cried out.

Two new robed figures suddenly appeared from underneath the drawbridge. Somehow they had clambered onto it from the moat wall. Rikard thought it an impossible task until he saw one was Grandmaster Suri-Yi. The two newcomers' Orlisium swords pulsed blue and green. They took up a position next to the general and near Naram-Sin.

"That's not the princess!" shouted the young man. "And the prince is no royal. He's an impostor."

Before Rikard was able to fathom the words, swords flew from sheaths, and the six black-hooded warriors forgot about threatening the royals and leapt instead at the Tasburai. General Volek kicked Rikard in the chest, knocking him onto his back. The general turned and ran back through the hooded warriors and towards the safety of his own guard.

"Don't leave me!" whined the prince.

The princess had thrown off her outer robes, and Rikard finally managed to get a look at her. She was dressed in a white tunic top and pants and carried an Orlisium sword. Though she resembled Princess Elsta in her fair features, it was another young woman.

Hallbjorn picked Rikard up off the ground. "Hurry, Captain. Raise the drawbridge," the Bear instructed him before pushing him into Bolt's arms.

As he and Bolt ran, Rikard shot a glance back across the drawbridge. The six hooded warriors and the young woman fought the two Tasburai. Meanwhile, Hallbjorn the Bear blocked the way for Naram-Sin.

"Raise the drawbridge," shouted Lieutenant Bolt.

54

CLASH

Adan knew it wasn't Princess Elsta. He had seen her fall from the cliff above the Sjorn. Still, he didn't expect the impersonator to be his close friend.

When she threw off her hood and came for him, he momentarily froze. Then he rolled away from her downwards sword thrust before the weapon slashed against the metal girders of the bridge and sent out sparks.

"Saphira, it's me!" It was all he could cry as he deflected the blows from the Hawarij.

Her expression was blank. It was as though she didn't recognise him. He could have been the next criminal she was bringing in for crimes against the republic.

Three Hawarij occupied him, backing him onto the edge of the drawbridge. Only a step remained until a drop into the reptile-infested moat. *I have to get off this narrow drawbridge. I'm being crowded out.* He saw from the corner of his eye General Volek waving his army forwards across the drawbridge. Then he noticed two Nostvektian officers run to the palace. A moment later he felt the drawbridge being raised. It was a good idea, but he wished he wasn't on the drawbridge.

The Hawarij were good fighters. They were well drilled but far from proficient. Suri-Yi danced with three of them, blocking and parrying their blows. It was just a warm-up. Naram-Sin was waiting. He was the one man she feared. It was not because he might defeat her but because of what he had done to the Tasburai Order and what he was going to do next.

As she toyed with his acolytes, she saw him bring Hallbjorn the Bear to his knees. The giant's face was bloodied, and he looked spent. Naram-Sin hadn't even unsheathed his sword, Fire, but she now saw him reach for it. Suri-Yi rolled under the next strike and fired a kick into the ribs of the Hawarij, who fell back and down into the moat. She thought she heard the sound of the reptiles slithering into action at the sight of food.

She sprinted towards Naram-Sin as the drawbridge began to tilt. Her momentum carried her faster than expected. She worked it to her advantage and leapt into the air while swinging Shamshir.

Naram-Sin sensed her. Instead of bringing down Fire upon the defeated form of Hallbjorn, he spun around, and their two swords clashed. Sparks flew. Naram-Sin rolled back as she flew over him.

The drawbridge's incline steepened. More Hawarij had leapt onto its edge and now came sliding down. This included Adan and the Hawarij he was fighting. Hallbjorn rolled like a stone, knocking one Hawarij off the side. Suri-Yi counted five more Hawarij plus the five that remained. She'd have to leave them to Adan, Navrosk, and his men. *Naram-Sin will keep me busy.*

Suri-Yi and Naram-Sin tumbled into the area in front of the gatehouse. They and the others took the fight into the open quadrangle at the centre of the royal palace. It was a picturesque vista of flower beds and well-manicured lawns.

Rikard urged his soldiers forwards, but they were no match for the Hawarij. They picked Rikard's people off one at a time. Other Nostvektian soldiers simply ran away. Rikard stood his ground. He remembered his father's words: "Don't give a man a task to do unless you are prepared to do it yourself." Now he realised what it meant. So he stood in the thick of the sword fight with the Hawarij. At his side were the great bear, Hallbjorn, swinging his mighty axe, Brynjar throwing daggers in all directions, and his trusty Lieutenant Bolt. Hallbjorn had taken a considerable beating, but he seemed to be regaining his strength whilst fighting Naram-Sin's disciples.

A quick glance to his left, and Rikard saw the young Tasburai who had come with Suri-Yi was holding his own against a host of hooded adversaries.

He and Bolt were preoccupied with one Hawarij warrior. Trying to avoid being hacked by their opponent's sword, the lieutenant fell over and landed on his back. The Hawarij stepped forwards, and Rikard drove his sword straight at the enemy's stomach. *Surely I have him now.* The Hawarij twisted his body out of the way, and as Rikard was overstretching, he yanked Rikard's sword from his hand. The warrior now held his own and Rikard's blade. He twisted and twirled them both in a dizzying loop.

"Yah!" shouted Hallbjorn, ramming into the back of the Hawarij and driving him into the ground. Brynjar followed with a decisive cut and thrust, which left the Hawarij motionless. A look over at Suri-Yi told him she was in a dangerous duel with Naram-Sin, and no one seemed willing to get involved in the encounter.

"Thank you," Rikard said to Hallbjorn.

"Look out, sir!" shouted Bolt, pushing him out of the way.

The Hawarij blade flashed, cutting a gash in the lieutenant's chest. Blood burst from the wound, and Bolt crumpled to the ground. Rikard went to help him, and Hallbjorn and Brynjar repelled the attacker.

"I'm going to die, sir," moaned Bolt.

"Hang on, Lieutenant," said Rikard. He lowered Bolt to the ground and ripped the end of his cloak to press against the wound. It was a deep cut but not anything life threatening.

"You'll live, Bolt. It'll be okay," said Rikard, propping him against a small wall around a fountain. "Get him inside!" he called to two soldiers who were standing at a safe distance from the skirmish.

When he'd seen Bolt off, he found a group of five Hawarij warriors had pushed Hallbjorn and Brynjar back against a wall. Rikard seized his sword and the fallen lieutenant's. Without thinking he charged into the group, swinging both blades in all directions. He caught them off guard, and they lost their grip on the tree folk, allowing them to move away from the wall into open space.

Rikard's heart nearly stopped when he realised he'd broken their attack but had ended up alone and surrounded by three Hawarij. He had to delay them until help arrived. *But who?* The Hawarij exchanged glances with one another and moved forwards. All three Hawarij shook their heads. They raised their swords and brought them down at him in unison.

55

DEMON BLOOD

The Hawarij were well trained and too many for Adan to handle at once. Adan had been cut on the cheek and forehead and had other minor grazes on his arms and legs. *Ignore the discomfort,* he reminded himself. He kept trying to make eye contact with Saphira, but she wasn't having any of it. *What have you done, Saphira?*

Five killing blades flashed over his head and performed a dance of death. He blocked, rolled forwards, flipped backwards, ducked, and swayed. He was tired, and it was only going to get more difficult.

He had to find a new location with obstacles he could use to his advantage. This place was too open, and every time he tried to finish off an opponent, the figure would drift away, recover, and come back. In tighter surroundings, Adan could finish off a downed opponent. Behind him was a circular building. He dived under the next sword strike and kicked the Hawarij in the back as he sprinted for it. He noticed three Hawarij had surrounded the Nostvektian captain, so he diverted his course. Adan sliced the back of the first Hawarij's neck and the back of the second's knee. He couldn't do more than that, but at least it would give the captain a fighting chance.

Adan burst into the building. His heart sank. It was a sealed well house with no way out except the way he'd entered. It was devoid of any tools or fixtures. It only had smooth walls, a pail, and the well. He turned to leave, but he was too late. The Hawarij and Saphira piled in, shut the door, and bolted it with a firm click.

"No, Adan, you aren't getting out of this," said Saphira.

They were the first words she'd spoken to him since the fight began, and they sounded like the words of a stranger. This was not the caring girl he'd known for so many years.

"Why did you go over to them?" said Adan.

"It's the future. You and Suri-Yi, you're the last of the Tasburai. It's a dead order," she said.

"We have values. The Hawarij have none," said Adan.

"It's a matter of interpretation. Now finish him off," she said, signaling the others to attack.

The enormous well was in front of him. His back was to the wall, and four murderous blades were closing in on him. The fifth warrior guarded the door to ensure he didn't get out. Adan could hear them laughing under their hoods.

Within his head he heard another type of laughter—a cruel cackle. He shook his head as though trying to tip it out of his ear. He had seen what it could do.

"No!" shouted Adan.

"Don't worry. We'll make it quick," said Saphira.

"Get away, Saphira. It's not safe," he groaned.

The cackle within him grew into a wild laughter—a sort of inexorable certainty. Adan felt himself become trapped within a corner of his mind. Firmly locked away within a cage, Adan was told to be a silent observer and not to interfere with what was coming next. *It's better for both of us that you leave this to me.*

Vega stood tall and broad. He rolled his head from side to side and twirled the sword in his hand. The blade radiated red. There were two Hawarij on his left and two on his right. Easy. Something told him to kill the girl last.

"Adan, your sword," cried the girl. "What's happening?"

The others stopped to stare at the crimson blade.

"Demon blood," the girl whispered.

Vega plunged the sword straight through the belly of the first opponent before he even had a chance to raise his sword. He then shifted his position, twisted backwards, and opened the belly of the opponent behind him. As the man fell, Vega gripped his head and leapt into the next opponent, piledriving him into the ground. Behind him a blade came swooshing down. Vega rolled to the side, and the descending sword cut the man he'd rammed to the ground in half.

Vega laughed. He leapt onto the rim of the well and then backflipped high and over the girl and her accomplice. Landing, he stuck his sword through the third man's knees before plunging the red blade into his neck. The girl ran for the door.

"Stop! There's something wrong with you," said the girl. "I'm your friend. Saphira. Your close friend."

Vega didn't have any friends. There was only meat to slaughter. The fourth hooded opponent stuttered forwards uncertainly. Vega collected a sword from one of the dead men and threw it instantly at the fourth man. His opponent skilfully deflected it but not the next thrust, which came from Vega's crimson blade. The enemy crumpled to the floor.

The girl struggled frantically with the bolt. He came up behind her. She dropped her sword and fell to her knees. "I beg you, Adan. Spare me."

He wasn't going to fall for such a trick. He'd already seen her go for the ankle knife. Before she had the chance to reach it, Vega took off her head.

56

OLD FRIENDS

It had been a long time since she had been caught in a fighting embrace. It had been a long time since her skills had been tested as thoroughly as they were being tested now. It had been a long time since she had fought with Naram-Sin. There had been a period in their lives when they practised together every morning.

Naram-Sin has developed a new fighting style. There is less fluidity and softness in his movements. It relies more on rigid, short movements and hard hitting. It is a young man's style, but he is not young. It will be his undoing.

"You fight like an old woman," said Naram-Sin. He checked his position and came around to deliver a sequence of vicious attacks. She deflected them with ease.

"I *am* an old woman," said Suri-Yi. Naram-Sin leapt at her, sword slashing at a horizontal angle. She rolled under and stood up. "And you're an old man."

"I've never felt stronger," growled Naram-Sin.

Around her the fighting petered out. The few remaining Hawarij lay beaten on the floor. Hallbjorn stood bloody but victorious with his great axe slung over his shoulder. Next to him were Brynjar and young Captain Navrosk. *Where are Adan, Saphira, and the other Hawarij?* From the alleys and passageways, Nostvektian soldiers appeared, and the quadrangle filled with curious onlookers.

"Your Hawarij have been defeated, Naram-Sin. You should concede defeat."

"We have an entire army occupying this city, and once I defeat you, I will simply order the spineless fools to lower the drawbridge. Look at them. They fear me. They will do exactly as I say."

"You always relied on fear."

"I would rather people fear me than love me," said Naram-Sin.

"That is not the way of the Tasburai."

"I am no longer Tasburai."

Naram-Sin attacked with a sharp succession of thrusts and swings, aiming for her head and then switching to her legs. She leapt into the air and kicked him full in the face. Naram-Sin went onto one knee. She could have taken his head off with Shamshir, but she stayed her hand. He knew she had.

"Still some love left in there from the old days, Suri-Yi?"

The truth was there wasn't, but her heart did ache for how things could have turned out.

"Compassion maybe."

"Rubbish! We will crush this kingdom and you with it."

"You overstate your abilities," said Suri-Yi.

"Do I? This entire Nostvektian army is like fodder for us. They are weak and craven. They are no match for people like you and me. Come, join us."

Suri-Yi looked over at Navrosk. "Bravery has many guises, Naram-Sin. Sometimes all it needs is a little push."

Suri-Yi rolled forwards and righted herself as she approached him. Her sudden movement surprised him, and he stumbled back. Still, she had opened a wound above his waist. Naram-Sin touched his side, and his hand came away red.

"A mere graze," he said.

Droplets of blood fell on the grass. *More than a graze, and it will make him furious.* The cut had the desired effect.

Naram-Sin roared and swung his sword down at her. She ducked and moved sideways, flicking Shamshir out and making a deep gash in the centre of his back as he went past. He pretended not to notice, but it must have hurt. Naram-Sin threw off his cloak. Both wounds had soaked his tunic.

"This is nothing compared to what I will do to you," said Naram-Sin.

He rushed at her. Shamshir and Fire kissed, and sparks went flying. High and low, the swords wove a pattern. It was an endless motion of strikes and blocks. They were evenly matched, but he was tiring, and she knew it.

Suri-Yi sliced open another gash on the other side of his waist. This one was close to his organs, and he felt it. Naram-Sin tilted to one side, trying to protect himself. She used the moment to drive a straight thrust through his right shoulder, severing the muscle and bone. As she pulled her weapon back, she delivered a wide cut across his chest. His sword clattered to the ground, and Naram-Sin staggered back. Collapsed on his knees, he was there for the taking.

"It's not too late. Repent for your actions, and I will show leniency," said Suri-Yi.

A trickle of blood spilled from his mouth and dribbled down his chin. "I'd rather die," said Naram-Sin. "As will you." His eyes flicked skywards.

She looked up. Hundreds of arrows bore down on her from Volek's infantry. It was too late to run for cover.

In the next moment, she was knocked to the ground and saw a shield go up and over her. Navrosk was crouched beside her and taking cover from the arrows. The barrage rained down around them. Some split the shield. Arrowheads came through and bloodied Navrosk's hand, but he held firm to the shield.

The whooshing sound that had accompanied the iron rain stopped. "Are you okay?" said Navrosk.

"Yes. And you?"

"Only a graze or two," he said.

"That was very brave. Thank you," said Suri-Yi and placed a hand on his shoulder. "Come, let's get under cover before the next volley."

As she turned to go, she saw the body of Naram-Sin prostrate upon the ground and riddled with arrowheads. *At least he didn't die by my hand.*

They raced back below the arches on either sides of the quadrangle. If Volek had fired so indiscriminately, he wasn't too concerned about killing the Hawarij or the defenders.

"Bloody brave thing, Captain," said Hallbjorn, heartily slapping the young captain on the back and almost knocking him over.

Very few are born leaders. Most grow into the role with adversity and experience shaping their path. Today Kronnoburg has found a new leader.

She smiled at him. "Thank you, Captain. I owe my life to you."

"Now there be a first. It's usually us sorry lot who be thanking her all the time. Good on ya, Captain," said Hallbjorn.

Rikard had saved the life of a Tasburai warrior. A strange feeling of relief and a renewed sense of optimism welled inside him. This was a story he'd tell his grandchildren, if he ever lived to a ripe old age.

Rikard took cover behind a wide pillar and stared out at the battlements surrounding the royal palace. The next volley of arrows would be coming any moment. It would probably be flaming arrowheads.

"Why don't they fire?" asked Brynjar.

"Send a man up top to take a look, but tell him to be very careful. We don't want to lose any more soldiers today," said Rikard to a corporal crouching behind him.

He waited whilst the message was communicated around to the gatehouse. He saw a young lad scramble up the spiral stairwell. The lad cautiously scaled the last few steps and then looked across at him. Rikard gave the young lad a reassuring nod. All eyes were on this boy. He took a deep breath and tiptoed the final steps to the top. He remained below the wall edge for a few more moments, and then curled his fingers over its edge, and slowly raised his head up.

Rikard expected the lad to take a peek and then sit back down behind the wall. Instead he remained in the crouched position with his head fully exposed to Volek's army. Then he stood up in full view of the invaders.

"Crazy lad, he'll get himself killed!" said Hallbjorn.

The young soldier on the roof scratched his head and stared out at Volek's army.

"He's got a nerve," said Brynjar.

The lad turned around to face Rikard and flapped both arms out to the side like a bird trying to take flight.

"They've gone!" he shouted across the quadrangle. "I can see them retreating. They're leaving Kronnoburg. The whole army's leaving."

"What?" said Brynjar.

Rikard took a deep breath and slumped against the wall.

"We did it, Captain!" shouted the corporal.

Rikard burst out laughing. He couldn't believe their sheer luck. Why had such an implacable enemy left? Did they know Naram-Sin was dead? No, they had an entire army. What difference could one person make, no matter how lethal? Rikard didn't care. They had survived, and maybe he would be a grandfather one day.

He looked across at Suri-Yi. She wasn't laughing or smiling. She had a sombre look as though she had just heard news of a friend's death. He checked his exuberance. During the short time he had known her, he had come to trust her intuition. If she was concerned, so should he be.

57

LETTER

Suri-Yi knew the scenes of spontaneous joy around her would not last long. A victory over Volek's army—a retreat in the minds of the Nostvektians—was akin to winning, but it did not happen without reason. *The world is made of cause and effect*. Something had caused Volek to withdraw his forces, and it wasn't the defeat of Naram-Sin. There would be a subsequent effect on the Nostvektians, but she didn't know what it could possibly be yet.

The quadrangle filled with more soldiers and townspeople, and soon they were clapping, hooting, laughing, and smiling. It was a moment of celebration, but it would only be a moment. The long shadow she had felt for months loomed ever closer. Then she remembered Adan. He had been fighting five Hawarij on his own.

"My apprentice, Adan. Has anyone seen him?"

"Yes, the young man saved my life when I was surrounded by three Hawarij. He sprinted off in the direction of the well house pursued by the Hawarij. I...I didn't see him come out," said Navrosk.

Pushing through the crowds, Suri-Yi and the captain ran towards the well house and entered. It had been a massacre. Four hooded Hawarij lay dead beside the headless body of a girl. It was Saphira.

"Adan," she called out. "Are you here?"

There was silence. "Only the bodies. No one else," said Navrosk.

She knelt down and removed the hood of each Hawarij. They were all young men and women. They could have done so much good if their energy had been channelled in the right way.

Adan wasn't present. So where was he? By the time they exited the well house, the quadrangle heaved with people. The drawbridge across the moat had been lowered, and she and Navrosk walked across it and into the plaza outside the royal palace.

On the other side of the moat, three people met her. Two were familiar—Olaf and his daughter. Standing beside them was a battered and bruised Durian rider. Suri-Yi's heart jumped. It was the warner she had been expecting. Hallbjorn, Brynjar, and Navrosk joined her. The forest folk hugged one another, but then fell silent, staring at her. Everyone else remained within the royal palace grounds.

"Keep everyone back for now," said Navrosk to a lieutenant. "No one is to leave the royal palace 'til I say so."

The Durian slipped from his saddle, and his legs gave way as he landed on the ground. Olaf held him up.

"I carry a letter from Emperor Heraclius of Duria to Princess Elsta Mik, ruler of Kronnoburg," said the Durian.

"She is not here. Maybe she is...dead. I am looking after things at this time. My name is Captain Rikard Navrosk. You can pass the letter to me."

The Durian hesitated and looked around at all of them, but he was too tired to argue. He handed the letter to the captain.

"I also have an identical letter addressed to Grandmaster Suri-Yi of the Tasburai Order. Does anyone know of her whereabouts?"

"I am she," said Suri-Yi.

The Durian looked at her and then came forwards with a nervous shuffle. He handed her the letter, and she opened it.

She read the message. It was brief. Heraclius was always one for brevity. She glanced across at Navrosk. The young captain's hands shook. He'd just read the same words addressed to his queen.

"The letter is from Emperor Heraclius of Duria," said Suri-Yi. "On the birth of the new moon and under cover of darkness, Duria was attacked from the sea by the Magrog. Duria has fallen, and Heraclius has fled."

This is only the beginning. Every kingdom and republic will be invaded. This is how the Magrog fight. They spread like a plague through the land, covering it in death. All the people of the Avantolian peninsula would need to unite under one banner—the Avanist Republic, Krakonite, Kronnoburg, Athenia, Pathan, and what remained of Duria.

Can we still do this? Our real enemy has arrived, and we are unprepared. We have fought one another and squabbled over land and ideas. The Tasburai are no longer a force. I am the last of the Tasburai, but I must believe. For if the world were ending around me—flames igniting, oceans boiling over, mountains splitting apart—and I had a seed of grain in my hand, I would still plant it. For in that seed there is hope.

"So it begins," said Olaf. "The end of days."

CAST OF CHARACTERS

Ab Isaac	Member of the Shining Fist
Adan de la Vega	Apprentice of the Tasburai order
Bolt	Lieutenant of the Kingdom of Kronnoburg
Brynjar the Blade	One of the forest folk
Cordaro	Apprentice of the Tasburai order
Elsta Mik	Princess of the Kingdom of Kronnoburg
Eydis the Green	One of the forest folk
Fur	Apprentice of the Tasburai order
Gyges	Minister of the Avanist Republic
Hallbjorn the Bear	One of the forest folk
Karlsen	Minister of the Kingdom of Kronnoburg
Klas Hakar	Captain of the Kingdom of Kronnoburg

Naram Sin	Grandmaster of the Tasburai order
Nezullas	Minister of the Avanist Republic
Olaf the Generous	Headman of the forest folk
Raven	Apprentice of the Tasburai order
Reider	Minister of the Kingdom of Kronnoburg
Rikard Navrosk	Captain of the Kingdom of Kronnoburg
Saphira	Apprentice of the Tasburai order
Sargon	Chancellor of the Avanist Republic
Serdar	General of the Avanist Republic
Sigrun the Hidden	One of the forest folk
Suri-Yi	Grandmaster of the Tasburai order
Theodoros Theseus	Prince of the Kingdom of Athenia
The Clerk	Keeper of the archives within the Oblivion Prison
The Shufi	Mystic of the Tasburai Temple
Torvin	One of the forest folk
Ulfheart	General of the Kingdom of Kronnoburg
Ulrik	Major of the Kingdom of Kronnoburg
Volek	General of the Krakonite Republic
Yaram Lim	Minister of the Avanist Republic
Ylva	One of the forest folk

ACKNOWLEDGEMENTS

To my wife, Faiza, you were a beacon of light and an anchor of stability – and most of all a comfort to the heart.

To my son, Yusuf, for his teenage witticism.

To my daughter, Imaan, for asking me what I wanted to be when I grew up. I was thirty-eight years old at the time.

To my parents, close family members, and friends for encouraging me.

To my editors, particularly Lorna Fergusson, whose editing skills I couldn't have done without.

And to all the writers whose works I've read, whose ideas I've been inspired by, and whose words have mesmerised.

Rehan Khan was born in Wimbledon, in 1971. His parent's home was close to the quintessential All England Lawn Tennis and Croquet Club and a bike ride away from Wimbledon Common. As a child he loved listening to swashbuckling tales of heroism and valor, as well as dabbling in science fiction. His debut novel is *Last of the Tasburai.* As his day job, Rehan is the Regional Consulting Director for a FTSE 100 corporation. He is also a Professor of Management at an international business school. Rehan holds a master's degree in applied social and market research, as well as an MBA in strategy. He lives in Dubai, with his wife and two children and can be reached at www.rehankhan.com

Made in the USA
Middletown, DE
07 March 2017